THOSE WHO
MAKE US

THOSE WHO

CANADIAN CREATURE, MYTH, AND MONSTER STORIES

MAKE US

Edited by

KELSI MORRIS AND KAITLIN TREMBLAY

THE EXILE BOOK OF ANTHOLOGY SERIES
NUMBER THIRTEEN

Publishers of Singular

Fiction, Poetry, Nonfiction, Drama, Translations and Graphic Books

Library and Archives Canada Cataloguing in Publication

Those who make us : creature, myth and monster stories /
Kelsi Morris and Kaitlin Tremblay, editors.

(The Exile book of anthology series ; number thirteen)
Issued in print and electronic formats.
ISBN 978-1-55096-589-6 (paperback).--ISBN 978-1-55096-590-2 (epub).--
ISBN 978-1-55096-591-9 (mobi).--ISBN 978-1-55096-592-6 (pdf)

1. Short stories, Canadian (English). 2. Monsters in literature.
3. Animals in literature. 4. Tales--Canada. 5. Legends--Canada.
I. Morris, Kelsi, editor II. Tremblay, Kaitlin, editor
III. Series: Exile book of anthology series no. ; 13

PS8329.T46 2016   C813'.608   C2016-904906-X
                                             C2016-904907-8

Design and Composition by Mishi Uroboros
Cover art by Bruce Rolff
Typeset in Fairfield, Copperplate and Akzidenz Grotesk fonts
at Moons of Jupiter Studios.

Published by Exile Editions Ltd ~ www.ExileEditions.com
144483 Southgate Road 14 – GD, Holstein, Ontario, N0G 2A0
Printed and Bound in Canada in 2016, by Marquis

We gratefully acknowledge the Canada Council for the Arts,
the Government of Canada, the Ontario Arts Council,
and the Ontario Media Development Corporation
for their support toward our publishing activities.

 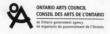

Canadian Sales: The Canadian Manda Group, 664 Annette Street,
Toronto ON M6S 2C8   www.mandagroup.com   416 516 0911

North American and international distribution, and U.S. sales:
Independent Publishers Group, 814 North Franklin Street,
Chicago IL 60610   www.ipgbook.com   toll free: 1 800 888 4741

*From both of us, to everyone who needs this book.
We know the power stories have, and every once
in awhile, they can have an emotional effect that
can take us by surprise. Please read with care.*

CONTENTS

INTRODUCTION

KELSI MORRIS AND KAITLIN TREMBLAY

In a lot of ways, it feels natural for two feminists to put together a book of creatures, myths, and monsters. For us, it all started with Godzilla – a myth, a monster, and a creature after our own hearts. For Kaitlin, Godzilla represented healing. Godzilla's penchant for revenge and effortless conquering of his enemies became a symbol of perseverance, and of learning how to rebuild a life from broken fragments of one. For Kelsi, Godzilla became a vehicle for venting social frustrations, the catharsis that comes from watching humanity realize we're not the centre of the universe.

This shared love of Godzilla movies became a bonding experience, and the foundation of a lifelong friendship.

The stories that create creatures and their myths play an important rôle in questioning and challenging the status quo. Monsters reflect what we see in ourselves – and how we see ourselves – as humans. They offer the chance to critique, to challenge, to see the best and worst in ourselves, and to grow. Some say monsters represent what is wrong with the world. We respectfully disagree. Monsters can represent those of us who don't belong, and stories about creatures, myths, and monsters can give us a space to belong.

Monsters have always been a safe haven for us, in the way that they represent non-normative beings who aren't accepted or understood within their society. As queer women, finding places to safely tell and share our stories – and for others to share and tell their stories – has always been our number one priority. And this is what *Those Who Make Us* means to us. They're not just monster stories; they're stories of trying to belong, trying to accept oneself, and trying to be understood.

With *Those Who Make Us*, we really wanted to challenge the idea of a national Canadian identity. Since Canada is one of the most diverse countries in the world, we weren't comfortable with the idea of saying, "This is what a Canadian identity is," or, "This is what it means to be Canadian." Being Canadian, and living in Canada, can be challenging, alienating, and isolating, at the same time that it can be supportive and inclusive. It is – and can be – many different things at once, and there is no way for a singular identity to reflect this.

This is why it was of utmost importance for the stories in *Those Who Make Us* to emulate this kind of living growth, this contradictory nature of Canadian identity. A nation is a living, breathing entity filled with people who clash, who mix, or who will never encounter each other, and this volume seeks to emulate this kind of living growth. Some of the stories found within will probably resonate with different readers for a myriad of reasons, while others won't, and this is by design. As a whole, *Those Who Make Us* speaks to the variations found within Canada. It's a Frankenstein-esque amalgamation of different genres and different voices, and there is no other way this anthology could have taken shape and still be true to its goal: sharing stories of sameness and difference.

The stories found within the collection sometimes have their foundation in traditional forms of fairy tales, folk tales, mythology, legends, and fables, but they all involve contemporary storytelling that goes beyond their foundations so that they represent personal or group identities, social commen-

tary, evolving cultural norms, and history/future history. There
are giants, there are dragons, there are new mythologies and
monsters, and, of course, there are trolls.

Like Canada itself, *Those Who Make Us* contains conflict-
ing, contrasting, and challenging stories that look at how we
understand ourselves and our place in Canada through the
creatures, myths, and monsters we carry with us.

The goal of the anthology was to give a space to stories
that reflect our attempts of understanding what we are as
humans and how monsters, creatures, and myths help us
understand what, and who, we are. These stories are personal, they are cultural, they are tragic, they are deviant, they
are delightful, they are weird, and they are wonderful. And
they are ours and they are also not ours. And we couldn't have
asked for a better anthology of stories to reflect this.

We hope you enjoy *Those Who Make Us*.

Kelsi and Kaitlin, 2016

A NEW BESTIARY

MICHAL WOJCIK

She was strange, even for a monster. Most people who underwent full biomodification chose a specific mould from a classical beast: a merperson, or a cyclops, or a satyr. Very few had themselves chopped and stretched into a full-blown chimera.

Only Melanie's face and parts of her torso remained human, the rest was replaced by raven wings, tiger-feet tipped with tiger-claws, her body a rippling array of overlapping scar tissue and fur grafted over re-grown bone. The surgeons had enlarged her heart by several chambers, elongated and toughened her major muscles, cut out her digestive tract and strung in a new set of guts, and turned her hair into a squirming mass of centipedes. The wings were purely aesthetic, too small to support her in the air, too large for anyone else to ignore.

Her amalgam of features resisted classification into one *gens* or another. Self-made monsters usually sequestered themselves into small communities based around their chosen templates, parallel societies signalling tastes and interests through the shape of a fang or snout. Melanie hadn't given thought to joining any; if anything, she spent more time among the unmodified than she had before her surgery. She challenged them with just her appearance, grabbed their attention and held it. Her job as a graphic designer at an advertising firm catering to normals meant constant meetings where she enacted the same little play over and over again with unmodded clients: terror becoming intrigue becoming acceptance.

The only time her interactions with people changed was her home life; the unmodded folk who'd grown comfortable speaking to her at work weren't so keen to have dinner or sleep in the same den as someone with bugs for hair.

So she rented a studio apartment with a centaur named Véronique, a monster who'd chosen a body unwieldy enough that her own chances of finding a herd were limited. They ended up together in this place because they didn't fit apart elsewhere. It wasn't exactly anyone's dream home: adapted from an old factory office, a mess of loose brick and plaster and exposed wiring, cold in the winter and prone to leaks in spring. Then there was the constant *clomp clomp* of Véronique's hoofs to keep Melanie awake at night. The centaur was an invariable insomniac.

Still, Melanie liked it. The loft had its charms; it smelled like a stable, hay and all. There was the neighbourhood too, full of derelict buildings where other monsters made their dens. A whole pack of dog-headed cynocephali hung out in the park across from the soccer field, where monopods hopped, and the roofs were spattered with griffin shit. Griffin-town indeed, a menagerie taken out of a medieval bestiary or a Renaissance wonder-book.

Despite her aggressive otherness, Melanie still sometimes wanted to feel like she belonged, somewhere, outside her profession. Even this island of monstrosity had its own cliques and guilds. Outside of its streets, the unconverted didn't all accept total biomodification; a vocal few resisted the encroachment of freaks in the downtown core with letters to the editors and rowdy marches. You could still walk through Westmount and see nary a blemmya. News stories popped up from time to time about monsters found crumpled in alleys, heads caved in by steel-toed boots. The perpetrators were rarely found, never convicted. There were no letters to the editors or rowdy marches then.

Going back to her family in BC was out of the question, not after the reaction Melanie's mother had when she'd first got whiff of what her daughter planned to do. The rest of her relatives had been equally horrified.

Melanie plunked herself on the couch and jacked into the VR feed. The implant immediately overlaid her sight with bright words and symbols she could directly manipulate with her brain. A multitasker's heaven – a procrastinator's too. Funny cat videos took up the upper quarter of her vision, and through the rest she glimpsed Véronique trot into the kitchen to pull a bowl of shrink-wrapped salad from the fridge.

"Bonjour, Mel," the centaur said while carrying the bowl into the living room. Half-hearted chat on their respective days followed, until Véronique said, "I just learned I am going to Toronto on Saturday. You will have the place to yourself. Is good, no?"

A cat jumping out of a box dimmed, the interface going clear when it sensed Melanie's attention drawn elsewhere. "New boyfriend?" she asked.

"Photo shoots," Véronique said. She must have still been smarting from her last tryst with that self-styled cowboy from Alberta (nice guy, a little *too* into horses, though). "These people who are into the Greek classics, they are always curious about what a centaur looks like in the flesh, want to take artful pictures."

"Pay well?"

"Oui." Véronique trundled up beside the couch and flipped on the holo for a live showing of *Latvia's Got Talent*, forked in a mouthful of grass and apples. She said in a far more tentative and embarrassed voice, "I had another oracle experience today. A *premonition*."

"Huh?" Melanie reoriented herself after fixating on the six-armed pole dancer dominating the holo, who might as well have been a superhero from the way she worked that pole.

"Something happened that I dreamed of. It came true. Only big this time."

Melanie suppressed a snort. "Not that New Age crap again, Véronique. It's just coincidence. Like the last time with the grilled cheese stand. If you have a dream about passing an artisanal grilled cheese stand on Saint-Laurent, it's going to happen because *you're in Montreal*."

"No no no." Véronique waved a hand in urgent dismissal. "I said it is *big* this time. I have this dream that keeps coming back for the last one, two months, that rocks are coming up from the ocean, and cities, ruined villes, forests. The trees drip seawater and leave puddles. I have told you about this, have I not?" She cocked her head and looked at Melanie expectantly.

"Yeah, and?"

"You haven't seen the news?"

"I *never* follow the news. You *know* I don't follow the news."

"Well, take a look. Today, it has *happened*, Mel. It has *really, actually happened*."

The interface awoke on cue, immediately slid over to the latest headlines and sorted to the most recent, sifted over to the science stories. A video bloomed open with a too-perfect announcer poised on the deck of a hovercraft, her curled locks whipping like Medusa's snakes in the wind. She cheerfully declared an abnormal geological event was taking place in the South Pacific Ocean. The first peaks of a new Terra Incognita had risen Cthulhu-like from the waters, forming a new chain of tiny islands. Melanie watched a little while longer before letting the interface lapse into clarity.

"That's…that's still a coincidence," she said, first unsure, then more firm. "The Earth's growing more unstable, everyone knows that. And it's just some islands, barely even islands."

"No," Véronique said. "This is just the start. Cities will come up from the sea, a whole new land. A land where monsters go and where we belong. Paradise."

But I like it here, Melanie thought, involuntarily, before discarding the notion as ridiculous, like all that other talk of monsters and re-enchantment, of spiritual awakening through surgery. So much chatter, so much noise. "It's nothing like that," she said quietly. "Dreams don't become real. Otherwise I wouldn't have needed to go to a biomodder to look like this. I would've just moulted my old body and been reborn with this one."

"That was before. There were not enough of us then," Véronique insisted. "There are all sorts of stories now of monsters curing cancer, granting wishes, flying. We are doing it, Mel. We are starting to change the world. And it will be so much better now."

Melanie yanked out the VR implant and said, "No," before stomping out of the room, leaving a track of claw-marks impressed into the kitchen linoleum.

Phantom islands kept on appearing. Certain scientists took to the holo to insist the archipelago would vanish in short order, that it was merely a ghostly protrusion that would grow weary of the world and sink back into slumber beneath the waves. Dead islands gone back to dreaming.

Only the archipelago was just a beginning, the first sentinel of a realm coming fully awake. The landmass grew and grew, satellite images tracking its daily expansion, the new soil like a slow-spreading coffee stain over the high-res map. New mountains, new plains, new valleys, new rivers. Navies gathered at a safe distance from the coastline to observe and, if pressed, plant their nations' flags.

Governments tried to impose a blackout on information coming from the continent, stating that it was empty and bare and that releasing any data about the land itself to the public could woefully exacerbate this volatile geopolitical situation. But it was impossible to stop the snapshots and 10-second video clips that first came trickling in through print or on unregulated corners of the VR feed, leaked by professors, scientists, sailors, and pilots. These, spread a thousandfold times across the net, were soon picked up by major news outlets once the classified nature of the material became meaningless: footage of empty cities built from cracked glass shining between the streamers of kelp and coral and barnacles that clung to the walls and died in the sunlight.

Véronique insistently showed these to Melanie, ignoring how Melanie recoiled from her attentions. The centaur's enthusiasm was unnecessary – Melanie had already seen them, couldn't stop herself from looking despite the images dropping a dose of dread into her stomach every time she did. She just didn't want to *talk* about them. At least, not until she'd made some sense of them herself without the distraction of mystic dogma.

Some monsters were already whispering about sailing there, Véronique said. Some had already gone, Véronique said. Monsters reclaiming the sphere from whence they'd come. Terra Incognita, the Antipodes.

The Forbidden Places.

On medieval maps the monsters dwelt on the very outmost edges of the world, and the belief went that the monsters' conversion to Christianity would mark the beginning of the Apocalypse. Melanie had read that in a textbook for a class she took at the University of British Columbia, back when she still lived on the West Coast. Back before her transformation. Now the thought gnawed at Melanie that the universe was settling into those old grooves. Soon enough the sun would shift into orbit round the Earth and the stars would affix themselves onto the heavenly spheres and begin scraping out music. Maybe some Johnny Cash.

She'd approached the idea of biomodding into monsters as a rebirth; now, all she saw was regression. A hum of religious fervour had taken over Griffintown, loud enough that Melanie avoided the other monsters when she rushed home from the advertising firm and locked the swiftly unbalancing world out of her apartment. She attempted to ignore the cynocephali who made solemn processions down the street carrying icons of dog-headed Saint Christopher before entering the park and howling in their prayer circles. She attempted to ignore the pensiveness that lay barely concealed in other monsters' eyes.

It was just a biomod, she told herself when she went to bed that night. It was Tuesday.

The ever-growing population of monsters hadn't summoned Mu and Lemuria from the ocean bed of the Pacific.

She hadn't done that.

She'd gone to the biomodders because she wanted to cross the crooked mirror. Become the monster that defined the human and, in the process, define herself. Back when she was just another unmodded person, she had trouble talking to anyone, stuttering away like a dying diesel engine into silence whenever she tried to carry a conversation with strangers, staying at home and eventually fading away from social circles. After spending so long feeling out of joint with society, rejected by it, she'd wanted to *own* that estrangement. Become it. That's why she didn't pick a *gens*. That's why the new body was her own design, not some indolent monk's doodle in a manuscript's margin.

That was why...

She drifted off into a heavy, dreamless sleep.

Her alarm switched from a gentle prodding to a more insistent hammer-beat and a dissonant snarl. Melanie rolled over, sheets damp and clinging to her skin, so wet she might as well have dragged herself up out of water. Surfacing. A heavy scent of sweat mixed with salt and roses greeted her in the world above.

Skin. Not fur and scales. Skin. She raised a hand, saw fingers long and thin and clawless. She pressed those fingers to her head, not feeling centipedes there but strands of plain old hair. She strung it out so she could see it shining gold in the morning light.

Melanie closed her eyes, took a deep breath, opened them again. The same hand hung there, the same hair stretched out there, the same sense remained that her body was thinner, lighter, weaker. Little tremors shook through her, like the kind she'd get picking up memories from dusty scrapbooks.

Packets of forgotten sensation wrapped around her in a snug sack of meat and muscle, imbibed her with now alien experiences of normalcy.

She spent a few more minutes in bed, ignoring the alarm that now resorted to blasting Coldplay to annoy her into waking. Then she slowly got up, keeping the sheets wrapped tight because she didn't want to see her body, not yet, and walked with the sheet to the washroom while avoiding looking at all the mirrors she'd specifically hung to remind herself of what she'd become and why, until she came to that one, the final one above the sink. Of course she knew what she'd see there, but it was still like looking into a photograph taken five years ago. The photos she usually avoided.

Melanie threw up.

Thank God Véronique's in Toronto, Melanie thought as she sneaked out the back way from the apartment, hiding her face and her body under an oversized coat. Everything she owned was oversized now, designed for a different bulk. She tried calming her beating heart, her weak little four-chamber heart, tried to stop the panic bubbling up inside her, telling her to find a biomod clinic quick as she could and revert to her chimera shape. She'd saved up for years to have that procedure, and it was a delicate one too, not an augmentation you'd leave to a standard biomodder on Peel or in Chinatown without experiencing horrific post-op complications.

She'd call in sick for work, that's what she'd do. Her voice had lost its reverb and growl but still sounded more or less the same, just softer (*weaker*). She could hide her metamorphosis, as long as her boss didn't try to put her on video – which he would, since Melanie had taken far too many unneeded sick days before. *Shit, shit, shit.* So instead Melanie went back inside and switched off her smartphone and anything else that could pick up the all-encompassing wifi that hung like a heavy mist over the city.

More of her thoughts turned toward biomods as she flicked switches, turned dials, pressed screens. The surgery had taken a week, and she'd needed months of recovery time. Her mind clicked through options – did biomodders steal into her house and revert her according to exact specs? No, that would have taken just as long as the initial modifications, maybe longer, not to mention that growing a custom skin to zip her in would have needed extensive body imaging beforehand. And then she'd have to lie in stasis for a while as her veins and nerves felt their way through the new meat and the nanobots knit her smoothly together again. But she was walking like she'd never had surgery, never changed into a chimera, like this had been her body all along.

On the street she kept her head ducked down, catching quick glances here and there. Barely anyone was out save a mostly unmodded couple (just the slight adjustment to the ears to make them elven) walking their dogs. *Maybe everyone's changed back...?* That thought immediately fled when a blemmya came out a door and down some stairs, his headless torso uncovered to reveal the mouth gaping in a yawn from his belly and eyes darting about on his chest.

Not everyone. Some monsters remain.

Melanie blinked away the oncoming tears.

At the Old Port she sat on a bench and watched the birds circling around an angel statue that surmounted one mansion's spire. She'd turned away from the St. Lawrence, away from any merpeople who might skim below the river's surface

like pale pink fish. Nobody cleared a path for her anymore
when she walked, and the few monsters she did encounter
passed without the expected nod of recognition and understanding.

There were markedly fewer monsters than she remembered from previous weeks.

They were still there, still forming little knots of strangeness, but they were muted, infrequent, and easily missed. Her
gaze slid over them, only able to hold for a second or two
before she had to look away. The unmodded folk she passed
by so casually before now became pervasive, oppressive, all
the more so because she was one of them. And the once-fel-
low creatures became other. Her body seemed to dictate what
deserved notice more than her eyes.

There were some people she saw in clothes that didn't fit
quite right, who shrank away from others as much as she did.
She thought of speaking to them, thought better of it. At least
for now, while she could still doubt that some kind of mon-
strous rapture had taken place, snatching away the chosen
form of those with little faith.

She'd left her persistent jack in the apartment along with
her phone, meaning she'd cut her mind from the network
entirely, and now her nose just took in city smells and ears just
took in city noise: traffic, exhaust, smoked meat, pattering
feet against cement, French and English and Swahili min-
gling, distant bells. There *was* something different in the buzz
and chatter, a charge in the air, colours grown brighter and air
grown richer and little tufts of white swirling about like
sparks. She reached out for one and watched the breeze spiral dandelion dust around her fingers.

At length Melanie wound her way past Chinatown to the
Plateau, over the cobbled walk to a well-lit pub called the

Bonaparte. Recently opened, Melanie guessed, judging from the jumble of furniture scattered inside, judging from the attempt and failure of conjuring an early nineteenth-century atmosphere with delicate white napkins and false gilt. It was yet another try at revitalizing the district to its former young urban professional glory through quirky themed restaurants and taverns.

One satyr sat alone by the window; the rest of the clientele were anatomically conventional. The largest group were probably students from McGill, what with the one man's moustache and plaid and the one woman's pink-pattern handkerchief wrapped round her hair. As Melanie shuffled by them for the bar she heard a snatch of their conversation. Something about Aristotle, about Paul Ricoeur, about time and narrative.

A beer came off the tap – Melanie nursed at it slowly, dulling her frictional nerves. Classical music warbled in the background, The Rites of Spring. She lost herself in the arrangement until the beer was nearly gone, until someone tapped her lightly on the shoulder.

"Hey, I *thought* I recognized you," a woman said and slid onto the next stool. No overt surgical modifications on her, but she had a hell of a lot of tattoos: tentacles that traced spirals round her legs and arms and neck, ending around her cheeks and disappearing behind her ears. They quivered and curled with each breath. At first Melanie thought it was a trick of the light, but no, it was a premium skin-swap, a living ink epidermis. The tattoos were an elaborate system of projected webbing that could expand, collapse, move. "Mel, right?"

"Yes?"

"Cheryl," the tentacle-lady said helpfully.

"Cheryl…" Melanie repeated. "Oh!" Another student at UBC, same program, but a different skin, then. Skin brown and smooth and clear of octopus limbs.

"So we both ended up in Montreal after all, huh?" Cheryl said. She ordered a tumbler of scotch and then examined Melanie with uncomfortable intensity before shrugging. "What a world."

Melanie put on a smile. It was a welcome distraction, at least, some aspect of the past that she didn't have to fear. They drank. They chatted, an airy kind of chat between near-strangers not willing to probe too far into personal details, sending out just the barest feelers. A chat Melanie wouldn't have possibly had before her operation without at some point lapsing into uncomfortable silence. At length they decided to ditch the Bonaparte, take a stroll up Mont Royal together and wile away the afternoon.

Cheryl had lost her job at a graphic design company earlier that week and had spent the day wandering directionless around the city same as Melanie had. Now, they passed under the gnarled trees up the trail ascending the hill, came to the long staircase and dutifully made their way up and up to the footpaths undulating along the hilltops.

"So you never went through with the surgery, then?" Cheryl asked, the conversation now finally crossing into the personal. "I remember you saying you wanted to do that, back in undergrad. Not that you talked much back then."

Melanie shook her head.

"But you live in Griffintown. Monster central."

"Yup. With a centaur."

Cheryl laughed. "Of course. Of course."

They came to a spur where the city spread out below in a slightly unreal haze, buildings arranged like dominoes, the St. Lawrence glimmering beneath the horizon.

"I can see why you wanted to, though. Me, I'm not brave enough for that. I was hyperventilating right before I got the skin done." She waved her hands toward her face, toward the tentacles gently writhing there. "Too attached to the body underneath, I guess. But there's something so intense about shedding the form you're born with and becoming something completely different. It's like, tossing away all the logic drilled into you when you grow up and giving yourself up completely to your dreams." She waved vaguely toward the river. "There's all these stories of monsters doing magic now. By making themselves imaginary things they're able to do anything we imagine, if that makes sense. Like this new continent that's showing up…they did that. Who else would've?"

A long silence followed. The wind rustled the branches and rustled Melanie's hair, even the little ones all up and down her arms. There was definitely a new smell there, a new taste, like crushed roses again, and she breathed it deeply.

"So why'd you change your mind? About the surgery, I mean."

Melanie barely even heard her. Not over the growing blend of sensations, not over her mind beginning to build a cartography of Terra Incognita and trying to dream up a home there.

Why did I change my mind? She hadn't changed her mind since the initial session strapped on the biomodder's bench, just gone in without realizing what it meant to become a monster. Get enough people doing the same and small shifts in the world's daily workings would swell, swell enough to force lands up from the bottom of the sea.

A sound like the beat of a vast pigeon's wings filled the air.

"She never changed her mind," a voice said, hers. "She just didn't understand. Still does not."

The hair prickled up on the back of Melanie's neck. She gripped the metal railing tight before chancing a look over her shoulder. From the way Cheryl had tensed, her tattoos becoming an agitated froth of cuttlefish, Melanie knew what she'd see there.

A chimera, its wings folding against its spine, centipedes coiling around a face that mirrored Melanie's own. Yet the tell-tale signs of biomodding were gone. There was no trace of scar tissue, of leftover skin outside of that face.

She was the ideal, the sketch Melanie had given over to the biomodders before they crafted her into its echo.

Melanie swallowed, hard. The monster smiled.

"You…you're—" Melanie stuttered

"No," the chimera declared. "You are my creator. The mind that birthed the monster. But you never became me.

"The world has changed, Melanie. We were not together as one, so I left you, like so many have done. I will find my way across the ocean westward."

The voice was the same, the way of speaking different. Deeper, a feral snarl beneath the words, but also a formal loftiness in the way she said them.

"Farewell, Melanie. I wished to see you one last time as you were, so you would realize what you chose to lose." Her wings unfurled and she sprang forward, launched herself toward the city below. One talon nearly raked Cheryl, who'd stumbled back in the dirt screaming, "Oh shit oh shit oh shit!"

Melanie, though, while her heart drummed deep (over-worked, too small), yelped and leapt as well. Her arms wrapped around the lower half of the chimera's body, *her* body, the weight dragging them tumbling against the railing. The iron bar crunched into Melanie's back, made her wince and cry out, but she didn't let go.

Her fingers roamed against the fur and slick reptilian scales as she tried to find purchase, but the usual bumps and ridges from the grafts she knew so well weren't there. The talons lashed out, claws too, scraping big tears in her clothes and drawing blood from the flesh beneath. But Melanie didn't let go. She crawled up the creature's body, trying to contain its powerful squirming.

They were wrestling. A brief thought back to the story of Jacob and the angel came to Melanie then, a sudden mad desire to laugh at the image as the chimera's wings thrashed about in the dirt and brought up clouds of dust and clots of grass while they fought together. Only Melanie found she couldn't laugh because she was already weeping, tears and great shivering sobs coming fast and hard. She realized she could no longer keep hold on that frame, not for long, which didn't stop her from trying, from gripping, from kicking, with that weak thin body of hers, until she had her face up against the other's. Centipedes tickled her cheeks and scalp. She stared into the eyes that weren't quite her own and they stared back.

"Don't leave me," she whispered. "Please. I need this. I need you."

The chimera's struggles subsided, not all at once but slowly, as if the will and strength sapped away.

Their chests heaved together in the sudden stillness. One body embracing another, Melanie's blood staining her clothes and smearing against the other's body.

"I'm...I'm a monster," Melanie said once softly, then louder. "I want...I will be..."

The other's lips parted. "You are."

It wasn't a kiss, not quite. Just a joining, one body partaking of another, moving together in something more than an embrace. Melanie's temples thrummed along with her heartbeat, stronger and stronger, putting pressure on her ribcage as the muscle grew and grew. There was no pain, just a building warm tingle soon surpassed by a sensation of utter joy as the skin transmuted on her arms and legs and chest, as new bones burst from her back and spread in a soft brush of feathers. Centipedes crawled out from her scalp, their little legs drumming against her skull. Muscles stretched out and grew taut, claws extended out from her fingers and toes, the latter crowding against the insides of her oversized shoes. By the time it was done, the last of Melanie's bones clicked into place, the other chimera was gone completely.

Melanie stood.

Cheryl's mouth gaped open; she was on her knees, poised as if in prayer or supplication. The tentacles were motionless.

"It's my own bit of magic," Melanie whispered. *Private metamorphosis, a second coming. I'm slouching toward Montreal to be born, is that how that poem went?*

She stalked over to Cheryl and extended a paw, helping her up to her feet.

"What…?" Cheryl whispered, trembling.

"I'm a monster," Melanie said. "We all are, or we can imagine ourselves as monsters."

"Oh?"

"We just need to accept that. That we live in a world like that now."

Cheryl didn't reply. Melanie gave her hand a light squeeze, then let go, turning back to the precipice and the city. She let her wings spread out to their full span.

"Wait!" Cheryl called.

Melanie turned back, lifted an eyebrow in inquiry.

"Where...where are you going?"

"I don't know. Not yet. But it's a choice I'll have to make one day, I guess," she said.

Then she spread her wings again and made a running jump over the railing, out into the air. And she *flew*, even though it was *absolutely, fundamentally* impossible for those wings to be capable of flight. Actually flew, over Avenue du Parc, over Place des Arts, toward the river before banking back over McGill University.

She wanted to explore this new, changed world first, before proceeding to its extremities, its unknown corners. Then she would fly toward a place where cities sat waiting in crystalline ruins that she might, one day, call home.

SUBMERGED

HELEN MARSHALL

Sarah was a sweet woman, and I never knew why she married me in the first place. Me with my small eyes and tarry-dark hair. Me, a young man still, but with nothing to my name, no luck, no ambition beyond hauling steel at the Manitoba Rolling Mills where my father had done the same before me. But she did marry me, and that is something I'll always be thankful for, no matter what came after and how much it hurt when I lost her. I knew I would lose her eventually, didn't I? From the moment I first took her in my arms. Nothing beautiful sticks around for long, not in my life, not in anyone's, and she was the most beautiful woman in Selkirk: small-limbed with hair soft as cornsilk. Not that I am bitter. I swore to myself when I first kissed her that I wouldn't be bitter about how it ended.

I watched them lower her body into the ground on December 4th, 1951, a bitter day, bitter with cold and bitter with heartache, me twisting that gold ring she had slipped onto my finger at Christ Church only a year or two before. I thought, there was this at least: she had never betrayed me. The only hurt she had ever done was dying before I was ready to let her go, choosing the life of another over her own – and who can blame a woman for that?

My father had loved Sarah nearly as much as I had. She had been kind to the old man, brought him tuna casseroles, meatloaf and chiffon pies, which all seemed like fine things to a man who had seen sliced bread and iced cakes rationed only a few years earlier. We didn't speak much before Sarah, my father and me. The grief of my mother's passing in '47 had nearly done him in. For a whole year he didn't say a word, not to me, not to anyone. And then suddenly, just like that, he started speaking again. He could've been a poet, I think, if it had been a place where people went in for that sort of thing. But though Selkirk had grown from the false-fronted, clapboard community my father had known as a child, it still looked on any sort of frivolity as wasteful. So they called him a drunk, which was about the worst thing you could call a man. For a while some of our more superstitious neighbours thought maybe Mother'd cursed him, for it was that sort of a town as well, the kind where long winters made pagans of even the most god-fearing housewives. So they said maybe Mother's ghost had taken his tongue to the next world with her and then sent it back with a spell on it. They whispered that he had betrayed her at the last, that she had always known about his carrying on. My father had been a good-looking man, the kind who might with nothing more than a glance of a particular type let a woman know she was admired. But he was an honest man too. Still, who knows what passes between a man and his wife? Certainly not his child. If there was aught amiss between my father and Mother before her death then certainly I knew nothing of it.

After Sarah was in the ground I feared what would happen to me, and to the little one as well: baby Joanna. My neighbours wouldn't come round or when they did they would be full of searching looks. If my hand trembled while I poured the coffee then they would tut kindly and help me with it. Afterward, though, the town would be full of their whispers. How would I care for the child myself? What did I know of raising a daughter? It got so I drove an extra fifteen kilometres along the Red River south to St. Andrews rather than facing the mischief of their gossip. Pretty soon I couldn't even do that. Whenever I set out on the road, I began to shudder dreadfully. Perhaps it was the look of the water moving so swiftly or the vastness of the sky which had never bothered me before. I had loved the flat land, its lack of shape, the way it interfered with nothing. But now I began to cower, tremors shook my hands, I felt like a field mouse underneath a great, black shadow. I was getting to be a hermit through no fault of mine. I wanted the company of friends, and yet I feared it too. The men I knew at the MRM loved their wives, but none of them to any great excess. They had looked distastefully at the little presents I used to bring Sarah, thought the attention might give her airs. Affection like that had no place out here, they said. I wondered if they were right. I had loved Sarah fiercely, but it hurt me to hold the child. I could not understand where she had come from. There was a general sentiment I should send her to Winnipeg where my mother's spinster sister could care for her better than I could.

My father must have heard about this, or maybe he had some intuition of it all on his own because after a week he began to drop by more and more frequently, bringing with him bacon and bread, butter, milk, onions, potatoes. Enough to keep me going. And he would dandle the child upon his knee while he spooned split pea mash into her tiny, wondering mouth. It was on one of these visits, after we both had a nip from the demijohn of whisky I kept at the back of the cupboard, that my father began to speak to me in that tone of his

I remembered as a boy, what Mother called his "romancing" tone, though she meant it in the old way, that is, as a kind of storytelling. As I said, I hadn't been close to my father until there was Sarah, and even then it had always seemed as if she were closer to him than I could ever be. Perhaps it's always that way between boys and their fathers. I had no friends I trusted enough to ask, those I had being the kind who were willing to laugh quick enough in the foundry but fell silent and stony if the talk ever turned to deeper passions. But with Sarah's death there was something like closeness forming between us, much as ice skims over a lake when the frosts come. It was delicate at first but it hardened day by day until it seemed six inches thick and solid beneath my feet.

This is what my father said.

Love is a wayward thing, you must know that by now but a known thing is still worth repeating from time to time. I loved your mother. Aye, I know what they say, them that talk but that's all it is. The talk of fools who never knew better. But even loving your mother as I did there was a woman I loved before her. It wasn't the same love, mind you, because there's no love you can stumble into twice. And if there's another that comes after Sarah you'll know how it is and if there isn't – well, a man can make a life out of anything he pleases. There are those who keep their love in a little box or a jam jar with its lid screwed on so tightly, just like that, but it was never that way with me. I reckon it won't be with you either. There will be another after Sarah, and perhaps it will hurt you at first to believe it, but I promise you can love two at the same time.

And now for this story. Well, it is about the waywardness of love, I suppose. Believe me or not, you can do with it what you may. When I was a child, Selkirk was a runt of a town, but one with big ambitions. It was just as the MRM was approaching its opening day that Great Britain declared war on the Kaiser. And good luck for us too, for the war would need all sorts of things that we could best provide. But when the first call for militia volunteers came, many of the men chose to enlist and the foundry was almost deserted. I had planned to serve, but they wouldn't take me on account of my gammy knee. Perhaps it was a good thing. In July of 1919, there would be a marching band, horse-drawn floats, and a dance held in the park while fireworks burst overhead to celebrate the end of the fighting. But in the beginning no one thought it would last much beyond four months. They said it was a chance to prove yourself. The old-timers all remembered their own conflicts: the Crimean War, the Riel insurrection, the Fenian raids. And they spun out these stories for the youngsters, eager for their own chance at glory. But by 1916, the first of the district boys had been killed overseas, and the reports of the trenches were hellish. While my school friends were dodging shells and bullets, I worked in the foundry surrounded by the women, one of the few young men left. And the women loved me something fierce because I was the only one among them – but they hated me as well for not being the one that they wanted.

One day the circus came to town. It was a strange thing, a holdover from the earlier days when Houdini had performed his famous Milk Can escape. But even Mr. Houdini had given himself over to the war effort, selling war bonds and teaching the Yankee soldiers how to slip themselves out of German restraints. There were brightly coloured caravans and tents. A man with a curled moustache hurled insults as you passed, but he did it with such a twinkling in his eye you couldn't help laughing. You wanted to shake his hand, you wanted to share a Coca-Cola with him, hear the stories he had about other parts of the country where the land wasn't flat and the sky wasn't empty and the men weren't coming back in boxes. This is an odd town, the man would tell me, a town full of nothing but women. Is it like this everywhere? I asked him, and he shrugged, saying: Everywhere is like everywhere.

They had fallen on hard times. Their strongman had run off recently. Some of the clowns too. They had scrubbed the greasepaint from their faces, shed their wigs, their long shoes, their suspenders and tights and all the odd get-up they put on to face the jeers of the crowds. Possibly they had enlisted. The man with the curled moustache thought that might be the case. Then their lion had died on the road. Their elephant went lame and he wouldn't stand on his back legs anymore. It was a sad affair, really, just this man with his curled moustache and a woman with a beard and another woman who could swallow swords and a set of twins who could hurl themselves through the air and do flips and such things. But we still paid for the show because he had a way with words and the women in the town were curious anyway. About the one with the beard. They wanted to touch it, they would pay extra for that. And the one with the sword. How did she teach herself to do that? Could they as well? Starting with butter knives? And the twins with their muscles as thick as cables, their breasts like iron lumps, their handshakes strong enough to crush a rock to gravel. They said nothing to these ones but they looked and they looked and they looked and when they left the tent I saw them measuring the girth of their own arms, wondering if they too might be able to fly through the air.

When it was time for the circus to leave I helped them break their camp. I may not have been a strongman but I had strength enough for that. They had nothing much to pay me but that didn't matter, the chance for company was enough and they shared with me the beans the bearded woman had set about cooking, which was kind for they couldn't have made much of a profit. We ate the beans with these long wooden spoons, and at the end of the meal the sword-swallower set about doing the dishes – one by one the long spoons disappeared into her gullet. The twins applauded like mad even though I could tell they must have seen the trick a thousand times before. After that I was ready to go, but the man with the moustache took me by the shoulders and he told me I'd been a good sport, a real help, and did I want a drink with him? One last drink for the road? It had been a long time since I had drunk whisky with another man. The antics of the 108th Battalion had turned the town against liquor of any sort, and by that time we were a dry county. But the work of the day had been hard, and the thought of a tipple reminded me of how it had been before, so I doffed my hat and I joined him in his tent.

The whisky he had was old but it was sweet and fiery and sore needed what with the chill of a long winter just beginning to dust the Red River with snow. And we spoke for a while, he and I, and he told me stories of the road and I had little enough to say to him so I simply listened. I wondered, for a while, if he might invite me to join him on the road, and I wondered what I would say if he asked me, if I would be willing to go. The tent was warm and the whisky was good and there was nothing for me here. But he never did ask and I couldn't bring myself to offer. After a while the man was nodding over his drink, his moustache was trailing in it, and I was beginning to feel a heavy sleep coming over me. Just then one of the heavy curtains twitched and from behind it stepped a woman dainty as a daffodil.

She was young, I thought at the time, though sometimes these things are hard to tell, and she had the same look around her eyes as the man with the moustache and so I reckoned he must have been her father. She was wearing a plain white nightgown. By that point I had spent some time in the camp and I had not seen her nor had she joined us for dinner with the others. And I thought perhaps the man had told her to keep to the tent when they were among strangers. She was a pretty thing and perhaps I would have done the same, though as I told you, there were few enough men around to bother her. Her father was snoring gently now, and she wrapped a warm blanket around him, but when she saw me sitting with him, she made a noise like she was frightened. I tried to calm her, to let her know I was harmless, and after we flapped our hands at each other for several minutes, neither of us wanting to speak, neither of us wanting to wake her father, finally she nodded shyly. I thought she would disappear then just as easily as she'd come in, and so I gathered my things about me. But before I left the tent I felt a tugging at my sleeve. Aye, it was her. She wouldn't speak, but she gestured for me to follow.

Behind the heavy curtain there was a bed. Only the one bed. I wondered if she slept there or if her father did. Or if her father was used to sleeping where he was with a demijohn in one hand and a blanket pulled up over him. And if that was how he slept, was it a good life he had or not? What did a life need to be a good life? What did a man need to be a good man? Was it enough to keep your daughter out of sight of prying eyes? To give her the one bed to sleep in? His daughter sat on the bed and there was nowhere for me to sit so I stood for a while in front of her until she made me sit on the bed next to her. What do you do? she asked me and I told her I hauled steel and shaped the ingots into whatever was needed. She nodded at that and she touched my gammy knee. I may have felt embarrassed at this or I may not, I don't remember. What do you do? I asked her. Are you a performer? She shook her head and smiled a small tight smile that made me wonder. One day, she told me, one day I will take the stage. What will your act be? I asked her. She looked up at me shyly now. Let me show you, she said.

Beside the bed was a small table and on the table was a shallow washbowl filled with water and beside the bowl was a knife. It was a good knife, one that would hold its edge. I had got to know about such things, working in the foundry. She took the knife up carefully in her right hand. I wondered if she was going to throw it. I had seen other performers in other circuses do something similar to that. They threw knives. They could hit any target they wanted. But she did not look like the type of woman who could throw a knife like that. In any case, she wasn't. She held up her left hand to me and then she placed it flat on the table. Come, she said, look at this closely. And so I stood up and I watched her as she placed the edge of the knife against the knuckle of her finger. Don't do that, I told her, but she didn't listen to me. There was that smile on her face, a very small smile and one that I thought now seemed quite sad. And she stood too, but her left hand was still on the table and the knife was still on the knuckle, and that was when I realized she needed all her weight for what she wanted to do.

She began to cut. Very slowly. She didn't make a sound the entire time, but she rocked back and forth until the steel bit through her bone and when it was done, she made a sound of happiness. And then the finger. Very carefully she took the finger off the table. There was no blood; I expected blood, anyone would expect blood, but there was none. Only a notch in the table and her holding the finger in the hand that had held the knife. And now for the trick, she said, and with a look of utter concentration she placed the finger in the bowl. And I stared at the finger and I stared at the finger and I blinked because then there was no finger at all – there was a minnow: sleek and grey and swimming in wide circles. My name is Sedna, she told me, and this will be my trick, now make a wish. I couldn't help it. I made a wish. I wished for love. She leaned forward, and she kissed me very gently on the cheek. The kiss was so tender and sweet I swear I began to cry. Will it come true? I asked her. Yes, she whispered. It was a year and a day later that I met your mother.

Your mother wasn't the first woman I loved, though I think my love for her was no less for what came before. It wasn't that the girl who travelled with the circus was pretty or that she was the first girl to ask me to sit beside her on a bed. It wasn't that I could hear her father snoring lightly in the other room or that earlier in the day I had watched a woman comb her beard until it shone and another who could slide a blade down her throat without blinking or twins who had taught themselves how to soar. All women, I knew, could do these things. They had been doing them all their lives, these tiny heroic things. But the girl beside me was different. I had seen the way her breathing hitched before she jammed the knife into the bone. She must have done this trick before. Many times, maybe. But still she feared the knife, and fearing it, went ahead with the trick anyway. Whence had come that bravery? Whence had come that pure faith in the miraculous?

That it would happen again when it had to? You can keep it, she told me, if you like. She gave me a glass bottle to carry it home in.

That was the first time I fell in love. I do not know why her father never let her perform, except, perhaps, that it is not the sort of trick a crowd would pay money to see. It went too deep for that, aye, it cut the watcher and the performer both. She could feel the knife. Her face went white with the pain of it. But still she did it. In the end it could not last between us. She loved the road, the wide open spaces, and she would not have been happy if she had stayed in Selkirk.

My father didn't stay long after he told me the story. The frost had begun to settle on the fields. It made the stones glisten, hard and white as baby teeth. He seemed exhausted, shy almost. He gave me a look afterward like he was testing what was between us, wondering if it was strong enough to hold in the face of the things he had said. I had no answer for him. But afterward I stared at the two glasses, his and mine. It had been some time since there had been need for two of any-thing. Thinking this made me feel small and strange and alone, out there with nothing but a bit of tin and timber between myself and the darkness. But perhaps that has always been the way of it. Small comforts are all we ever have. A skin of rime over a freezing lake, a thing we might pretend is solid earth, if we want to.

That night as I tried to sleep, a memory came to me. There was a story I had been told by a man who worked for the MRM as a surveyor. He had spent time in the North. And the story he had told was about a woman from those lands who married a great hunter. On her wedding night, she went to strip away his clothes and underneath she found, not the flesh of her husband, but the rank feathers of a seabird. She could not love him. When her father came to take her away, a great storm battered their boat and flung her into the ocean. She clung desperately to the side of the boat, calling "Father, Father, help me in lest I drown!" But it was her father who would not let her into the boat. He hacked at her hands with his knife, desperate that she would kill them both with her struggling. This story haunted me as I slept, terrifying me by turns with its loneliness and violence, the salt taste of tears. There was betrayal at the heart of the story, but I could not fathom who had done wrong and why.

I woke in a sweat that drenched my nightclothes. The babe was crying. Without thinking I plucked her from her cradle and held her to my chest. I knew then that if I could not love her, then I must surely send her away. None would fault me for it, not even my father. She deserved love, she deserved love enough to feed on and fatten. If I was to starve her of that then it would be better to let her go. I could feel the seashell curve of her ear against me. Its smallness filled me with panic. How fragile she was! How easily crushed beneath my weight! What was this thing my wife had cradled within her? A marvel, an ingot, a dream in the darkness.

As she quieted, I touched the cornsilk softness of her white, white hair. There now, I whispered, and sleep. Her fingers curled around mine. I kissed their dainty bones, light, practically weightless. The sound of her breathing was like something underwater, struggling to surface.

THIS COULD BE YOURS

ANDREA BRADLEY

When Tom came home with a set of keys, Bill figured he'd invested in an apartment building or a StoreAll, a business with a guaranteed income. It was their retirement plan, after all. They were getting too old to eff around.

"Don't slag it till you've seen it," Tom said. So Bill hauled himself into the truck and drove off to his future.

Bill's future turned out to be a parking lot. The keys (to the office, Tom'd said) opened a booth not big enough to piss in. The view was a pothole ridden polygon of chewed up asphalt, squeezed between a Chinese food place and a methadone clinic.

Bill fixed Tom with his meanest troll look, the one that could knock the smile off a kid three blocks away. Tom fixed *his* meanest troll look right back at him.

"Wot," Tom said.

"*What*," Bill hissed. "What I want is an explanation. What I want is to hear you say you didn't just sink our savings into an alley off Dundas West."

Tom's fat lips curled up in a distant approximation of a smile. He opened his arms wide like the parking lot messiah.

"Charging tolls on vehicular traffic is in our blood. It's proper troll business, innit?"

In hindsight, it was easy to see where they went wrong. For one thing, parking lots were not proper troll business. Trolls were supposed to work in the shadows, under bridges and down wells. They were groping hands in dark recesses and faces in the window at night, a story to tell children before a warm fire. Before Tom sunk all they had into the lot, they'd gotten by on odd jobs, anything needing absurd strength or a hideous mug, which mostly meant *discrete* jobs. Troll jobs.

Needless to say, customer service did not come naturally to them. Neither did seeing their hand when it was an inch from their face, meaning that Tom had some trouble admitting he was wrong. He had a different theory about why the lot barely broke even.

"Taxes," he said. "If someone'd told me about the bleeding taxes, I never would've bought this place."

"What, you didn't think we'd have to pay taxes?"

"Look around you," Tom said. Bill looked. He saw the faded paint lines, the overflowing bins, the rats and users scurrying in and out like the tide. He saw grey rain falling on dull concrete, a few parked cars. He saw the same thing he saw every day of his life: a sad heap of nothing.

"There's no water, no power, no cops, no nothing. This place isn't even on the map. Wot exactly would make me think we'd have to pay taxes?"

For the dumber brother, Tom sometimes made a lot of sense.

For eight years, Bill and Tom sat in the booth, shoulder to shoulder, day and night, watching the paint lines fade. They made enough money to pay the bills and keep the rain off their heads, nothing more.

Life was bearable, barely, until the day that Bill saw the sign.

He was walking home from a shift at the lot, Tom-less for once, his surroundings streaming past him like white noise. He was thinking about the pork cutlet on its Styrofoam tray in the fridge, and whether the day had greyed it beyond edibility. He was thinking about his cast iron troll stomach and how eight years ago he wouldn't have worried about a little grey meat. He was thinking about how life turns you on yourself, when the sign hit him.

It flapped off a telephone pole and plastered itself like a dead parachutist, spread-eagle, across his face. Bill peeled it off, muttering appropriately. He held it out for the benefit of his near-sighted eyes.

Green hills. A flowing stream. An old stone bridge. Underneath, the words, *"This could be Yours!"*

"Wot the…" Bill said, slipping into his childhood accent.

He turned the pamphlet over, but that was it, a picture of a bridge in the old country. Thrown in his face. Bill's brows came together. He crumpled the paper in one fist and looked around. He was alone on the street. Young's Convenience was on his right, the bars pulled across the windows. Row houses leaned in toward the store like conspirators. Everything closed in on him, all concrete and cracked.

Bill walked the rest of the way to the sound of his own teeth grinding.

The pamphlet did not stay crumpled long. Bill tried to throw it out, but just thinking about that bridge set his veins thrumming with longing. He pulled it out and smoothed it on the kitchen table.

It was a troll bridge, he had no doubt. But did any of them still live that way? Hunched beneath a bridge in the miserable damp, waiting for something fat and meaty to cross. Tearing into fresh flesh, collecting coins, living off the land...

"Wot's that?"

Bill slammed his palm on the table.

"Come on, I saw it, dinnit I? Open up." Tom reached down to pull up Bill's fingers and then they were at it like ten-year-olds.

"Shove off!"

"Not. Till. You. Show it!" Tom pried Bill's fingers off one at a time and ripped the paper in two, dancing back from the table with his half held above his head.

"That's mine, now give it back." Bill reached, stumbling clumsily on oversized feet.

"*This could be YORS*'. You buying a timeshare, Bill? Without consulting yor own brother?"

Bill stared at Tom, at his misshapen potato nose, his mean eyes, the spit dripping off his fat-lipped, gap-toothed smile. He saw what people saw when they looked at him. A dumb oaf, good for nothing more than growing an ass and collecting cash from people too cheap to park downtown.

He saw his wasted life.

Not long after, the Chinese food place closed. Bill stared at the barred up windows, gnawing on a sheep rib, wondering what he'd do without $4.99 chow mein. Tom farted beside him. The hammy stench drove Bill out of the booth.

"I was eating," he protested. Tom shrugged and Bill threw his bone at the plastic window. Ventilation in the booth was subpar. Bill had at least ten minutes before the atmosphere in there was breathable again, so he set off down the block. He walked with his head down, like a bull, assuming anything smaller would get out of his way. And so it was that he nearly ran over the two women portaging their canoe. Luckily, his head was thrust so far forward that he saw the canoe floating below his nose before his body crashed through it.

"Watch it!" The girls stumbled sideways and Bill reached out on reflex, lifting the canoe off their heads.

"You're the ones with a boat on your heads," he muttered. The girls did the thing that humans do when they see him standing at full height. Their heads tilted back, their chins retracted and their eyes opened wide. Bill could see their thoughts like ticker tape running above them. *What is wrong with that man he is so ugly don't stare stop staring I need to stare if I'm gonna figure out how it's possible to be so. Freaking. Ugly.*

"Where d'you want this?" he asked, breaking through their circling thoughts.

One of the girls blinked, blushed, then stared down at her feet. "We're taking it in there," she said, pointing at a door in a red brick building that Bill passed at least once a day. A shuttered bank about two blocks from the lot, obsolete since the Instacash set up shop. He'd never given it a second glance. The other girl kept her eyes on Bill. "How are you doing that?"

Bill looked up at the canoe over his head, held in one thick hand. He shrugged, then lumbered through the open doorway. A stack of chairs stood at one side of the room. On the other side, a bar. Except it was nothing like the bars Bill knew. There were no amber bottles lined up, no smudged glasses stacked in puddles of water, no dusty taps jutting out. Instead of all that, there was one squat silver machine, with levers like arms sticking out and stacks of tiny cups lined up beside it. There were jam jars, filled with strange little pebbles that looked suspiciously like rabbit food. There was a wooden sign behind the counter that said, *"The Portagery. A Vegan Cafeatery."*

A sick feeling squeezed into Bill's gut. He turned around slowly. "What is this place?"

The girls' answer buzzed in his ears. He heard the word "espresso" and that was enough.

"Hey, thanks for helping with the canoe," one of them said as he shouldered past her into the street. "You dropped this." She pressed something into his chest and Bill grabbed it absently, breaking into a run as soon as he hit the sidewalk. When he reached the booth, Tom was standing outside.

"Drove meself out with me own..." He stopped as Bill doubled over beside him, breathing like a spent horse. "Wot's knackered you?"

"We...can't...stay...here," Bill panted.

"Wot you mean, we can't stay here. I don't advise going in there." Tom pointed at the booth.

"No. Coffee shop. Opening..." Bill straightened. "A block down. They'll drive us out like always. Best to move on before...you know what."

"A coffee shop. It ain't exactly pitchforks and torches." Tom squinted at Bill, his gaze dropping to his hands. "Wot's that?"

Bill looked down at the paper the girl had given him. Half a stone bridge looked back at him, with the words, *"be Yours!"* beneath. He shoved it in his pocket.

"Nothing," he said.

"Roight. Anyway. It won't last a day. Who's going to go there? 'im?" Tom pointed at a junkie bent under heroin's weight, the sole other occupant of their lot.

"Maybe," Bill said, anything but sure.

Within a week, the Chinese restaurant was a neighbourhood gut wound: a deep gash spelling the death of all its kind.
The old Polish guy who fixed deep freezers, the Korean rub n'
tug, the cabbage roll place – one after another, they all closed
shop. It wasn't long before the rats and users were replaced
by baristas and strollers. The bars came off the Chinese
restaurant and a sign went up.

Kikoga
/kik/ōgə/
noun
1. Kickboxing and yoga fusion classes.
2. An awesome workout.
3. Because sometimes you need to fight for inner peace.
Try two weeks unlimited for $20 and get a free bam-
boo neck towel!

A steady stream of tattooed twenty-somethings began to
flow through the lot, rolled mats on their shoulders, sipping
algae-green drinks in plastic cups and thumb-hammering
their devices. Bill watched them pass by the booth, grinding his teeth to powder. The owner of the kikoga studio
watched him back, eyeing the lot behind half-closed blinds.
Bill could read his thoughts as clearly as the coffee shop
girls'. When he approached the booth, Bill was ready for
him.

"Hey guys, I'm Todd." He stuck his hand through the little window. Bill thought about snapping it off, sucking out
the marrow, and throwing it back in Todd's face. Instead, he
waited until Todd retracted the hand, irritation flickering
across his brow.

"So, uh, you had this place long?" Todd asked.

Tom grunted. Bill stared stonily ahead.

"Ahh, listen. I'm going to speak from my heart here. You've probably noticed the studio's doing really well and as much as I think cars are obsolete planet-destroyers, we could really use the parking space. So, you guys ever think of selling?"

Bill looked at Todd, at his tanned skin and too-white smile. He looked at the arch of his eyebrows over his blue eyes and thought of bridges. He thought about punching those blue eyes black, one after the other.

"No," he said.

"No?" Tom asked.

"Huh." Todd made a sound through his nose, part disbelief and part disdain. "What are you boys planning on doing with it?"

"We're starting a farmers' market." Bill slammed the window shut.

"So wot yor telling me is, some fat farmers are going to set up shop in our lot and we ain't going to have room for cars neither? Have you lost yor bleeding mind?"

Bill wiped Tom's spit off his cheek. He put his hands in his pockets to keep them from knocking his brother. He found the tattered pamphlet and clenched it tight. Tom wouldn't understand, not if he took a year and a day to explain. It was no old country bridge, but the lot was theirs. Bill wasn't letting it go without a fight.

"First off, they're paying us. And we're not being run out. Not again."

"But you hate this place. You been wanting to sell since the start."

"Yeah, I hate this place. And I hate those skinny-necked, hairy-faced, grass-eating, know-it-all assholes even more. We're not being run out, not by them."

By "them," Bill didn't just mean the kikogis. He meant everyone. All the young professionals and new parents who were driving out the old guard. The first generation immigrants. The addicts. The trolls. They didn't come brandishing pitchforks and torches. They didn't burn. They were water, tearing at rock with implacable fingers. They were change, and above all things, trolls hate change.

The farmer's market turned out to be an excellent idea, at least in human terms. Sure, the lot was closed to cars every Saturday, but the market brought people into the neighbourhood. People who liked to buy arugula with dirt still clinging to it for three times the price of the boxes of triple-washed greens at the grocery store. In other words, people with money and cars. They came for the market and discovered kikoga and underground theatres and glass-blowing studios. They came back on days when the market was closed and they parked in Bill and Tom's lot. Business had never been better.

If trolls could be happy, then Bill and Tom were happy. Most days. Their newly found financial comfort meant nothing on Saturday mornings, when the soil grubbers began to set up shop. Tom was too offended to put up with any of it, so he spent Saturday mornings drinking lager at the Ukrainian men's club. That left Bill to keep watch.

The bee guy was always first to arrive, with his glass hive, jars of raw honey and $50 candles. Next came the bread, the microgreens, the artisanal flowers, bespoke fruit leather, and lavender popsicles. The goat always came last. It was free range, which meant the goat lady had to set up a pen, with a fence and bales of hay for it to perch on. She sold things off a table. Bill wasn't sure what because he didn't trust himself to get close enough to find out. As soon as the goat showed up, Bill's day was ruined. He'd spend the rest of it in a stare-off with the yellow-eyed beast, daring it to come out of its pen. By lunchtime, he would be shaking and sweating.

Their tenth Saturday in operation, Bill was so focused on the goat that when a knock came at the window, he nearly put his fist through it.

"Oh!" A grey-haired man stepped back in surprise.

Bill breathed deeply. He ground his teeth and opened the window. "What?" he said.

The man fidgeted, clutching a basket of apples. "I was just wondering what you're selling."

"Selling," Bill said.

"In your booth here. I didn't see a sign so I thought I'd just ask."

Bill stared at the man. He was thin, a herbivore from the looks of him. Probably one of those people who ran for no rea-son, with little juice packs strapped around his waist. Bill thought about the days when people used to run from *him*. When they didn't have time to pull on tight shorts and lace up shoes and find a portable snack. When their screams would set his heart singing, the blood rushing to his ears, and he would laugh. They would both laugh, him and Tom, because the faster the people ran, the sooner they could feast on every last blank-eyed goat in their yard. They didn't have to scheme to come up with money or food. They had nothing to trade for it. They bullied. They took. They killed. Bill was a troll. It was time he started acting like it.

"I'm not selling nothing," Bill said. He spoke so quietly, the grey-haired man leaned in to hear. He peeled back his lips in a hideous grin, showing every last one of his fifty-six teeth.

The man ran.

Everyone ran.

It took five minutes for the lot to become a scene of chaos, greens flying, tables upended, fruit mashed to pulp beneath dozens of feet. The only one who didn't run, who couldn't run, was the free range goat.

The police investigation went nowhere. A monster, some said, or a gun-wielding giant. Todd said he saw the whole thing from his studio, but his story made just as little sense. He said it was the parking lot guy, as if one guy could cause that much destruction, as if a man could devour an entire goat in the time it took for the first responders to arrive, leaving nothing but a bloody spine attached to the skull. The Bloody Market, the papers called it. For a week or so, the city was on high alert for wild animals, and then time buried it at the bottom of everyone's newsfeeds. Whatever happened, it worked out for Todd. The kikoga studio got its parking lot.

As for Bill and Tom, the farmers left enough money in their booths for them to retire a second time. They found work on an Italian ocean liner that would take them home. Bill was surprised to find that Tom had kept his side of the torn pamphlet. He taped them together and stuck them above his bunk. At night he gnawed on a goat leg, staring at the old stone bridge. The troll bridge.

THE MERMAID AND THE PRINCE OF DIRT

ANGELINE WOON

In the end, he threw me into the Ottawa river. He leaned over the sun-kissed railing, looking for me, burning his hands and a band of skin across his chest as he did so. He tells me he still aches from the burn. I tell him it's because his heart's on fire.

He says he saw a cold glint of silver in the water. It could've been light reflected from the scales of my fishy tail. Or it could've been his imagination: the light, as well as the splash he had heard, coming from a long way down.

Cars roared behind him, supplemented by the high-pitched, angry hum of the metal grids, a teeth-grinding noise characteristic to the Alexandra Bridge. They drowned out the placid lapping of the river beneath. His internal seas crashed against his head, broke in his gut, thudded in his heart. I was gone.

He was supposed to join me; just one leg over the burning railing, then the other, bringing along the rest of him, and, lo and behold! A kingdom of magic awaited.

But then came dizziness. The river was too much for him, too deep, he thought.

The summer sun bid good day, and he lost all chance of finding me in the darkening water. He mounted Moby and drove on to our empty home.

Spare some change? Thanks. Hey, wanna hear the rest of my story?

Home. Could be anywhere, couldn't it? Doesn't have to be a place; you can feel at home with someone, or yeah, an idea. Wild, huh. So long as it's like, a bubble you can sorta sink into...

Anyway, growing up, my sisters and I were nomadic; we travelled from hunting ground to hunting ground according to season. We didn't set up shop. We didn't root ourselves to anything. That wasn't what the tails were for.

Some people get a sense of belonging when they're in a group, among family. My sisters did, they loved each other. I was the odd one out; the youngest fry – a big surprise to my mother, I can tell you. I got left behind a lot.

At times, I lagged on purpose. I thought elder siblings were like sand, ya know? They got everywhere, like, in my face, on my nerve, and in my way! Great Poseidon, the ocean was crowded with big sisters and their inane chatter. Oh, look at my mother-of-pearl, look at my hair, look at...

It was enough to make me gag.

I'd often stick my head out of the water just to get away. Pretty soon, I learned how to hold my breath in air and to climb on rocks like seals. I'd look at the sky, the birds, and the waves. I wondered what was there, far beyond the ends of the sea. My sisters told me it was Land. Well, Land seemed static. Dead. It made me wonder what a world is like without movement. Scary. But yet, I was drawn to contemplate it, time and again on the rocks.

One or more of my sisters would show up eventually, once they figured I was lost. They'd yank me into the water by my tail, like I was some naughty little seal cub, then they'd fall on me like sharks at a feeding frenzy: "You've made us late, the whales will be gone and what would we eat, huh?" or, "What if someone saw you from the boats? If they catch you, we'd never get you back." Nag, nag, nag, nag, NAG!

Why won't they leave me alone? I thought. But that wasn't their way – and geez, were they ever set in their ways. We're mermaids, they said, we stick together. We hunt and eat as one, or we're the one hunted and eaten! It was all about survival, man. Tooth and, er, more teeth. Nature stuff. In any case, my sisters would never abandon me. It was the one thing they had going for them.

After a while, they got tired of stopping everything just to look for me, so, to prevent me running off on my own again, they assigned two siblings to follow me around. These two took it as punishment. I did as well.

In revenge, they mocked me, asking me if I were looking for a prince on the rocks. Oh, a prince wouldn't care to fall in love with *you*, they said, and swam circles about me. That puzzled me, because as far as I knew, princes were food, no different from whales and sharks. Why would I want a prince to fall in love with me?

I asked, "What is 'fall in love?'"

They twittered and laughed at me for being a silly little know-nothing fry. I bet they didn't know either, heh.

Oh yeah, in case you haven't caught on? I'm a real mermaid. Half-human, half-piscine – you know, *fishy*. For real, not like those girls who wear plastic things to the pool to get away from men, tying up their legs like that. A real, honest-to-goodness mermaid with a tail.

One time, there was a behemoth of a fight between a kraken and a whale. My two prison guards, er, sisters, were distracted. That gave me an idea, and faster than a squid can squirt, I was away.

Unfortunately, they caught up to me. I realized then that if I wanted some freedom, I was going to need a better plan. I had to go somewhere far away, somewhere they wouldn't want to go.

I'd been thinking about land for a while, and been tired of my sisters for longer than that. But more importantly, Something had happened to me, Something good and fascinating that I couldn't understand. All I knew was that I had to go on land to find out what it meant. And the only person who could help me do that was the sea witch.

Ironically, it was my sisters who had told me about the sea witch in the first place. Stay away, they cautioned, from those shallow waters. In particular, they warned, do not under any circumstance go near that rocky outcrop.

. But why not, my sisters, I had asked, my eyes wide open, my lips trembling.

With ominous tones they told me that there be a witch with powers to take away my tail and turn it into legs. They had shuddered after saying that.

I asked them what legs were and they said, little fry, don't ask silly questions.

Flaming fishballs, they were so stupid. I couldn't wait to get away from them.

It took some doing to get away from my guards. I had to wait until we were hunting near the sea witch's domain. Like before, I took off, but this time, I headed for the shallow waters as quietly and quickly as I could. They spotted me leaving, but once they saw where I was heading, they milled about in fear and confusion. I headed for a hole in the rocks, covered ominously by fronds of vegetation and bones – it was obvious what the place was – and shouted to the sea witch, "For half the length of my hair, keep me hidden from my sisters' sights, so that we may bargain further."

I still can't believe that worked.

Anyway, I told the sea witch I wanted to walk on land. I told her that I wanted to see what it was like, if it was a dead thing, or if it was alive, like the sea. After all, there were things that came from there, that floated about upon their boats.

The sea witch heard me out. She sucked on her talons for a bit and stroked her gills. Then she laughed. I thought she was going to tell me to go away and not talk about silly things, the way my sisters would, but she grabbed my tail like she was going to spank my butt. And, she pulled – that nerve, you know, the sensory one that tells you where you are when you're in the water? Oh, you wouldn't know about that. Imagine if someone went and stuck their talons into your back and snagged your spinal column. Yeah, now you get it, haha, so, she pulls and she pulls and... She did this thing, and, it was like I had a big fucking zipper running up me, splitting my tail in two.

That's how I got my legs.

Damn right it was painful. It hurt so fucking bad that after, when she stuck breathing bags and tubes into my chest, and sewed up my gills – look, you can hardly see the wounds on my neck – I didn't notice the pain as much. That's how much it hurt.

She smacked my ass. Told me to get going. So I toddled out of the water into a shitty little seaside town, stocked with oily men smelling of dead fish. I must have been in shock, because it took me a while to notice that that bitch, the sea witch, had taken my voice! She *had* said there would be extra payment later on for services rendered, but I thought it would've been standard stuff. Tradeable items, like lice off a great white, the eye of kraken, or the life of a prince or something. Easy payment plan.

Only, it wasn't.

Speaking of princes... I met this guy at the corner grocery store, where I watched him grip, knuckle-white hard, the handle of an empty shopping basket. He seemed to be building a philosophy of toilet paper. I didn't blame him. Man just wanted something cheap, so what did furry creatures with glassy eyes, like mounted fish, have to do with wiping ass? Which of them should he trust? Soft or strong or supreme, all kinds of sibilant words just for a sh—

Anyway, everything goes down the toilet in the end.

"Tough call, isn't it?" I broke in.

His gaze travelled down. There I was. Girl in motorized wheelchair. He had a glum sort of face, like an escargot missing its shell. I've seen happier, less-confused faces on a flounder. Well, he was like that before I showed up! Could've been the toilet paper, or, more likely, the lack thereof. Could've just been his face.

"I'd get the one with the kitten. No, the other one, about to get flattened by a piano. That's it. The usual price is a fucking joke, but it's on discount at the moment. A good catch, if you ask me. Toss me one, please."

He passed me a pack of the (temporarily) cheap, but soft, strong, and supreme toilet paper. I saw him hesitate, then take one for himself.

If I had known then that he had just set himself up for a week of breakfast at St. Luke's and dinners of mac 'n cheese from the food bank, I would have discouraged him. But apparently, he tells me later, my "eyes like seaweed twinkled at him in expectation" and he felt he needed the fancy toilet paper as a conversation piece. What a sweetheart.

Anyway, I told him my name, Annalee, and asked him for his.

Liam.

"Like the prince? Not even half of one? Haha. Joking. I have a thing for princes," I said. "You see, I'm a mermaid."

Bastard left me on aisle 8. So I powered up Moby – that's my wheelchair, recently overhauled with new batteries and tires, and man, that baby could do up to 6 mph on a straight, clear aisle. Too bad the aisles weren't exactly empty. Toot toot. Schools of fish can dodge me, why couldn't humans? It was Saturday afternoon, and there were the usual line-ups for taking away our money, so I caught up to him three laden shopping carts and four full baskets away from freedom.

"Mermaids love princes," I continued, as though he hadn't, a moment before, bade me a hurried goodbye. "We pluck them out of the water, when they're drowning."

He shuddered and took a half-step away. I should've toned it down maybe, but she who drops the trident hath not cod for dinner.

"Sometimes we rescue them even when they're not drowning, maybe having a pleasant little swim out in the sea. Some of us try to snag princes by actually causing them to jump into nasty waters. Sirens, you know. Totally unethical bitches. Can you swim?"

Great Poseidon's seahorses, what a loaded question! I found out just how loaded, much later, along with everything else.

At that point though, Liam merely stared, for the longest time, at the *Old Farmer's Almanac*, sold beside the payment counter among the candy, gum, and blazing tabloid lies. The cashier rang up two cartloads of groceries before he responded. It was like I wasn't there.

He unfixed his eyes from some celebrity's cleavage, or maybe it was the roast turkey on *Canadian Living*, and told me that, no, he did not swim. Then he chuckled. A rather alarming prospect after all that gloominess. He said – don't you laugh – that he walked on water during winter.

OK. So *I* laughed.

(Liam says my laugh is like an otter's bark. Like the ones he saw during a school trip to the Biodôme de Montréal a long time ago. Heh.)

"Oh, Liam," I said. "Why do you want to walk on water? You should swim in it. I can teach you. You'll be one with the waves. It doesn't matter if you don't have a tail. People swim all the time without tails. Though, I admit, tails are nice things to have."

I must have looked at my legs then, wistfully, and with great longing. I can't remember, because we'd reached the cashier and busied ourselves with packing and paying. I lent Liam a quarter because all he had in his pocket was fluff and expired bus transfers.

Liam says my otter laugh and that look of longing when I looked at my legs made him stay with me the rest of the afternoon.

But I'm getting ahead of myself. Let's go back to when I first got my legs. There I was, fresh out of the sea. Walking, yes. On land, true. But I couldn't speak, I couldn't sing. Bet you didn't know that a mermaid's life, her very survival – escape from predators, the control of great beasts during a hunt; life and death stuff – depends on her voice? On her siren song? You did? Huh. Good for you.

Well, it didn't matter anyway, not in that town. People treated me good there, despite being a stranger. Not sure why. Anyway, while I couldn't sing or speak, I still had a mouth, right? I used it. For what? Geez. Use your imagination.

In that town, I could also dance. I danced like I was in water still, sweet and slow, in and out like the tides. Liquid. Ah. And all that while, it felt like I moved on burning, freezing, diamantine sea urchins. I wasn't used to it, see? I wasn't used to having feet.

I danced, made some money, and as soon as I could, I went looking for somewhere else to live. Somewhere more alive.

Don't ask me how I ended up in Ottawa.

Liam, who had also stumbled, somewhat confusedly, into Ottawa, found out about the scales the first time he ran his hand under my skirt, up my thighs, across sand, across broken shells, rotting seaweed and driftwood, across the desolate beaches of my legs, polluted by an oil slick.

"It's not as bad as it feels," I said. "I've got mild ichthyosis vulgaris." Why did I say that? I'd already told him I was a mermaid, it sounded like a fucking apology. Maybe I was just nervous. We'd known each other, what? A month? A week? Um, wait – it was less than an hour.

His roving hand returned to port, innocent and flaccid of intentions, and he reached for the toilet paper, still in the plastic bags beside the couch.

I got mad. "You're not going to catch anything, you dick. It's a genetic skin disorder. If I don't moisturize, my skin turns to scales." It's not a disorder. It's my skin. My gorgeous, scaly, mermaid skin.

He pulled far, far away, out to sea, where the big ships sailed, his with a broken mast.

"Useless dollar store crap moisturizers." I grabbed Liam's hand and placed it somewhere slick. I gripped firmly and leaned over to glare at him. "Make up your mind. If not, see if I put out next time."

He made up his mind. And, I might add, didn't regret it. Then he chose that moment to muse out loud that all in all he had considered it quite pleasant, despite the faint odour suggestive of fish. It reminded him of sea scent.

"Say what?" I asked.

He said, you know, smells like the hand-washing liquid.

"You mean the stuff that's not quite blue nor green, but teal?"

He supposed that was what he had meant.

"That weird blue-green globby thing that we're supposed to believe will sanitize our life? The one we get from the dollar store, in bottles where the labels have pretty pictures on them mimicking expensively designed bottles, so we can pretend we are better off than we are?"

Er, yes? He asked if that was a problem, the scent. Women were all like that, weren't they? They smelled like the Atlantic, he said.

The Atlantic! He hadn't been near that body of water, nor women either, it would seem. Rivers and canals, ye-es. Lakes and ponds, ye-es. He was of the royalty of dirt, born of farmers who harnessed freshwater (which was anything but fresh by the time they're done with it).

"Sea scent, my briny ass," I said, ignoring what he said about women. "The people who make this hand-washing crap, the ones who name the things, have they actually been to the sea? The sea smells like salt and dead microbe shit. Even under water. That's not sea scent. It's high fantasy."

He was forced to agree with me. After all, he wasn't a fair judge. He had never seen anything as grand as the ocean, he said. Never anything that undulated away into eternity.

He had never *been* grand, this prince without land.

But he was, ya know, kinda *my* prince.

You want to know what made me want to come on land in the first place? I said already, I saw Something and couldn't understand what it was.

Wait. What? You think…a prince on a fucking boat? For fuck's sake, who gives a fuck about princes and their fucking Olympic yachts? I bet they learned to swim in their fucking Olympic pools, building their fucking Olympian muscles. I could wait forever and never have to rescue one, thank fucking Poseidon. Unless he had cramps or something. Or a norovirus. And then I'm not sure I'd want him.

OK, sure, I was sort of dumb before. I thought princes were food (maybe you don't want to go too deep into this?). But after I came on land, I found out they were men. Still not impressed.

Look, mermaids are pretty democratic beings. The individual is only important because they add to the group. Got that? No? Whatever. The key is that we don't elevate ourselves with land (don't have it), money (also don't have it) or titles (laughable and related to the previous two).

Now, a real prince, I think, is the sort of person who exudes unadorned kindness. The real shit, not sorry-ass stuff like giving patronizing handouts… Say, you wouldn't happen to have a smoke on you, would you? Chocolate bar? *Coffee Crisp*! My favourite. Thanks.

Where was I? Right. The Something. You seriously really wanna know what it was I saw?

Here goes. I saw a man on a lobster boat in the Bay of Fundy. He was red and flabby, and swore to God Almighty. He dropped traps into the water, chummed with fish guts – herring, it tasted like – mixed with molasses in a little net. So, you know, I fell in love with the idea of men on legs, all because one of them bought me lunch.

Lame, huh?

For some reason, that made me think of Liam. He'd grown up on a farm, you know. He used to swim a lot, as a kid. To swim, he had a choice of many ponds – each dominated by fearsome fertilizing geese that messed up everything in their path, including, on one memorable occasion, Liam – and the Lake.

The Lake was pretty, and made up the cottage-country part of Liam's otherwise remote hometown. The water was clear and clean. Thus, Liam saw everything, and was terrified, that time his legs had been caught by the skeletal branches of the ghost grove that lay beneath.

He said he had visited Heaven. He was sure of it. He just didn't recall much, not even memories of china dogs. The china dogs came into it because the feeling of going to Heaven was much like that time they had gone to Simcoe when he was three years old, to visit Great-Aunt Jane, famous in the family for her dog figurine collection. All he remembered from that trip had been butter tarts. Try as he might, he could never remember the china dogs.

After the Lake, Liam no longer swam and was averse to bathtubs. Showers were barely acceptable. He avoided skating, even, because of the possibility of falling through the ice.

All I could think of, when he told me his tale, was that he must have seen something really awful in Heaven, to fear it so. I don't think he saw china dogs, they're nice.

Anyway, he'd seen Something too, but I don't think it make him feel as great as my Something made me feel.

My voice? Of course, I can talk now. Look, I mentioned sisters, right? They're – what would you call mermaid chauvinists? Mermaidists? Fishists? Those people, anyway. They believe that a mermaid isn't a mermaid without her siren song. I mean, for me, the song is a survival tool I carried with me. It was a part of me, not all of me. To them, the song was everything. The song was more important than the backend. You know, the tail? They couldn't stand it (swim it?) that I had done gone given up that beautiful singing voice of mine.

A short while after I got my legs, when I was still dancing in that awful joint in that dinky little town, a few of my sisters got brave enough to go to the sea witch.

Before the sea witch, they beat their gorgeous breasts and pulled their lustrous hair (additional mermaid must-haves), and tried to make a deal.

The sea witch listened to them.

Said she, "Well, I reckon that if she wants her tongue back, you could return her legs."

My sisters loved the idea! It would solve their problems at one go. They came and told me the deal, thinking I'd jump at the chance. Thinking I was tired of being gawped at by horrible things on two legs, that I was tired of the pain of moving on legs.

But I wasn't going to dance forever, that was just for money to get out of town. And sure, the legs still hurt. But otherwise it felt so right, especially when I walk about bare-foot in dirt. It made me feel at home, for once.

So I signed at them, "No fucking way."

Had my own plans, you see. I was going to find my own happy ending.

So I did leave that no-name town, ending up somehow in Ottawa. And I met Liam on aisle 8, and he, the silly guy, said to me he wanted to take care of me. I was like, what? I told him I could damn well take care of myself, I didn't need another sister. He got rather upset about that, and sulked about for a bit. He said it was what people do for each other when they like each other.

"Is that love?" I asked. Honest, I had really wanted to know. He clammed up and I couldn't get any answer about that point from him. I thought, well, what's the harm in giving it a try, maybe I'd figure love out. So we moved in together.

We shared an apartment on the third floor of a high-rise, in a building that used to house junkies, where, once upon a time, those driven beyond desperation would fling themselves off of the Brutalist balconies, leaving behind a legacy on the street below. Things were different now. People weren't driven to such desperation, only to the kind of resignation where they sit about, yes, in one piece, but hollow and with empty eyes. I don't know. Maybe things were better in the old days – we had more heart.

The people who lived in our building had bedbug bites, cats, dogs that looked like pit bulls but were said to be boxers, and Yorkshire terriers that may as well have been clones, the way they yapped and looked alike.

The place swarmed with construction workers, because the new owners wanted to fix it up so they could double the rent and attract a better class of people. Not us, in case you haven't guessed. We were both on disability, and while the place wasn't exactly a turreted castle, at least the elevators worked...most of the time.

Who am I kidding? It was a cloaca pile.

The balcony made up for the inside, and was wide enough to fit the wheelchair. I loved sitting there, listening to seagulls scream as they followed the stream of the street, looking for – who knew what? Fish that swam in tar? Sitting there reminded me of those moments of peace away from pesky elder siblings.

Sometimes, Liam came out and sat with me.

"I feel like I'm on a high rock over the open seas," I said to him once, with my eyes closed. "I love the feel of the wind in my hair. I love the sun on my skin, but not too much, because I burn. Doesn't this make you happy, Liam?"

To sum up his speech: he replied that happiness was never much of a consideration for him. Money, or the lack of it, made up his mental state. Further, he seemed plagued with the fundamental inability to believe that such things as joy existed for the likes of him. Others, perhaps, but not Liam. Because Liam was the boy who went to Heaven, and the man who could almost, but not quite remember it. A lot of work went into chasing the memory of something profound day after day, not knowing if he'd recognize it when he saw it. Every time a potential Heaven pops up, the klaxon goes off in his brain, lights start flashing and people yell at him with advice. The people in his head, that is.

He suffered the repetitive drumming, thumping, grinding construction that drilled into his head. Drilled so that his brain split open to the world, side-to-side and front-to-back. Rat-a-tat-a-tat, said the jackhammer. Rat-a-tat-a-tat, said the man in the yellow hat. Rat-a-tat-a-tat, said my man one day, through gritted teeth, in the throes of his agony.

And he reminded me that on that day, we'd just been to the office of the provincial disability support program. The well-apportioned office, whose carpeting did not smell of cat dander and stale beer, had a wall-to-wall painting which to me, was a metaphor for the frenzy and violence that followed a whale hunt, but, after prising apart the artist statement, seemed to be about the painter's revelational relationship with his addictions. Same thing. All Liam saw was a migraine.

Further, the case worker, some new lady with carmine nails and a suspicious smile, had stared pointedly at my legs, saw that I couldn't be faking it, looked disappointed (I swear she did), had then turned to Liam and asked, "What's wrong with you?"

Judgemental bitch. You won't last long. And hey, you've got lipstick on your teeth. Nyah.

It had bugged me that she only saw the wheelchair, though really, she wasn't the only one. Can't tell you the number of times I wanted to yell, "Lookit me here. Here! I'm a person," but anyway, that's another story. At least she didn't give me any shit over my cheques. It bugged Liam that she gave *him* trouble. So he was a bit grumpy at that time. I got it.

But I asked him, "Don't you believe in fairy tales?"

He asked if I meant a happily-ever-after. Because if so, no. If I'm talking about love, he's not too sure if he knew how to do *that*. He wanted me around, wanted to take care of me, but what was love? Heaven in a butter tart?

However, he said, he was moved by my sense of conviction, and that my faith "shone from nacreous eyes, with a fervour reminiscent of the saints depicted on stained-glass windows" so he'd think about it. I think he was a little high from the painkillers.

Maybe I was a little high too, or maybe I was irked by his bitterness – I mean, I had to put up with all that shit too, and I was trying to be happy – because I said, "Humans fall in love because they have souls. Mermaids don't have souls. When we die, we don't go to Heaven or to Hell. We go back to the sea. We become the sea. Whadaya think about that?"

He looked thoughtful, and a little cross-eyed, and asked what mermaids do for love.

That made me laugh. I barked like a cute otter.

"Dearie, mermaids don't love each other. We just get born, eat and shit, fuck and die, and turn into sea foam. Sea foam, for Poseidon's sake. What's sea foam but whale sperm or something."

For a moment, his eyes cleared. He said that it seemed that regular people, those without tails, did the same thing. He wasn't too sure about the sea foam.

Another week went by. He was high again from the painkillers. He said maybe the sea foam thing happened to regular people too. Who was to say that it didn't? Who was to say that the afterlife wasn't a wave, beating fanatically upon the shores?

Sea foam. Sea spray. Weird glowing globs of waterless sanitizers that smelled of teal hand-washing liquid. Sea spray that smelled of dead microbe shit.

That was what was waiting for me.

I don't know what made me think my sisters would leave off easily. They had wanted me back, even though I'd showed them the finger (maybe it would have been more effective if they'd understood what it meant). They still thought they could get me to trade my new legs for my tail and song.

The attention was touching, but no way was I going back. I'd just got enough cash to leave that gloomy town, and my future was sparkly.

Now, in the stories my sisters would have killed my prince. But, haha, I didn't have one at the time, the lucky dog. My sisters went back to the sea witch.

The sea witch, she said, "Nice hair, sisters. Give me that. All of it."

My idiot sisters protested. The hair was important too.

The sea witch sighed. "OK, give me most of it. But it won't be enough, because now I want the legs, too. I'll be nice. Just half. Your little rebel can keep the other half, either the left, or the right, or cut off at the knees. I don't care. Your choice. Have a good one."

Truth is, I didn't give a shit about singing again. Or heck, talking. Walking takes you places. But you can't argue with people like my sisters. They know what's best for you, get it?

One day, they showed up with their hair in bobs and pixie cuts, and sang to me until I fell asleep. When I woke up… Voilà! C'est no legs below the knees. You know what they said to me? They said, "It hurt you to walk anyway."

Bitches.

I had thought that Liam and I were solid, like iceberg… No, that's not quite right. Too brittle, too cold. We were more like the earth beneath us, warm and, well, earthy.

The pain came suddenly. All over. One day I was fine, the next I looked in the mirror and what I saw there was like a shark unravelling in formaldehyde. I began to understand Liam's migraines, how he behaved the way he did sometimes due to the pain, because I too wanted to blame everyone for my sickness.

Couldn't pin it on a god, too far away and I had no soul. My sisters? Blamed them for everything anyway, but they too were too far away, in the past and locality, so it didn't stick. Poor Liam received the brunt of my accusations.

I thought, maybe, it was all about love. But what did I know about love? I mean, come on, I once thought lobster bait was part of love (help yourself to this metaphor, can't stand to look at it myself).

All I understood about love was Liam's daily kindnesses to me. The stuff that made me re-evaluate my definition of princes. He did simple things, like rearranging items in the apartment so I could reach them without having to depend on someone all the time. Like raising the floor of the balcony, so I could get my wheelchair out there without a problem. Doing the laundry, changing the sheets…

I chafed at some of the stuff he did. I didn't want to be babied. But then he pointed out that I had to do the cleaning, the cooking, and the grocery shopping when *he* was sick. There was a synergy between us, he said. It all worked out in the end.

Or it did for a bit anyway, until I got sick. Then I wondered, maybe that wasn't love.

I thought, well, mermaids didn't have souls, right? Humans did. Mermaids lived in water, humans lived on land. What if, to live on land properly, to be human, one had to have a soul? And to have a soul, one needs to love, or be loved. Since mermaids didn't love, I had to depend on the other.

Why was I still sick then? Was it because Liam didn't love me enough? He said those kindnesses of him were a sort of love, and maybe the only kind I could get from him.

I wondered then if maybe Liam didn't love me enough because he wasn't properly motivated. Maybe he didn't actually think I was a mermaid.

Did he buy the explanation that my scaly skin meant I was a mermaid, and that being a mermaid, I had no soul? Or did he just think it was a skin condition that other humans have? That I sat all day on Moby because of some accident that had happened to me, and I had blocked it out from trauma? That I'm making everything up as some healing fantasy? That I, too, had a version of Heaven and clamouring voices in my head?

Somedays I thought maybe I did.

So I couldn't even hate him for thinking that.

When it got really, really bad, I went to Liam in the shower, while he was naked in mind and body, so that I could hear, really hear what he thought about me being a mermaid.

I showed him a handful of hair, that had come out of my head in clumps. "Look at me. I don't have a soul, nothing to tie me to this place. I need love, Liam, and you don't love me enough. Look."

"I thought mermaids don't love either way," he said.

"They don't come on land either."

"I give you that. So how would loving you help?"

I explained my reasoning, and his face was an unfeeling blank. I gasped like a fish out of water, whether from anxiety, or my sickness, I didn't know. And in the midst of all that, a thought came to scare me further. It may be too late to be loved, to get a soul. It may be that the only thing that may help is the sea witch, but... I had a prince now. What would be her price to make me whole again?

"Let's go to the doctor," said Liam.

"No, there's a long wait time."

"We've put it off long enough. You're really sick, Annalee. They won't make you wait. We'll go to Emergency."

We didn't go to Emergency. I went out to the balcony and he finished his shower. He took a long, long time. Odd. He'd always been afraid of water before. There were no seagulls that day to take me away, so I thought about Liam's lack of reassurance.

"Why didn't you tell me you loved me?" I said, to my slightly damp prince, when he finally came out.

"How am I supposed to answer that? If I said I loved you enough, and loved you more than enough, here's proof that I don't." He leaned forward and brushed my cheek, and ran his hand through my hair. He sat back, staring at the dull lock of hair in his hand.

"It's my sisters' fault. If they hadn't done what they did, this wouldn't happen," I said. "If they hadn't chopped off my legs, I would grow into the land. I'd be able to ignore the call of the ocean."

"Not everyone has legs, Annalee."

"Did they come from the sea? No. So who's to say it isn't the reason why I'm sick?"

"I thought it was my fault," said Liam. He had his secret smile on. It was a sad smile.

"Oh, my God, the air is hurting my lungs," I said. "This is tearing me apart."

"I wish it wasn't," he said.

No one had spotted the madman in their midst. No one had seen anything, had done anything. Yet, in their horrific, heart-broken pain at my "death," they, the media, the public at large, ate up the news with ghoulish delight. They called Liam names. They wanted to bring back capital punishment, just for him.

Of course they were afraid. They did not want the same things to happen to them. Let one man throw his common-law wife from a bridge, and soon we'd all be screwing gay dolphins. Bye-bye civilization!

What gets me is that all along, they've always only seen the wheelchair. All of a sudden, I'm somebody?

Liam couldn't speak. He couldn't understand anyone. They probably sounded like seashells over his ears. I imagine he sat shackled to a leg of a recalcitrant table in a grey, grey interview room, listening to the sounds of the ocean he had never seen. They must have questioned him, in a loop, expounding clashing opinions and theories for a motive.

Disability checks? An accident? Murder-suicide pact, forgetting one vital component? Or just plain evil? Pick one, said the Good Cop, for the sake of a cup of lousy coffee. Pick one, we'd all like to sleep.

Just like TV.

You know, I saw it. I saw that it was going to happen. There had been a rapid succession along the street: a seagull, a lady on a bicycle with a red tuque, and a grey car.

I remember frowning, and chewing on my thick, plaited hair. I mulled over it for days. When Liam asked me what was wrong, I told him about the sequence and said, "There's a message for me. Whatever it is."

"I think it means that people use the street and birds fly over them. Now, if a squirrel had come by on a bicycle, and a raccoon in a car after hot-wiring it, I'd stop to think twice."

I glared at him like he was escargot marinating in garlic. "It's a mermaid thing," I said. "You wouldn't understand."

And how could he? A mermaid has mermaid thoughts. Seagulls were bringers of messages. Red followed by grey meant violent death, or maybe passion then peace. A small vessel followed by a larger vessel meant big things were going to happen. But I'm not an oracle, and I was all alone and playing at being human, so I couldn't ask anyone what it really meant. I had never before yearned to speak to my sisters, to find out what they knew. Was that what was making me so bitter all of a sudden? The realization that maybe I wasn't even mermaid enough?

All those people thought Liam had killed me, because they found out he'd dropped me into the river. They thought that way because that's how things happened on TV.

I think Liam agreed with them, the social media commenters and the police, because maybe he had TV thoughts too, notwithstanding the Heaven hiding in his head. Perhaps he nodded for their benefit, nodded, like a seabird bobbing upon the water, placid on the surface, frantic paddling beneath. Poor Liam.

Could I blame him for abandoning me? He was scared. I don't completely understand that feeling, it was one I never had the luxury of exploring.

I've always ignored warnings, those from my sisters, or from well-meaning folks who only saw the girl in the wheelchair. To be fair, sometimes you need to listen. But sometimes, life isn't about staying safe, but about doing stupidly risky things – the kind of things that makes life worth living.

But I can say shit like that, cos, "I'm a survivor!"

I'm not saying *you* need to go down the difficult path. There are all kinds of dying, ya know?

He tried to cheer me up. He tried to show me that he loved me. He wrapped me up, nice and warm in blankets because I was shivering; and because I asked him to, he took me to the wide pedestrian walkway on the Alexandra bridge. We stood and looked at the boats on the river beneath. It was late evening, and the sun was drifting, lingering, waiting to set. Few people were about.

"Those are gorgeous," I said, pointing. "There, in the water, the rocks standing tall, like pillars. Tufas. I see them, rising out, reflecting – red, white, and gold. Oh, hear them sing. A song a wind chime would make if it was made of shale. Listen, when the waves touch the pillars... Listen. They're just rocks, you know. Beautiful rocks. They're not alive, but they sing. They don't have souls, do they? How weird would it be if they did? Where is my soul, Liam? Where?"

He didn't reply with words, but I felt a slight squeeze on my hand. We stayed there together, me on Moby, staring through the bars, Liam leaning against the railing, until it got a little darker, but the sun stubbornly clinging to day.

"They're not really there, are they? The tufas," I said. "I don't know if I've ever seen tufas. Was it a dream I remembered? Is this all a dream?"

He shook his head. "No, there aren't any tufas. And no, this isn't a dream. I don't think."

"Oh."

"Where," he said softly, "is our happily-ever-after?"

"We're not there yet."

I was lying, he knew. And the voices in his head, what were they saying? Where was that Heaven I wanted for us? Suddenly, I realized that my time there, on land, was over. I couldn't continue on, not in that form.

"Liam, if you love me, you'll throw me into the river now."

"Don't even joke about things like that."

"I'm not joking."

"I love you, Annalee. But..." He looked at the river beneath.

"Tough call, isn't it?

"This isn't like choosing toilet paper," he said.

"You don't believe that I'm a mermaid."

"Annalee, I do believe you. I've been with you all this while."

"Yes! You cleaned up after me, and took care of my dinner, and made sure I was happy."

"Well, then. I don't understand."

"You let me *pretend* to be a mermaid. See. You can't deny that. You want it to be true too. You don't want this world to be the kind of pathetic place that prints images of soft kittens on plastic packages so that people are persuaded to buy pulped dead trees. You don't want to believe in the sad truth of a girl in pain. You want to believe in something other than the mundane. You're chasing, chasing, chasing after your Heaven, like a dog chases his tail, but unlike the dog, you're afraid to catch it."

"I don't know what you want. Do you want me to believe you or not?"

"I want you to believe the right thing for the right reasons. I want you to believe, truly believe, that I am a mermaid. Then maybe you'd find that this, *this* life is your Heaven, and that it's OK."

"How the heck do I do that?"

"Drop me into the water. Watch me revert to type." I was pretty sure that that was what would happen.

"You're crazy!"

"Help me, Liam. I can't do this by myself."

"No. No! Why are you—?"

"Help me. Please. And…come with me." It was selfish of me to say that, but I wanted him with me. I suddenly realized that I couldn't do without him in my life. I'll keep him safe from the sea witch. There are other things to trade with besides princes.

Liam didn't speak for a while. Cars rushed by at intervals, thump, thump, thumping, the high-pitched humming of the bridge, hurting.

"What is the alternative?" he asked. "If…if I don't do what you say. What else is there?"

I smiled at him. "In another world much like ours, you are a sane, evil bastard. That makes me a sick, pathetic fool. Believe, Liam. Let me go into the water, and then come with me. I'll take care of you."

"How? How would that work?"

"I…I don't know. Just come with me, please? You didn't know how to take care of me either, before, but you figured it out."

"Yeah, I did."

"The sea witch would help. I know she would. Here's an idea. You could give her your memories, the ones of Heaven. She'd be able to get them out. She likes shit like that. And you don't really want the memory, do you? Wha-daya say?"

"Um. How do you know you'll become healthy again? A healthy mermaid, I mean."

"I don't know if we're ever healthy, I mean, what with sea lice, fungal and bacterial infections, and squids, octopi and careless turtles, and don't forget the oil spills and plastic, and—"

"You know what I mean!"

"Look. I don't know if I'd go back to what I was. Maybe it's straight to sea foam for me. But I know what will happen if I stay. So...Liam?"

"OK."

He took the blanket from my lap and folded it with care. Then he picked me up from Moby, with no effort at all. I'd lost so much weight. I hadn't even realized. I clung to Liam, and he held me tight.

"I'm going to miss Moby."

"Annalee," said Liam, his voice urgent as he clutched me painfully, "What if I can't love you because I don't have a soul? Is that why I'm like this? Maybe that's why you're sick. I'm not human enough."

"My dear, dear prince," I murmured in his ear. "In that case, maybe this is the best for both of us. We're both of a kind. I am sea foam. Soulless I may be, but I love you."

He lifted me onto the railing. My truncated legs dangled over the water.

Now, it was time for our happily-ever-after. He held me and didn't seem to want to let go. I wriggled violently. "I love you, Liam."

And I was falling, falling, free.

He called out my name. He said he loved me.

There was a desperation to his cry. A ring of truth. Maybe, facing my loss, his heart opened. Maybe he thought I wouldn't be able to hear him, and that absolved him of his inhibitions. Maybe he found that he had a soul after all. Whatever reasons he had for saying those words, I knew he meant it. Finally.

Amazing how many thoughts you could cram into such a small, significant moment between a bridge and a river.

Still, he didn't come after me, not for a while. He tells me that in his cell he had wondered if he would have liked the Atlantic. Every day, during exercises in the yard, he would wonder what I was doing. Cavorting with other mermaids? Swimming with the dolphins? Sometimes he thought I had gotten sicker and died. He wondered if I felt as cold as he did, as he sat in that north-facing cell, day after day. It was so cold, he says, he could walk across the water in his paper cup.

I never got around to teaching him how to swim, so he worried about that, if he needed it in the Atlantic, or if it would come naturally. He learned to take longer showers, and the fear of Heaven that he had picked up as a child lessened in intensity, until one day, it wasn't there. In its place was the strong wanting to go to the sea, to be with me.

He wanted, he says, to walk on water, to fall into the water. He wanted to break upon the shores, like a giant heart beating, together with everything, with me.

He wanted to dissolve into Heaven.

OK.

Once upon a morning, dull and grey, there was a prison cell that faced north. In it, they couldn't find the man, Liam. Upon the empty cot, was a pillow, wet, wet with the sea.

TYNER'S CREEK

NATHAN ADLER

Oose-Tynuck splashed through the shallows at the creek's edge, the water sparkling in the sunlight, minnows running from his bare feet, pink toes gripping the rock and sand, water so ice cold it hurt his bones. That ache that slid up his calves and made them sing. The fount of the little stream was subterranean, which meant it came out of a cave under the ground where it stayed cold all year round, even when it was the height of summer. The closer you were to the springs, the colder the water became. Could have been frozen solid if it hadn't been in constant motion.

He scrambled up the small embankment on the other side – the short stride of his legs made it difficult to clamber back onto solid ground, but he managed it, just barely. It wasn't a very big river, barely a stream. A brook really. Too small to have a name. But Tynuck was still growing, and he knew that one day he would be big enough to step across this brook without even trying. His birch-bark bucket full, he struggled not to spill any of the fresh water he'd collected.

He'd gotten mud all over his leggings, but the sun would bake it dry, turn the mud to dust and then flake off with his every movement. The water sloshed over the top of the mkaak as he walked, the birch-bark *bucket* sewed together and sealed with bear fat and pitch so it was waterproof. It didn't leak, but it was still tricky not to spill any. The water was heavy. When it was flowing out of the rock, burbling nicely and sparkling in the light, it didn't look heavy. But as soon as he scooped out a portion it seemed to pick up a lot of weight.

The sun was hot on his face, and sweat beaded, even though he'd only made it a short span in the direction back to camp. A drop of salty water trickled off his forehead and dripped into the bucket. Ripples in the sheen distorted his reflection. *Eww, gross* Tynuck thought, *this water is for cooking!*

Oh well. He pictured the radiant smile that would surely be on his mother's face when he returned with his cargo. Sun bathing her in a corona of light, backlit so the frizzy split-ends of her hair caught in the light like spider webs. Aate would appreciate his efforts to fetch the water. She would be proud of him. He was seven winters old now, and he wanted to prove that he was old enough to collect water. She'd never allowed him to do so on his own before.

He wished there were somewhere closer for them to gather water, but this area of land was high in elevation and dry, lacking in streams, ponds, or rivers – with only a few marshy areas where the water was stagnant and not fit to drink. The springs were the closest source of freshwater on the plateau, Ghost Lake was too far. Tynuck didn't mind. He was a big boy now, and his mother trusted him enough to go to the stream to gather water by himself.

He paused to wipe the sweat from his forehead so more of it didn't drip into the bucket before beginning the steep ascent. It was a very steep hill. He noticed movement in the distance, and saw his omishoomeyan, his *stepfather* coming down the hill toward him. A cold fist gripped Tynuck's heart. He wanted to squirm back into the shallows like a snake, hide in the reeds and bulrushes. What did *he* want? Tynuck's face felt hot, not from the heat, but like a medicine bundle squeezed tight, forcing the contents into a tighter and tighter space until the bag ripped open. He almost dropped the birch-bark mkaak, but managed to lower it gently to the ground without sloshing too much over the sides – though the waves rocking back and forth continued to make the bucket dance.

Chaboy didn't like him. Gshkaadiz. *Angry*. Chaboy was always angry with Tynuck.

No matter what he did, he could never do anything right.

"Why are you so stupid?" His stepfather towered over him. Then speaking in a soft, kindly voice when his mother came back, "You're a good boy, Tynuck." Tynuck could see through the fake kindness. It was a lie. Chaboy was only kind to him for show. He turned nasty again the second they were left alone. His face was a mask. It changed so quickly no one else saw it. They were all fooled. Only Tynuck saw through the mask.

"Chaboy doesn't like me."

"Oose. Don't be silly," his mother said. "Your stepfather is a good man, a good provider. He wants to be your De-De. It will take some time getting used to. That's all."

But Tynuck knew this wasn't true. Chaboy hated him. His eyes squinted, crinkled around the edges, lip curled back from his teeth like a snarling dog, face twisted up. Lopsided. Like Oose was something that disgusted him. That was his true face.

"There you are." Chaboy came close, teeth gritted in a smile. Chaboy actually seemed happy to see him for once. Tynuk didn't trust it, that smile. Feared it was some trick. His legs felt weak.

Chaboy grabbed him by the shoulders and began shaking him. Then shoved him down. *Oof!* The strength with which Tynuck hit the ground forced the air from his lungs. It didn't take much. Chaboy was a grown man, and Tynuck was still only a boy.

Tynuck scrambled to his feet and turned to run, tears stinging his face, making his vision blur. He ran toward the nameless creek but Chaboy caught up with him in the shallows. Grabbed Tynuck's foot as he ran, making him fall, so he tripped face-first with a splash, half of his body submerged in frogs' depth water. The sand and grit of the river-bottom imprinted into the flesh on his palms. He kicked and struggled, but Chaboy was too strong. Tynuck's head was forced down. No deeper than a puddle, but bubbling like a kettle when he screamed. He couldn't breathe! He couldn't breathe.

KAAW! KAAW! KAAW! KAAW! KAAW!

The weight of Chaboy's hands on the back of Tynuk's head let up for a moment, as his stepfather turned to look at the crow, cawing like crazy up in the branches of a tree. Tynuck gasped, drawing in air frantically now that he was able to raise his face from the stream. Chaboy was trying to kill him!

Tynuck didn't want to lose this brief opportunity to escape, in case the attack resumed. He had to get away. He had to get away. Chaboy had palmed a river-stone, his body turned, and his arm extended as he aimed for the noisy bird up in the tree. Tynuck crawled, scrambled to his feet, taking off toward the embankment, and toward the village. He didn't look back to see if Chaboy had hit his mark.

Heavy hands wrenched Tynuck back, and his legs went out from under him as momentum carried him forward. *Oof!* The back of his head banged against the ground. Hard. He was staring at the sky again like an upended turtle, the wind knocked out of him. Chaboy's face swam into view above him, smiling, mask-less, looking down at Tynuck upside down. There was a large rock in Chaboy's left hand. Tynuck raised his arms to protect himself as the large stone descended toward him, growing larger as it filled the field of his vision. He turned his face away, every muscle in his body clamped tight, preparing for the blow.

The rock hit him. The world went red. Then black. Blood flowed.

Chaboy lobbed the bloody stone into the creek, gathered the boy in his arms and carried the limp form a few yards away, placing the body where the banks were steepest, and the shore littered with stones – much like the one he'd used to cave in the boy's skull.

He'd never liked the little shit. Always whining and crying to his mother, and stealing all her affection from him. He had no intention of rearing another man's son. And as long as Aate had her dear little boy, she was uninterested in bearing more children. He wanted to father his own sons, strong sons, not be tasked with her onaabeman's child. The child of her deceased *husband*, like a ghost trailing after.

The blood flowed down over the rocks, co-mingling with the waters at the river's edge, where it slowly became diluted, curling away like a red ribbon of smoke. So much blood flowed from his skull, it was shocking that so much blood could flow from such a small form. He'd killed many things. All manner of fowl and game, he was a skilled hunter – elk, moose, deer, beaver, marten, porcupines, pheasants, duck, geese, loons. His family was never short of meat. This hadn't felt all that different from killing any other animal.

Except the blood was surprising.

The way it flowed, as if the boy's heart still pumped, as if the blood still circled through his network of veins, branching out from his head in a series of red rivulets, the stream tinged brackish brown.

His mother had placed far too much confidence in the boy. He had fallen from the bank and hit his head on the rocks. An accident. Nothing more. A sad occurrence, but not exceptional. The land was a dangerous place.

In a nearby tree, that damned crow cawed again, and Chaboy looked up at it. The sole witness to his crime. Aandeg tilted his head, looking down at Chaboy, and crowed, a long cawing sound like a rattle. Chaboy rinsed his hands in the water of the cold, cold stream, chilling his fingers to the bone. Then turned to collect the bucket, washing the ground where he'd hit the boy, spilling out the contents – the boy's hard work – to clean the blood and brain matter. The evidence washed away from the site where Oose-Tynuck died. Then Chaboy layed the birch-bark bucket at the top of the steep embankment.

The boy's body lay bleeding out into the creek below. The network of blood extending out from his head like horns, like the antlers of some beast. For a moment, the atmospheric pressure seemed to shift, as if Chaboy had dove into Ghost Lake, and the weight of the surrounding water was pressing in on him from all sides before lifting as he rose. For a moment, he felt stretched and distorted, before reality reasserted itself around him. It was odd the way the blood continued to flow, long after Tynuck's chest had ceased to rise and fall, rise and fall, his heart surely stilled by now. But the flow was continuous, and if anything, seemed to blossom and grow as he watched. Probably owing to the fact he'd positioned the corpse head-first on a slope, so all the fluids drained downward. That was probably it. The flow of blood would slow once all the fluids had drained out.

He walked away, to finish his hunt, pleased. With that unpleasantness accomplished, he would now possess all of his Aate's affection, and she would now be more amenable to bearing his children. He would have sons of his own to raise.

After a successful hunt, Chaboy returned to camp a few hours before dark, carrying slabs of moose-meat on his back in a bundle of flesh, a young bull-calf tied together with intestines, the way people carried their children in a dikinaagan, a *cradle-board*. He passed first through the forest and then through the high-ground plateau, where the stands of trees clustered together like islands here and there on the more open areas of the plain.

By the time he arrived, their summer-camp was already in a disarray. No one was working or going about their various tasks and occupations. The boy's body had no doubt already been discovered. Aate had been the one to send Tynuck to the creek bed to fetch water after all, so she would have known where to look when he didn't return.

Aate was sobbing, her head on the shoulder of wizened old Maingan, scrawny as tree-branch limbs.

Maingan squinted at him.

"What's all this now?" Chaboy asked.

"Where have you been?" Maingan asked. Aate abandoned Maingan's shoulder to throw her arms around Chaboy, her face streaked with tears, the long strands of her dark hair sticking to the moisture on her cheeks.

"Bizaan. *Shh-shh-shh.* What's this?" he soothed Aate, and then turned to Maingan. "Hunting." Chaboy lowered the bundle of meat to the ground at Maingan's feet like an offering, tied tightly together with sinew and intestines. Maingan's eyes widened at the sight of the dead calf. Nostrils flaring. It was against proper decorum, disrespectful even, to hunt such young moose.

"He's deeeaaad," Aate wailed. She spoke more, but her words were incoherent, too choked by her own despair.

"Who's dead?" Chaboy asked, looking toward Maingan. He let some of his actual apprehension show on his face, to give his question legitimacy. The lines on Maingan's face softened.

"Oose-Tynuck. He never returned. Aate sent one of the other boys to fetch him from the creek. He must have fell from the bank. Hit his head. Tynuck's dead." The low continuous keening from Aate was getting on his nerves. He patted Aate's dishevelled hair and held the woman tight.

"Oh my dear. I'm so so sorry." He turned Aate away from the wizened old Medicine Man and led her to their roundhouse, whispering comforting nonsense words in her ear. Following the unfortunate passing of Aate's late onaabeman, her *husband*, Chaboy had moved in shortly after the 12 moons of her mourning had elapsed, in order to help console her through that difficult winter. Maingan stood his ground, watching them as they walked away, face creased with lines, as if there were more wrinkles etched onto his face than there had been yesterday.

Nosy old man. When Chaboy emerged from his endaad, his *home*, the old man was still waiting.

"I need to speak with you."

Chaboy nodded his head soberly in assent. These were terrible times, terrible times.

"I've instructed everyone to leave the boy where he lies for the time being."

"Why?" Chaboy asked, finally allowing some irritation to slip through in his voice. "We need to prepare. He deserves a proper funeral. It's cruel to make his spirit wait."

"I'm going to hold a Shaking Tent. Something about the boy's death doesn't feel right. I need to speak to the manitous." And for the first time, Chaboy felt a twinge of real alarm. He didn't want the old man talking to his *spirit guides*. Who knew what they would have to say? Not that he had much faith in Maingan's abilities – always predicting the weather – incorrectly. Stupid old man. Chaboy nodded again, unable to come up with a suitable reason to delay the ceremony.

"I've already begun fasting." Maingan turned, and it was Chaboy who watched this time, as the old man walked away.

Chaboy watched the construction of a small burial hut being built around the child's body, to ward off predators, though this would not be the gravesite. Oose-Tynuck could not be moved until after Maingan had finished fasting for three days, not until after the Shaking Tent ceremony. Funeral rites were being delayed, put on hold for this foolishness.

They had had to move the little house back from the edge of the stream, not once, not twice, but *three* times, as the level of the waters continued to rise, mysteriously, as there had been no rain. But since the source for the spring was subterranean, something else must have been causing the flood. Swelling the small creek like winter snow melt, until the waters rose far above their normal bounds.

The little creek had become a river. Trout leaped from the waters. New life congregated on the banks to drink, to grow.

Tynuck's Creek was now teeming with all manner of animals and plants, fish, fauna, and fowl. This change did not go unremarked.

Someone was stationed with the body at all times. A fire was lit. Family, friends and community members came to put down tobacco and say their prayers.

"It is weird." The old magician shook his head. The corners of his mouth turned down as he overheard talk of others from the village.

"Isn't it marvellous?"

"It can't be a coincidence."

"The swelling of the stream. The child's death. They must somehow be connected."

"Maingan is correct in calling for a Shaking Tent. He is wise."

Standing on the embankment, the image of Tynuck came to Chaboy's mind: skull caved in, the blood continuously flowing, branching out like a fine network of lightning arching across the sky. Valleys filling between the peaks of the rock, interminably swelling the waters. Foolishness.

The boy would have bled out and the flow would have stopped days ago. Chaboy was tempted to rip apart the little wigwam perched at the edge of the engorged stream, to find out. But he knew this was folly. There was nothing to see. Unless he wanted to look on the boy's corpse, surely beginning to rot by now in this heat.

On the third day of his fast, Maingan would perform the Shaking Tent. And then they could be finished with all this foolishness.

Far below the tiny stream carved a silver ribbon through the forest. This was one of Euwen's favourite places in time to visit, back when the water was fresh and new, and the ice had retreated from the land. Wings extended, Euwen skimmed across the tops of the trees. Some of their leaves had already begun to turn as the light shifted, despite the continuing heat of the summer. He pulled his tail feathers forward and flapped his wings to bring his body into position as he came to alight on the branch of a tree overlooking a small creek. Barely a rut in the ground really, though the slight tinkling of sound was soothing. The wind blew and attempted to ruffle his feathers though they all remained in place, not a single feather gone astray.

Best thing in the world to be was a crow. Better than the two legged or four. Or the sleek-scaled fins of the things that lived in the rivers and lakes. Though Euwen knew Nimosh, *Dog*, would disagree. Euwen wouldn't trade his wings for anything. Two legs, fins, or four. Two wings were better than four legs on any day of the year. If Nimosh had wings then maybe he would agree. Maybe he would understand. The best thing in the world to be, is a *crow*.

Aandeg.

That's what Anishinaabeg call him. Though he preferred to think of himself as Euwen. The king had named him. No one else had ever thought to give him his own name before. He puffed out his chest, and refolded his wings so they were nicely tucked. Euwen tilted his head, watching a two-legged Anishinaabeg gathering water in a birch-bark pail. They were wasteful beings, always leaving food behind. Though rarely willing to share. Greedy two-legged beasts.

Euwen watched the two-legged child struggle across the small stream, carrying the bucket heavy with water now. Maybe the child would leave some scrap behind, some morsel. Wasteful beings.

Euwen loved them.

This is why he often he visited a withered old man, who was king for a brood of roosting crows. But that was far in the future from here. Euwen was always willing to accept an easy meal. Though he knew most humans were not generous. Far from it. His beautiful blue-black plumage was mottled with a splatter of white where bleach, tossed maliciously from a jam-jar, had sprayed his feathers. Not all humans were so generous, or kind; some were outright malevolent. And greedy. Greedy. How he loved them. Wasteful.

But he'd learned to be cautious.

Another human appeared on the hill. It walked toward the young one. Euwen didn't recognize either. Friend or foe. Neither was the withered old man. The king. They were unlikely to feed him morsels of flesh, though they may leave scraps behind. Greedy. Greedy. Wasteful. It was worth waiting for a moment or two, to see what they would leave. His eyesight was keen. He felt sorry for the beasts below with their poor vision, blundering around in the dark, almost blind. And they had no feathers!

A commotion below. The wiigwas gourd, with its captured spring water was rocking back and forth, sloshing, threatening to tip over. The grown man had knocked the young one to the ground. Was holding his head, face down in the water. KAAW! KAAW! KAAW! KAAW! Euwen called out in alarm. The man turned, stone in hand, and the boy scrambled to escape. Euwen easily evaded the projectile. But by the time he had resettled on his perch, the boy was once more pinned by the weight of his attacker. The man raised a rock above its head. Mad beasts, always throwing the world into chaos. Disturbing the balance of the day with their violence. Dumb beasts. KAAW! KAAW! Euwen called out again. But it was already too late.

The young one was dead. Head smashed in with the rock, brain and bodily fluid leaking out onto the ground. KAAW! Upon hearing his call, the two-legged Anishinaabeg again looked up at Euwen. Their eyes met. Brown-black to red. Too much of the whites of his eyes showing. Eyes too large. Pupils dilated to gather in the light. *Darkness. Madness*, Euwen thought. He was glad he wasn't human. Irrational beasts.

Murder! Murder! Euwen called. KAAW! KAAW! He launched himself into the air, pushing off with all his might for maximum lift-off from his perch, extending his hind limbs for propulsion, and then flapping away from the creek and the mad gleam in the human's eye.

Worst thing in the world to be was a human. Useless beasts. Their original instructions came from Wanabozhoo. No wonder. Such foolishness. Such a one as that, the *Hare*, with a forked head. It was his fault for making them. Anishinaabeg. For-nothing-man. Such flawed beasts.

The best thing in the world to be is a crow. No matter what Nimosh said. Allowing himself to be *owned* by humans. What kind of creature did that!? Worse than a Boozhence, that *Cat*.

To the king! To the king! Euwen flapped his wings, headed to the withered old man who was the king of a murder of young male crows. They roosted in a dead cherry tree. Far, far away from here. He would find refuge there, refuge from the mad eyes of the two-legged beast, and his bloody deed. Far away from this time. Far away from this place. Flying direct, the way only a crow can fly, if a crow only knew how. Across time as well as space. Not every crow could master this. Not like Euwen. The First Crow. Crow of Crows.

Euwen had been around for a long time, and he would be around for a lot longer. What was distance to a time-travelling crow? He could traverse great distances in space as easily as time. Why other beings felt obligated to live by so many rules, Euwen didn't understand.

Euwen had briefly considered pecking at the brain matter of the dead boy, but dismissed the idea. The mad one would surely murder Euwen as well, if he got too close. It would go to waste. The brains. Poor thing. He could always come back later for a taste.

To the king then! To the king!

If the king could listen, Euwen would tell the tale. The entire murder would know of this murderous deed, before the end of the day. He'd raise a ruckus, he would. A murder. The others would hear of this. His brothers. They'd always know to avoid the human beast, with the gleam of madness in his eyes.

He was no friend to fowl. No friend to the crow.

They gathered around, watching the tent as Maingan, the djessakid *seer,* began banging on his drum, and singing and calling to his manitous, imploring them for their assistance. Chaboy hated to think of what secrets they had to tell — though he had never trusted such things. It still made him shift, unable to sit still while the ceremony commenced. Maingan's high, ululating voice emerged from the tent, and rose to the stars which were just beginning to appear in the quickly darkening skies. Medicines were burned, and the smoke from those too drifted out.

The jiisakaan, the *shaking tent* was not large, a round-house just big enough for the old man to enter. Saplings of spruce and birch bent into a frame, and secured with more saplings of spruce and birch hoops. And layered with birch bark, so that once Maingan entered, the opening was sealed, and nothing of what happened within could be seen from the outside.

Various sounds were heard emerging from the tent as Maingan continued to sing and drum, sounds which could never emerge so perfectly from a human throat, and the small birch-bark enclosure began to shake as the spirits entered, shaking whether from spirits or from the fervour with which Maingan performed the ritual – first a growl, like that of a mountain lion, then a hooting sound like an owl, and finally a *cawing*. A cawing sound, exactly like that of a crow. A fist gripped his heart. Chaboy could hear the beat of his heart in his ears. *Lub-dub lub-dub lub-dub*. Thumping. Thumping, despite the raucous noises Maingan was making inside the tent. Even Chaboy was getting caught up in the ceremony.

The drumming came faster and faster, like the tempo of his heartbeat in his ears, and Maingan's voice came louder and louder and more urgent as the tent shook as if blown back and forth by a strong wind, though the air was still, and the tent was filled with a cacophony; the cacophony as of a murder of crows. Dozens of them must have been in there. Wings flapping, beating chaotically along with the drums, along with his heartbeat, and the djessakid's ululating cries. Finally, the tent came to an abrupt stillness. Silence.

Maingan emerged from the Shaking Tent.

He looked directly at Chaboy. His eyes were red. He tilted his head to the side. And let out one single rattling-cawing, like no human voice could mimic, so perfectly as to be indistinguishable from the real thing. Exactly like the sound a crow would make.

THE SHUCK

ANDREW F. SULLIVAN

After a while, you know how they died just by the smell.

"He left his watch in the sink. Filled it with water first."

The man did not kill himself. We wade through pizza boxes, rat feces, and empty cans of mushroom soup, the last few drops leaving behind putrid whiffs that complement the greasy outline where the body used to lie on the couch. The couch itself will be taken away and incinerated tomorrow. So will the clear plastic bags of congealed underwear, busted socks, travel magazines, and tangled extension cords. Icy vistas and soggy jungles splayed out on the floor. The smell clings to everything inside the house, a thin film of loss. Angela has already started to wash the kitchen walls with industrial soap. We will all stand in the shower for hours tonight, trying to wash it out. We will call people we love and ask them to remember things, anything really.

"A heart attack...at forty? No shit."

This is what happens when you are alone long enough. The smell is thicker and heavier than a suicide. If it's an apartment, the landlord usually calls us. He calls us because there is no one else to call. He calls us because the property is no longer making him money and the other tenants are complaining. If it's a house, it's the neighbours calling, the ones with the very high fences. There is a new smell they can't place – until they do. Someone reaches out to the family, to whatever shard is left over from an old Thanksgiving dinner that ended in a stabbing or a bottle of gin bounced off someone's head. An estranged uncle, a forgotten sister, a son who doesn't care what we do with the body, just clean the place out.

And so we do.

The van is parked out front, but there is no logo. We don't make a fuss. A crew of five cleaning out the dead, cleansing all the fallout from abandoned fathers, neglected mothers, and wayward sons. We find hard drives full of evil, folders of letters never sent, pictures of families that are more like fables. Every one of these homes is betrayed by its smell.

I usually deal with the human element. Anton and Dennis handle the biological hazards, the rats and roaches lingering around the edges. The cats who have finally tasted human flesh. The bats in the attic and the songbirds in the rafters. Angela covers the surfaces, the deep cleaning. Her fingertips are always pink. Sometimes at night, she holds them up to mine and I have to ask her if they're burning. She gives off so much heat in the dark. She is my furnace.

Caleb is in charge of sorting through what's left. He tries to find the pieces that haven't been ruined yet. Anything worth saving is passed along to the family members, donated or auctioned off somewhere. Free weights. Televisions. Jewellery and collectible *Star Wars* figures. The rest is thrown into the fire, any fire that will take it. He is sorting through mail and old photo albums when I pass him in the living room.

"Just a lot of nature shots, old fields, houses, pets. Is there a pet here, Tasha? Looks like there were cats and dogs before, but no one said anything about it. And I don't smell the shit."

"I don't either," I say. "I think just the tenant. Paramedics didn't notice anything."

The couch is lost. The body had been here for at least a week. I struggle through the stacked garbage bags up the stairs to the bedroom, cataloguing the mess to conquer. The previous tenant had taken to blowing his nose on the walls, arcs of fine blood now misted brown onto drywall.

I find what I am looking for huddled in the pink bathtub. Its presence chills the room.

Massive black paws dip over the side of the tub, a large head with floppy ears and wide black nose sniffs at the air when I enter the room. He doesn't always linger like this.

"Go home," I say. "He's gone."

The Shuck pretends it can't see me. Its thick hide rises and falls as it pants. Four hundred pounds of canine wheezing and snuffling, half-hidden by a shower curtain. Its fur is black and shimmering. Your hand can slide right through the coiled flesh. I don't tremble or flinch. I stand tall surrounded by the pink tiles. It is sated, for now.

"He's gone," I say. "You can't feed anymore."

The beast rises to its feet and stands almost above my waist. It bows its massive skull and passes through my white coverall, my jeans, my flesh. A cold wind.

It continues down the hall behind me and out through the wall. No one else can see it here. It walks through them without a sound. Its howl carried away by the breeze, by a conversation, by the rattle of the radio or someone's inner monologue reciting an argument.

It only comes when you are alone. Alone within yourself and all you carry.

A speck of dust in the air after the light goes out. A growl from below. And a smell.

When my mother died years ago, we all returned to the old valley up north near Sudbury, to the house filled with her face, our faces, all of them peering down from the walls to examine our red eyes and raw knuckles. You could watch my brothers ageing on the walls as you walked down the hall toward the bathroom. There was only one-ply dangling from the toilet paper roll.

The line for the wake stretched around three sides of the funeral home. The sea of hands passing, shaking, weaving, sweating in the summer heat. No smell of rot. A clean death, someone said and someone else coughed into their hand. I still shook it. I shook them all.

My brothers and I all stood in a line, Dad at the end. He didn't see the beast beside him, didn't hear it panting in the spaces between prayers and promises and weeping. She was only 57 when it came for her, the casket closed because he couldn't bear to see her, to deal with it himself. An infection in the blood is what the doctors told us, but they only shook their heads when I asked for more. There was nothing I could change. Nothing clean about it.

I spent the night in her old house, now his old house, alone, studying for exams, rewriting my name in the top corner. Tasha, repeated over and over until it didn't mean anything and the black dog stopped pacing outside in the hall. I knew then he was asleep and I could close my eyes.

The next day, walking through the graveyard, Dad caught up with me.

"You can leave if you want, you know. I can see you don't want to be here."

He didn't notice the heaving dog behind him, the beast almost as large as him. He couldn't smell the stench, old milk and wheat and blood seeping through its fur.

"No one wants to be here. It's a funeral for fuck's sake," I said, trying to walk away. He slipped a hard hand around my wrist, closed it tight. For years, I had only came back for Christmas. His hands were too familiar. They recognized the old cracks, the spots I couldn't cover. I was alone here. It was night again. Even under the sun, sweating through my dress, sweating in all the worst places, sweating in broad circles under my arms, it was night.

"I know your heart," Dad said, the words sputtering out of his mouth. "I know your heart."

I pulled away, kept walking, keeping pace with the crowd as we skittered between tombstones, toward the open dirt maw across the field. My brothers were pallbearers. My father did not give a speech, just tossed his dirt into the hole. And then I tossed mine. And then I left.

I know your heart.

That is what I do best. I leave.

Angela presses hot fingers into my spine, runs her dexterous hands over each node. She finds the spots where I carry the weight of the day, the families asking for our help, for our discretion, our ability to make their shames disappear. We are a service. Lethe Restoration. No symbol on our uniforms, no logo on the truck. A small website on the Internet. Discreet.

"Maybe let Caleb handle this. Give him some time on the phones. I heard that McCaul lady yesterday, I mean, everyone could hear her. Grief, whatever, that lady was a shit bird."

This is what they want most from us. This is what they pay us to do. To keep whatever secrets their dead leave behind. Or to mop up the mess when no one else will claim them.

"It's fine. It's part of the process. She'll pay just like everybody else. The dirty laundry has to go somewhere and she does not want to touch it."

"And that is why your neck is so fuckin' twisted, Tasha. Feel that. Here. Put a finger on that. Hmm? How does that feel?"

"Like a rock. A pebble."

"Yeah, under your skin, you think that's healthy? You think that's wise?"

I grunt and roll away onto my side of the bed. Our apartment is close to empty. Angela would call it minimalist. It is better this way – we are well-acquainted with hoarders. Twenty-seven years of *Entertainment Weekly* and *Newsweek* toppling over to trap an old woman in her powder room. A man with a fungal infection in his brain after every pot and pan and plate became a litter box. The woman in her mid-forties who drowned in her own diapers after the toilet stopped working. I don't miss stacks of books on the floor or overflowing laundry hampers. We only have two sharp knives in the kitchen and four plates. We only have what we need for now.

"You can't just roll over and pretend we're done here."

Sometimes I see the Shuck on street corners, heaving shoulders and thick black coat standing out under the sun. It is always following someone, always attached to a new victim. Even in the crowd, that person is alone, an island separated by some vicious currents beneath the water, things that we can't see. The Shuck can smell it, feeds off it, follows like a loyal pet, but the beast is something more like a parasite.

"But I just did. And we are done."

"You're an asshole, Tasha."

Sometimes the Shuck lingers even after it has all become too much, licking the ground around the splatter, panting beneath a length of rope hung in a closet or dangling from a shower rod. It lurks around the scene, its hide flashing between the bright warning lights and caution tape before the cause of death is determined. It struts down hospital hallways and barks at the windows outside church basements hosting support groups, asking them to have another drink, another swallow, another lurch into their veins.

The Shuck always needs to feed.

My dad's mother is the one who first explained the Shuck to me. A single tree on a moor somewhere on the island that she came from, a single tree and her own father dangling from a branch high up, so high no one could reach him from the ground. And a dog in that middle distance, pacing beneath the body and the puddle of shit beneath it. A big black dog circling the moor, silent and cold. She said they must have brought it with them, across waves and through storms. A harbinger, she said. A terrible bedtime story, my mother said.

A lie, Dad said.

"I am an asshole," I say. The fan keeps the noise of the street at bay, lets us believe we are the only ones in this place tonight. It keeps out the drunk screams and shouts on Saturdays, the cranking lifts of garbage trucks on Wednesdays and the nightly huff of the late bus hydraulics. It keeps out the doubt when you're alone and even the Shuck can't make itself heard.

"I know. I'm the one who said it."

I wrap my arms around her body, feel the heat push its way into me. I am cold, but I can feed off of her heat. I can thaw. She flicks her hair into my eyes, but I don't pull away.

"Yes, you said it. But I can be other things too."

I push my body into hers, my lips into her lips, and it is in this place that the Shuck cannot find me, cannot smell my breath, my loss, my loneliness. I know the Shuck is out there though, down in the subway somewhere, stalking a platform, waiting for someone, anyone, to jump.

⁂

The new job is a widow in a penthouse overlooking the city from a hill, staring down over the streetcar wires and specks of people down to the waterfront. Her son is the one who phoned a few days ago, claiming she refused to see him for the last two years after he married a woman from a Catholic family. She called him a Papist, called him a betrayer.

He seemed to genuinely miss her, but we don't offer a discount for legitimate grief. It was the doorman who found her while delivering packages after she kept ignoring the notices, the doorman who found her slumped down in the shower, curled into the fetal position. So many of them are found naked, stripped bare for no one. She left behind a thick brown stain on the bath mat. We parked the van around the corner to avoid making a scene.

"She really liked dogs, I can tell you that much," Caleb says, going through her hard drive. The rest of us are moving furniture. There is not much mess here, except inside the bathroom. The usual sex toys are tastefully arranged in the bedroom, primarily glass and steel. The reams of old letters disparaging relatives, husbands, the women on the charity board, all are ordered in neat folders in the living room. We ride up and down the elevator with old armoires and a writing desk from the 1850s. A moving van has been ordered by the son.

Anton and Dennis sort through the clothes and try to make themselves busy. There are no biological hazards here. Angela scrubs and scrubs away at the floor in the bathroom, a mask pulled up over her face. My white coveralls are spotless. I sit in the bedroom on a bare mattress, a few stains from old romances scattered over the flower pattern. I sit waiting for the dog I know should be here, to shoo it away once again. Sometimes it gets its fill before we arrive.

None of the others can see it. My mother never could. Sometimes I ask Angela if she feels the cold, if there is a wind cutting through her too, but she just tells me we're wired differently. She runs hot at all times. She always needs more fuel. A lot of rice and noodles in the kitchen.

"Where are you, you mutt?"

The smell of loss is still here, even without the Shuck. Thickest in the bathroom, even with all the cleaning. A stroke in the shower – it is so easy to die in the bathroom, so many unfortunate places to fall, so many hard unyielding surfaces to hit on your way down.

Only the kitchen is more dangerous.

"Where are you?"

When my phone vibrates, I hesitate. Another recluse in a tower somewhere discovered this morning, a floor littered with what looks like cheese, but could be pus. A dead man on a balcony waving to his neighbours. A noose in a split-level over the stairwell. A pile of used matches beside a bed, a bent spoon and curses carved into the bed frame. Fuck you all. It vibrates again.

"Hello?"

"Tasha? You at work?"

My brothers tell me he won't see anyone. They tell me he has the door barred against them, that he is cursing, that he still has that old shotgun, that the grass is growing up over the porch. The pheasants he used to raise behind the barn are tearing each other's throats out, feeding on the blood. The septic tank is flooding. They tell me he won't see them, won't see the doctor, won't see the priest. Dad doesn't trust the voices on the other side. He doesn't trust what he can't see.

My brothers stopped visiting after Mom passed. They took their cues from me. They heard enough to know enough, but they don't ask questions because they have circled the same drain. They are worried though, worried about a scene, a mess, their consciences most of all, I suspect. I listen to them rant and rave, their voices whistling past one another.

I wait for the Shuck to appear here, to shoo it away once again, to keep it from waiting outside my door. These confrontations keep us equal, keep the distance real and viable. Cleaning up the leftover people, the bodies. Just bodies. Keep people like Angela safe in the dark while I lie awake and count steps up to the roof of the building, metres to the ground, measuring the physics of impact and the probability of passing pedestrians in the middle of the night.

"What am I supposed to do about it? He gave up a long time ago. You know this. I know this. Fuck. Come on. Ancient asshole that he is, he knows he has nobody left."

There is a pause on the end of the line that says please, that asks for more.

Everyone is so hungry.

"I'll come up tomorrow," I say. Their voices fill the phone again, but I hang up.

Angela is standing in the doorway with a string of teeth on a wire. A necklace.

"She kept this in the water tank behind the toilet bowl."
A string of baby teeth.
"Throw them out."

The house lies at the floor of the valley. It was once painted blue, now faded to grey and distended with benign additions. The pheasant coop is quiet. They have all finished one another off or escaped under the loose chicken wire. I park my car out by the laneway, make my way through the grass that reaches up to my knees. My brothers stayed back in town, drinking, talking to each other in the back room of their shop, surrounded by half-built engines and retired motorcycles. Parts bikes, they say. We just harvest the good bits.

The old oaks behind the house do their best to block out the sun. I continue wading through the grass. My phone sputters on and off with reception out here. I can't rely on it to help me.

"You don't need to go, you don't owe him shit," Angela said last night. She wouldn't touch me, just sat in the corner of the room, the silver stilts of the chair wrapped around her legs.

"Just think of it as clean up then," I told her, packing a bag, ignoring her words, wondering where the dog was lurking. Lethe Restoration had another job that started this morning, seventy-five cats in a basement after the owner fell asleep forever watching *Law & Order*. Her walls were covered with portraits of Jerry Orbach. The floors were covered in scat and cats that could not go the distance. Animal control had been notified. It would be a joint operation.

I told the daughter she would not have to worry. We would take care of everything.

"And do you know when you'll be back?" Angela asked, her voice chasing me down the hall. "Do you know when this shit stops? Tasha. Listen to me. Does it ever stop?"

It doesn't. It never does.

I try the front door, but he has pushed a table or the couch to block it. The windows are papered over, fading headlines, fading faces. Reds turning to pink. Accusations in bold print. A sound coming from inside the house, the place itself sputtering to tell me nothing, nothing at all. The Shuck waiting here for me, its weight palpable, its cold present even in the summer. Its smell calling me like it called to Dad his whole life.

I smash a window with my right hand wrapped in an old T-shirt. The kitchen is empty. I tear foil and newspaper down from some windows to let in the light, find dust stacked on the counters, find coffee cups arranged in swirling circles on the floor. I kick them into the corners. Ceramic explosions to get his attention. A voice upstairs, calling for someone. Not for me.

The phone line has been cut.

Sometimes Dad would come home from the school, hands already clenched into fists. My brothers and I would sit at the window, watching him walk back and forth across the yard, watch him headed toward the hill above us, the elm watching over the house. I asked my brothers about the dog with him, the beast almost half his size, and they told me it was just a shadow I was seeing. But I knew what shadows were, knew that they stretched out at the end of the day. The dog did not stretch. The Shuck was not a shadow.

It sat beside him like a lap dog when I came home alone after soccer practice, when he sat in front of the television, yelling at the Blue Jays. It raised its head whenever I walked in the door. It was there when his voice would whisper in my ear to be good, to be patient, to be quiet when we had company. It paced the front yard when I came home late one night with Kevin Higgins, came running up to the car door, howling and barking at the full moon. My father had stood on the porch, swaying, cursing. I told Kevin to go home. To never come back.

"I know your heart," Dad bellowed from the porch, but I thought he was talking to Kevin.

"You can't scare me like that, you know. You're mine," his voice said as I fled to my room, the same room I head toward now, taking the stairs two at a time. Our faces still line the hallways, our growth charted by Sears two months before every Christmas. I hit twelve and I stopped growing. I hit twelve and the Shuck started to follow me too.

His body barely fits in my old bed. His beard is grey, thick, and full of old food. The bottle in his hand is empty. He has soiled his pants and isn't wearing a shirt. This is not new.

"Who said you could come in here?"

Kevin Higgins did not come back for me. My mother did not come back for me. She stayed in the ground, buried deeper than I wanted to dig. My grandmother saw the same thing when she looked out into the night. She told me the Shuck did not understand distance or faith. It did not know oceans or skyscrapers or touch screens. It only knew the weight inside you, how to be alone in a crowd of people, how to lie in someone's arms and remain entirely apart.

"You see him, don't you? Tasha, you see him, don't you?"

After the school didn't need him and Mom didn't need him, Dad tried raising rabbits. He tried raising pigs. He tried raising pheasants, but sometimes he put two males into the same cage, got stuck watching them tear each other apart, afraid to stick his hands inside. Anything to ignore the Shuck. It waited peacefully. It waited because that is what it was born to do.

"Yes. He's here."

The Shuck is in the bed with him, its massive body sprawled across Dad's stomach. It gazes at me with empty sockets, heavy breathing. Each exhalation chills the air between us.

"You were the one who knew."

I never should have told him I saw the dog, that I was like him. Dad followed me after that, his car parked behind mine at baseball games and bush parties. Lurking outside my door, asking me if I could see it behind him. What was it waiting for, he asked sometimes. Why were we bound like this together? His hand around my wrist, his other hand on my shoulder.

"Make it go away. Make him go away."

The Shuck climbs to rest its head on my father's chest, breathing directly into his hazy eyes, soothing his bright red brow. I don't move from the doorway. I don't speak.

When I told them I was leaving for school, he ranted and raved, slammed doors up and down the hall, kicked my brothers out of the house. My mother hid in the basement. The Shuck lurked behind him in the hallway as he held me up against a picture of his mother, as he shook my face in his hand. "You would do this. I know your heart. I know. It's a faithless thing."

The Shuck pulls itself further up onto Dad's body. All the windows here are covered with newspaper. I begin to tear the paper down, the light pricking at the darkness on the bed. The dog melds with the body. Dad's eyes begin to close. Dad's eyes begin to clear. He nods at me.

Soon, all I see is the Shuck in the bed. Its stomach is distended. It is full. It is waiting.

It has always been there.

I walk back down the stairs. You can always tell by the smell. Cancer. A heart attack. A suicide by pills, by knives, by rope or a bullet up and out through the skull. I smell the fear here. This is how he died. Fear clenching his throat until he could not breathe. Hate degraded until every shadow was a nightmare. Until every knock was reason for paranoia. There is always something coming for you.

I shove the kitchen table out from the door and step outside. The sun is still in the sky and I head toward the hill, the same one he used to pace before dinner. I head toward the highest point I can find, an open field with one old elm tree stranded among the hay. Behind me, I feel its presence, the weight of the Shuck plodding behind me. It has waited so long. It had skipped out on other meals to find me here. Toward the top of the hill, I gaze up into the branches, waiting to find bodies in the family tree, waiting to find someone like me.

At the top of the hill, I finally have reception. Angela picks up on the first ring.

"I need you to bring the van. The whole team. Tonight."

The Shuck walks up to me, nuzzles its head against my waist. Stale sweat and old urine.

"We're already on our way."

I run my hand through its black fur. I rub my knuckles between its ears. The Shuck gurgles and pants. The tree above me stays empty. The house remains a hole. I pet the beast's head again.

I can almost forget the smell.

WHERE WILL THE SEAS ROLL UP THEIR THUNDER

KATE STORY

Am I close enough? The microphone is built right in, is it?

Clever little technologies they have these days.

So, you're here about the Bell Island Boom. What made you want to talk to me in particular?

Smart? Well, odd, or eccentric, that's more what I'm used to hearing about myself. Or worse. But smart. I like that. It's true, I always have my nose in a book. Always was like that. I used to love reading those old science fiction paperbacks. They had a soft feeling, the pages, and a musty smell. Must be the cheap paper. Do you read much? I used to go into St. John's to get the books, because you couldn't get them here, not on Bell Island. Not a bookshop in the place, me love. My brothers called me "Bookworm," because I always had my nose in a book. Original jokesters, my brothers.

I was very fond now of books about Mars. Martians. There are so many of them. *Barsoom. Red Planet.* Have you noticed how we humans seem to recycle ideas? Like this idea, that somewhere and sometime on Mars there was this vast civilization. There's a sadness to our imagining. A sadness to it all, yes, nostalgia. Nobody does nostalgia like Newfoundland. *Take me back to my western boat. Let me fish off Cape St. Mary's...*

What's that face, me duckie? Don't you like my singing?

Take me back to that snug green cove, where the seas roll up their thunder...

All right, all right, I'll get around to the Boom. We'll start at the beginning. That's what your high school teacher wants, right, for the project? Names and dates and all that.

My name is Susan Fitzgerald. I was born in 1935, and...

Yes, 1935. I am eighty-two years old.

You look disappointed. Aren't I old enough? What's that? Someone told you I was a hundred?

Not me, son, I'm not a hundred. My. I haven't laughed like that in a long time.

You're here now, aren't you? Have another cookie.

1978, now, that's when it was. I'm old enough to remember that, certainly. How old do you think I was when it happened? Or aren't they teaching you math anymore?

Very good, I was forty-three. Still fairly ancient.

Well, it was very unexpected. For most people that is.

Yes, it was a Sunday morning. A lot of people were in church.

No. I was down on the beach. The Grebe's Nest. The Grebe... A grebe is a bird, a migratory bird. It summers here, raises its young, then travels vast distances, almost unimaginable, all the way over to Europe...migratory. Migratory... Your mother's from here, isn't she? From this town, from Wabana? Before her people moved to Portugal Cove, after the mine closed, yes I knew your mother. I'd have thought she'd have taken you down to the Grebe's Nest at least once.

I used to lie in the grass on the cliff tops overlooking the Grebe's Nest, grass and wild strawberries, roses and vetch, and stare up into the sky, and wait for ancient aliens to come get me.

I knew if I wished hard enough, they would come. Because I was special, chosen. Oh, yes, we seem to recycle that idea too, don't we? These ideas that come up over and over again, like being chosen… Does the mouse dream the dream of the cat?

The Grebe's Nest is over that way. No, we can't see it from here. It's a bit of a walk, up past the Number Two mine, along Carter Avenue and past Mr. Crane's place, then it sort of peters out into a path. It's a lovely little sandy beach, sheltered, and many of the rocks have fossils…

Didn't I say? Just that it's shaped like a nest. That's all. It's a little crescent moon of a place. Magical. A lot of people say that about it, not just me.

In the old days, miners living nearby used to supplement their income with some fishing, and they'd bring their catches into the Grebe's Nest. It was an easy place to drag a dory onto shore. But the cliffs are high there. I'd say over a hundred feet. They attached a cable and they'd send their catch up in tubs, to the top, pulled by a horse. Then row around and home again. You could get to a nearby beach just by walking, but that beach is rough and rocky, unsheltered – no good for boats. So in the 60s, after all the Bell Island mines closed, the miners had a lot of time on their hands and a lot of mining experience. Not to mention a lot of explosives. So they blasted through the point of land that separated the Grebe's Nest from the path. Maybe a hundred and fifty feet, the tunnel. No, I wouldn't exactly call it safe. Maybe that's why your mother hasn't taken you there. We can go after we finish talking, if you like.

Which we'll never finish doing if I don't stick to the point. Sunday morning, right. April 2, 1978. There was snow on the ground. I was down in the Grebe's Nest, and everybody else was in church.

Everything got quiet. The wind dropped. The sea even seemed to pause. And then, the air filled with this ringing. Like a tone, like a bell.

And then I saw something in the sky. It could have been a meteor, yes.

The Boom rocked the island, like an electrical shock. It shook the island, me duckie. They heard it sixty miles away. That's a hundred kilometres.

Electrical appliances burst apart. Blue flame shot out of electrical outlets. Animals fell over dead. Buildings were rent asunder. The explosion was loud, the loudest sound anyone had ever heard, louder even than the German torpedoes back in 1942… I'll tell you about those later, me love. No, I don't believe they ever found an epicentre to the explosion. All that was left – other than some dead chickens with blood seeping out their eyes and beaks, and some burnt-out appliances and startled people – were some holes in the snow, and two small hollows in the ground.

Mr. and Mrs. Bickford's wee grandson saw a great globe of light, hovering above the ground. But nobody else saw anything like that.

What's that? A beam of light? Yes, there was a woman over across Conception Bay swore she saw a beam of light shooting up from the ground. But I believe they didn't hold much by her testimony.

Certainly there were lots of stories.

You've heard about Mr. Warren and Mr. Freyman, have you? People got very excited when they came. Yes, that's right, from the Los Alamos Scientific Laboratory in New Mexico. They started asking around.

Because of their suits perhaps, people thought they worked for the U.S. government.

It turned out they were tracking…lightning superbolts, that's right, you've done your homework. They told everyone that they were satisfied the Boom had been a lightning super-bolt, and they went back to New Mexico.

Yes, it struck near Lance Cove. Pretty much the opposite end of the island from the Grebe's Nest.

No, I didn't speak to them. I was in hospital in St. John's. See this hand? Yes, that's a burn. I still can't close it properly.

How did it happen?

A burn, what do you think?

No, I never thought anything like that.

Who's that? Nikola Tesla, who's that?

I see. A doomsday device. But who'd develop a doomsday device?

Well yes, I suppose the U.S. or the Soviets might have had an interest back then… But who'd shoot a doomsday device at Bickford's old farm?

Ah, the iron ore. Yes, me son, Bell Island's riddled with it. Great blood-coloured layers of it all through the rock. It's heavy. Here, hold this in your hand. Heavy, isn't it? That's the iron makes it so. But there's a flaw in your theory, I think, me duckie. Iron ore isn't a magnet. Just try and draw something with that rock you're holding. It's *magnetic*, certainly, and it can be magnetized, but it's not in and of itself a magnet. So I don't see how it could inadvertently draw this superweapon and…

Hematite, yes. Really? It means "egg"? Now that is inter-esting. Very, very interesting.

You have got my attention.

How do you spell that? Oolitic hematite. Half a second, I'm going to write that down. O-O-L-I-T-I-C. And it means egg, egg stone? Goodness. Sedimentary rock, yes, you can see that. It looks different from the main island of Newfoundland, doesn't it? The rock around Portugal Cove is light and dark, gold and grey. Bell Island's red, rising steeply from the sea, tall cliffs. Wonderful soil, here. The coast is very regular, you'll have noticed. Almost no indentations or coves. It's a big egg shape itself. Almost like someone dropped it into Conception Bay from space.

But that's not an uncommon kind of rock here on Earth. You'll find it all over the world. Here, the bottom of the Aral Sea, Egypt, Saudi Arabia, Russia. And China, yes, China has a lot of the stuff.

They opened up the first iron ore mine on Bell Island in the 1890s, a surface mine. That's right, that's why most of us are here at all, the mining. They went down under the ocean, under The Tickle. Conception Bay. It's the biggest submarine iron mine in the whole world. It's as big as St. John's. Have you taken the tour? You should come down on my tour, I'm one of the guides. Yes, I am the oldest Bell Island Mine Museum tour guide. Although Mr. Carter's getting up there. Anyway, come on the tour. I think you'll like it.

We were one of the world's major producers of iron ore. Oh, yes, during the Second World War we had ships anchored here. When I was seven years old, they torpedoed and sank four warships, right there. Look out the window and you can see where they were anchored. Seventy merchant mariners lost their lives. And one torpedo struck the DOSCO iron ore loading dock. The Germans didn't mean to bomb the shore; it was an errant torpedo. But it turned out to be the only location in North America to be subject to a direct attack by German forces during the war. Even if it was a mistake, yes, it was still an attack. The whole island shook.

Where was I?

The Grebe's Nest.

No, I wasn't supposed to be there. I was supposed to be in bed. I wasn't a very good little girl; don't use me as your model. You know what Catherine Aird said: "If you can't be a good example, then you'll just have to be a horrible warning." She's an author, mysteries...never mind. Anyway, when the Germans attacked I was down in the Nest with a headlamp I'd filched from my father, who was a miner of course; almost everyone on the island worked in the mines back then. I was visiting my eggs.

Oh. The eggs.

I didn't mean to tell you about that.

But really, what's the harm? It's all going to come out sooner rather than later.

What do you think is the real reason two physicists came to visit us here on Bell Island after the Boom? You might know better than I. They were into a particular branch of physics as I recall, something...

Plasma physics, that's right. Something to do with lightning.

Yes, that makes sense; if plasma is electrically conductive, it responds to electromagnetic fields. Infinitely conductive, I see. Really? And it can form filaments and beams?

Could it form a passage?

That's a very interesting idea. Space is filled with it, is it? A network of currents that transfer energy over large distances...I see. The solar wind is plasma. It's the most abundant form of ordinary matter in the universe?

I think you have just explained something I've been wondering about for a long, long time.

Well, you will think I'm crazy. But you've explained it to me, how they can get from Mars to here. That's been the sticking point for me all along. But if they can ride this solar wind, like a passage…

My eggs. Or what comes out of them, anyway, that's what I'm talking about.

They weren't *my* eggs. I just called them that. Of course I don't lay eggs, what are they teaching—

Down in the nest. The Grebe's Nest.

You can see the layers of iron ore in the cliffs; there are all kinds of fossils. And there's this one place, about ten feet off the beach, that looks like a great big nest full of red eggs.

They're about the size of your head, yes, bigger than an ostrich egg. And they're red like the stone around them. In fact, you could just imagine they were strange egg-shaped formations in the stone, something that got fossilized back when the rock was part of North Africa, five hundred million years ago, and it was on the bottom of the sea.

They were there for anybody to see. I first noticed them during the war. I was only seven years old. But I always had my nose in a book, and I had a lot of ideas, and I noticed something that nobody else seemed to about the stone nest in the cliff.

Snow or ice never stayed on them for long.

I made myself a little tower of flattish rocks so I could climb up and touch the fossils or whatever they were.

The egg things were warm to the touch.

On the surface it looked like a hundred and two of them. Yes, me love, I counted them. I took a real interest in those stones. And when those torpedo attacks occurred, when the island shook, it seemed to me that for a brief moment, that nest of stones sent out a ruddy glow. But that soon disappeared, and afterward, I could never say for certain if it had happened or not.

I used to go down to the beach very often and visit my eggs. Climb down the cliff, down the old cable. This was before they blasted the tunnel, you see. I got a reputation for being odd. As if I wasn't odd enough already for reading books about Mars.

I felt Chosen. The eggs had chosen me.

My dreams changed. My dreams became long, and dark, and full of strange music. I got so that I just loved going to bed, because with my head full of the eggs' humming, I'd dream.

My mother said she'd never seen anything like it. Before, it'd been like pulling teeth to get me to bed. I was the baby of the family, and I guess I always felt like when I went to bed I was missing out. I'd scream and cry when I was a youngster, or worse, I'd sulk. Mother used to say my sulking was like a fog. "You don't have to make a federal case out of it," she used to say. Federal case. Newfoundland was a country back then, its very own country. Oh, you know about that, do you? I am glad they are teaching you something.

But yes, now I loved going into my little room and...sliding down. Not like sleeping. It felt less like dreams, and more like dipping back into one long dream. A long sleep, shared by many minds at once, minds that...communed. I'd feel like my body wasn't my own. It'd stretch, it'd be enormous. Full of energy; *made* of energy. I'd remember soaring through long, lazy strands of ice-blue cloud. Vast, languid beats, great wings made of lightning. Living between and around...this. What we call reality. A red land. Dry. Terrible mountains, and glaciers burning cold. Thin air. Heat, and...

What's that, me son? The eggs?

Well, yes, I kept going down there and reading to the eggs, talking to them, telling them about my life. Sometimes I'd hum, and it seemed to me that they hummed back. Maybe I imagined it. I was lonely, a lonely little girl, I suppose.

I never told anyone a thing about them. I knew they'd think I was touched. Touched. Nuts, crazy in the head, that's what touched means. But now I'm telling you. I think it's time to tell somebody.

I am quite sane, if old. I've passed all my memory tests. I still have my driver's license. If that doesn't prove sanity, what does in this society, I ask you.

Next, all the mines were closed. Every mine on Bell Island. There was lots of competition from all over the world, and we'd never made sure that local people owned the mines, that's why. So everybody was all set to leave. There were over twelve thousand people living here then, can you imagine? Now there's only about two thousand of us. I was pretty ancient by that time, the 1960s. I was around thirty or so. And everyone was leaving. My parents left; Dad was about ready to retire anyway, and they went into St. John's; Mother always did like to shop. My brothers left. One to CBS, one to St. John's, two out to Alberta to work in the oil fields.

I stayed. I wasn't married or anything. The eggs took care of that. I didn't have time or inclination for dating or courting or whatever it's called now. I stayed, and got a job here and a job there. Had to commute back and forth on the ferry for a few years, because there was no work to be had on the island. I cleaned houses. And I kept visiting the eggs. It was easier, because by then they'd blasted the tunnel.

I'd wake up slowly in those days. I'd have to set my alarm very, very early to be ready for people, for work. Sometimes it'd take me an hour just to stand up and put on my clothes. I couldn't move too fast. My eyes took a long time to adjust, too. Funny things, these human bodies. So small and meaty and chilly.

Then it was 1978.

My dreams went black and cold. It was a whole long dream, a dream that lasted for months before the Boom. It was, I realized slowly, a migration. The dreamer was migrating from the red place, the home place, the dry place, riding the electric wind. The long black airless cold, the between, gradually gave way, and the watery world came into focus. Watery world – that's us, the Earth. We have a lot more water than Mars. So.

So, we're coming up to the Boom again now. Goodness, that's like me, I can't seem to help but tell a story in a spiral.

The Boom, I was down on the beach, and when that bolt hit, the nest just...came apart.

That's right. The eggs, or stones if you want to call them that, fell out onto the beach. Some of them, anyway. There were far more of them than I'd thought. I'd only been able to see the front of the nest, you see, that was the hundred and two I'd counted. But more than that fell out. Far more. And in behind, you could see they went back far, far into a sort of perfectly round, smooth tunnel. I'd say there were thousands, at least. Although without taking them all out it'd be impossible to tell.

The Boom dislodged them, that's right.

I got even more curious, then.

Oh, yes, I took tools to them. Chisels and hammers and everything I had until I broke one, and what came out...

See this scarring across my hand? And the way I can't really close it? That's from what happened. Liquid fire. Magma, maybe. I'm lucky I didn't lose a finger. If I hadn't been wearing gloves...

I scooped up a few of the ones that had fallen out of the nest, all I could carry, to save them from being washed out to sea...

But that's probably enough for your report, now, isn't it.

The dream? Well, I'm sure I'm simply foolish.

The dreamer came close, came closer still. The watery planet filled her awareness. And she plunged into the atmosphere, following the filament, the path between our worlds. She plummeted toward Bell Island. I don't know, I just felt it was a she. She came from Mars to awaken the eggs. She impacted the island, and sent a jolt right through the magnetic ore to the nest on the other side. She jolted them free.

The Bell Island Boom came from Mars.

Well, yes, that's an interesting fact too. Mars is full of hematite. It's one of the most abundant minerals in the rocks and soils there; NASA has proven it. That's why it's so red, red like Bell Island. They seem to be attracted to hematite, to need it. I don't know how to understand their being. I'm just Susan Fitzgerald who reads too much science fiction and is touched in the head.

Certainly they must live for a very long time. Thousands of years, maybe. Maybe they never ever die.

Well, of course I have a theory. Here it is. If you look at the stories, it seems like there is a cycle of perhaps six thousand years. Think of all the legends. Chinese, Persian, Slavic, Indian, African, European. Water Serpents. The Leviathan.

Dragons.

They come here to lay their eggs. They hatch here; I think they need water for the first cycle of their lives. And there's lots of prey here. The young need food to thrive. Here, have another cookie.

And then, when they're ready, off they go, back to Mars. Where there's all that nice red magnetic rock. They are, or become, beings of energy, perhaps. That's what I think. Living plasma, that's a good idea. Sentient energy.

They commute between planets, riding the solar wind. Migrate. Like the wee grebe.

So. Soon the eggs will hatch, and we'll have the first cycle of dragons here on Earth in over six thousand years. And I'll be alive to see it! I hope so, anyway. That will be exciting, won't it?

If we live through it.

I am not sure they worry too much about us. I mean, we're not all that relevant, except as a source of nutrition.

Anyway, thank you for coming and interviewing an old lady, even if she isn't fully a century old.

What? Oh, you noticed that, did you? I didn't finish telling you what I did with the fallen eggs. Very perceptive of you.

Well, to be honest, they're here.

No, not on the cookie plate. They're in a metal trunk, under my bed.

Do you want to see them?

They've gotten hotter than before, and sometimes, they move. Just a little rocking motion. My dreams have gotten longer now. Does the prey dream the dream of the hunter? Soon I'll have to retire, just to keep dreaming.

You're right. That's them, that sound, rattling around in the iron trunk under me bed. Don't worry, it's been happening for months. Do you want to see them? No?

All right, me son. Go catch that next ferry, you'll just be in time.

What an exciting time in history. To be alive to see it!

Where the stars shine out their wonder, and the seas roll up their thunder.

Yes, thank you, glad you enjoyed the cookies. Goodness, can't you run fast.

Goodbye.

Goodbye.

FOSTERING ARTISTIC TALENT

ANDREW WILMOT

"All publicity works upon anxiety."
—JOHN BERGER, *Ways of Seeing*

i.

The room is dark and smells of salt and industry, like a port at night. Soft rectangles of teal blue circle the room. Between each, other materials are housed – gallon containers of paint, frames and scraps of wood not yet assembled, five enormous rolls of unprimed canvas stacked upright like carpet in a furniture supply warehouse. In the centre of the room, a twelve-foot square concrete dais and a garden hose coiled neatly nearby.

A window of light appears in the ceiling – a silhouette descends through a hatch, down a rickety wooden ladder. The figure approaches the centre, stands atop the dais; reaches for a chain.

Pulls and a spotlight ignites. A man surveys the aquarium tanks that line the room. His long, ashen dreads are tied in a single, thick vine. He wears a black apron with a pouch in front; slips a rubber, elbow-length glove over each hand, rolling the ends up past the keloid scars that crosshatch his fawn-coloured skin.

He – Samael – lays a large square of canvas on the concrete dais, using metal woodworking clamps to position it flat against the cool, damp surface. He reaches for a gallon tub of white latex paint and a flat, two-inch brush, and proceeds to prime the canvas. As he works, he replays in his mind the interview conducted earlier that day with an agitated, uncertain young man called Fairweather who annoyingly insisted on addressing Samael by the wrong name. As a rule, Samael was not generally fond of interviews and had only agreed to it at Gregor's request.

"*Mister Lüst*," Fairweather had called him, before ascribing frustrating, couched labels to his work: controversial, confrontational. "*Unconventional.*" Samael rejected such assertions – his work was avant-garde; calling a successful work of art "unconventional," he thought, was a form of linguistic cowardice.

Samael finishes priming the canvas – a near-perfect square of white with a two-inch perimeter. He leans over the material, presses his thumb into the paint at the very centre, leaving behind a faint impression of a thumbprint like a topographical map of a mountain – his signature. He wipes his thumb on the apron and goes to the wall of aquariums behind him.

He stands between two glowing teal tanks, racked by indecision. He settles on the one to the left and reaches into the water. From within, he removes a wiggling, half-metre-long cephalopod. Its moonlight-blue body shimmers in the dim studio light. With his other hand, he grabs its eight tentacles and bunches them together to keep the creature from thrashing free.

The artist carries the squirming cephalopod to the dais and places it above the centre of the freshly primed canvas, right over his thumbprint. Beneath direct light, the creature's dark, slick skin begins to change; colours materialize, churning beneath the surface – ocean blues, orange and crimson segmented by tracks of abyss-black. He observes as its tentacles sweep across the surface as if rooting to the canvas itself.

He unsheathes a fine-tipped brush from the apron's pouch, spins it around – its reverse is sharpened into a spike. Drives it through the cephalopod's large head, right above the canvas' centre. He's careful not to pierce the material beneath. The creature shudders; its tentacles stiffen. Samael retracts the brush; a clothesline strand of paint veins the weapon to the wound. The creature's skin comes apart at the seams. It dissolves; its innards seep into the canvas, flattening into the shape taken prior to death.

As the paint sets, Samael uses the sharpened tip of the brush and carefully lifts the empty, transparent skin of the cephalopod from the canvas. He tosses the limp epidermis into a nearby trashcan.

Staring at his work, Samuel notes the creature's insides reveal a symmetrical design – a mirrored pattern. The centre a large oval surrounded by eight crescents, impressions left by the tentacles. Where its beak had been, a trigon of white.

In his hand, the brush continues to drip.

ii.

Samael wakes the next morning, searches with his right hand for something that isn't there. He opens his eyes, sees that the other side of the bed is empty, sheets thrown back.

He staggers into the washroom. Stretches in front of the mirror, throws out his chest. Across his torso and down both arms the bright scar tissue from dozens of self-inflicted cuts – his body is an imprint of past artistic ventures. He grabs a bottle of Advil from the counter next to Kimiko's oestrogen and takes two.

He shuffles down the hall in a T-shirt and sweats. From the kitchen, he hears an echo from the previous day:

"I'm not sure if it's as much a question of ethics as social relevance," says Fairweather. "Can you say that what you do has artistic merit?"

"What I do is no different than the hunter who kills to feed or clothe himself."

"Except that art is not necessary for human survival. And you didn't answer my question."

"You're telling me Picasso is not necessary – Pollock – Warhol?"

"Not one of whom conflated killing with creation – especially when it comes to the murder of intelligent creatures."

"Christ, the temerity…"

"There is mounting evidence that these creatures have, and exhibit, above-average—"

"Just because a cattle-ist acknowledges its surroundings doesn't mean it's 'intelligent.'"

"And what of the Coast Salish people who've stated that what you do amounts to little more than brash cultural appropriation?"

"Let's be clear about something here. These creatures are *tools*. They are not an identity. They don't even have a voice."

Entering the kitchen, Samael spots Kimiko leaning against the counter, drinking coffee as she focuses on the wall screen in the living room. Her long black hair is looped in a messy bun at the top of her head. She notices Samael and quickly switches off the screen.

"Think I came off pretty okay," he says, pouring himself the remainder of the French press. He glances to Kimiko, who takes a long sip from her mug and looks away. Samael approaches, puts his hand to her face. "You okay?"

She spies a dried half-moon of orange wedged beneath his thumbnail and steps out of his grip. "There was another one today," she says, dumping what's left of her coffee into the sink. She indicates to the kitchen table with a flick of her head. Samael walks over. On a sheet of newsprint, the words "MERCHANT OF DEATH" are printed in wide block letters. "It was taped across the front door."

"At least their spelling's improved."

"This isn't funny, Adewale. These people are dangerous, and they know where we live."

Samael waves the newspaper in the air. "This is juvenile bullshit. Probably some first-year philosophy students turned vegans. They can't do anything to us."

Kimiko frowns.

"What is it?"

"I wish you were just the tiniest bit concerned about this."

"You think I'm not?"

"I think you've got it in your head that you're invincible, and that simply isn't true." She glances at the scars on his arms. "You've healed, but that doesn't mean you can't get cut again."

Kimiko walks past, into the hall running from the kitchen to front door. She stops at the entrance to a small, dark room.

"Say hi to Kandinsky for me," she says, and disappears inside.

The shed is a short walk across the yard from the single-storey art deco home Samael and Kimiko share. Samael inputs a combination into the lock on the door and enters. The inside is small, filled with landscaping equipment – shovels, rakes, a lawnmower. A brown rubber mat covers the floor. He kicks over an edge, revealing a wooden hatch with a cast iron handle. He opens the creaking hatch and descends into the dark.

At the bottom of the ladder, he reaches to a small table, presses a button on an iPod set atop a large block speaker. Philip Glass' *Metamorphosis* begins to play. He strolls the perimeter as the music haunts, tracing the surface of each tank as he passes. He peers inside them, watching as the creatures, all different lengths and colours, respond uniquely to the music. Their bodies gleam, the chromatophores in their skin triggered by each new sound as if the individual cells were themselves undergoing a process of direct pigmentation. He glances to the centre of the room and his piece from the night before, the colours of which are still setting. It would be ready for mounting in a week, maybe less. That will please Gregor, he thinks. At the very least it will give Gregor something new to sell.

At the room's apex is a tank twice as large as any other. Samael can see the cephalopod inside twisting against its too-tight confines. The way it rotates, it resembles an enormous drill spinning in place, its skin a kaleidoscopic veil of too many colours to quantify. Whereas the others appear segmented, their colours singular and separated, this creature's body is tattooed with thousands of small circles and lines, each a different tone or shade than what surrounds it. It's as if a star chart has been drawn into its DNA.

Samael puts his hand to the large tank and kneels. "Hello, Kandinsky." And for a moment he thinks the creature is staring at him, as if wanting to respond. The thought quickly dissipates; the creature continues to undulate colour within its cramped housing. "Soon as I can, buddy, I'll get you out of there and into some new digs."

From behind, a tentacle thrashes against glass. Samael rises, looks to the other side of the room where a relatively new addition – an eight-incher – is caught in its final throes. As he approaches, the young cephalopod sinks to the bottom of its tank. Then, like a piece of tissue over an air vent, its skin detaches and billows to the surface amidst an abstracted oil spill of primary colours.

As the music moves into its second and third movements, Samael takes the loose skin of the recently deceased and throws it away before dumping the tank's contents over a grate in the concrete floor in a corner of the room. He rinses it out with the hose, and then takes a last look at the other tanks and their gently rippling guests before heading back upstairs.

Thirty minutes later, Samael stands in the alley behind the Commercial Fish Market in East Vancouver, smoking a cigarette, leaning against the trunk of his navy Accord. A door opens and a tall woman with cartoonishly muscled forearms enters the alley. Her dark brown hair is netted into a bun; she wears a large white apron splotched pink and red.

"I thought you quit," says Nehir.

Samael stamps out the remains of his cigarette. "Didn't take."

"Too much stress." Nehir's accent is strong; Samael can't tell if she's asking or inferring.

"What do you know of it?"

She grins mischievously. "Only what I see on TV. I hope you had insurance." Samael nods; rage draws a line across his face. Nehir spits to the ground. "Fucking protesters. You are back on the horse though, yes?"

Samael pulls a roll of twenties from his jacket, passes it to Nehir, who stuffs it down the front of her shirt.

"Follow me," she says.

Inside the market, men and women busily unpack boxes of fish and other assorted sea creatures packed in ice. The floor is slick; Samael has to watch where he walks to avoid puddles. He follows Nehir to a small side room.

Several long wood crates are stacked one on top of another at the back of the small room. Nehir slides the top off the first. Inside, safely encased in expanded polystyrene, are two small steel and glass tanks filled with water. Inside each, a creature four, maybe six inches in length, shining luminous blue, like how a child paints a portrait of the ocean.

"They're young," Nehir says. "From the Tsleil-Waututh region, north of the city. They'll grow considerably."

"Yeah, about that. Last one I bought from you died this morning. I was checking the tanks in my studio and it just up and burst in the middle of a song."

"How much exposure were you giving it?"

Samael shrugs. "Five, six hours a day."

Nehir shakes her head, tsks. "They are like balloons. Fill them too fast and they will not survive. You must be attentive to their needs."

Samael slides the lid back in place, hefts the crate under one arm. "Worked so far," he says, impatiently. "They're not pets, you know."

"Neither are they tools." Samael turns to see Nehir offering a knowing glance. He exits silently, taking his purchases out back and placing them safely in the trunk of his car.

iii.

Samael wakes the following morning, his head and neck crying out in pain. He's in his studio, having fallen asleep seated upright against the rolls of unprimed canvas. The previous evening, after spending much of the day setting up accommodations for his two new palettes, he'd gone inside and crawled into bed only for Kimiko to demand he take a shower. *"You stink of them,"* she said, jumping out from the sheets. Offended, Samael stormed out, returning to the studio where he proceeded to lay out another swatch of canvas upon which he painted the first of his new additions. Its tones were muted, watercolour-thin; he'd barely given it time to take position before striking. If asked, he'd say it didn't matter; he just wanted to see its colours run.

The ceiling hatch opens as he struggles to his feet. "Adewale," Kimiko calls, a disembodied voice through the opening. "Phone. It's Gregor."

"Can you bring it to me?" he asks. She does not respond. He ambles to the ladder, legs stiff as if he has not walked for days.

At the top, he sees Kimiko leaning against the wall of the shed. She wordlessly passes him the phone.

"Gregor?" Samael says. "Wait, what are you – Gregor, slow down... All right, I'll be there as soon as I can." He sighs, lowers the phone.

"Another incident?" Kimiko asks.

"The Satellite got broken into again. Two of my pieces were torched. Fucking protestors and their appropriation bullshit."

Kimiko goes to the door. "I liked it better when it was just your blood you painted with," she says as she leaves.

Arriving at the Wallace Satellite forty-five minutes later, Samael is greeted by both his agent, Alistair Gregor, and the gallery's owner, Leanor Ortiz-Wallace, standing amidst a field of broken glass. Behind them, the shattered front window and a large stone on the gallery's floor, next to a smouldering pile of what Samael assumes remains of his work.

Leanor, wearing a tight black dress and not giving a fuck about the cold, crosses her arms as Samael approaches. "The Archivist, as I live and breathe. Good of you to join us. Fucking eventually."

"Always a pleasure, Leanor." Samael is unfazed; he's come to expect Leanor's distaste at his presence. It's not the politics behind his work; it's that his art causes her stomach to somersault. However, she has proven more than willing to sacrifice her comfort for the money his work brings in. *"Fucking celebrity culture,"* she remarked after his first six-digit sale. *"If there's blood in the water..."*

"You know," she says, "I think I preferred it when you were just fucked out of your mind and bleeding your own blood for your art. Least then I just had to mop the floor after a showing."

"You're the second person to say that to me today."

"Think maybe there's something to that?" she says scathingly.

Samael turns to his agent. "Where do we stand?"

Gregor exhales. "Insurance will cover what was lost, naturally. But we need to start thinking of another course of—"

Samael shakes his head. "No fucking way."

"Adewale, my boy—"

"Don't call me that."

Leanor scoffs.

Samael turns to Leanor. "Something to say to me?"

She circles him, her gaze alternating between the messy, achromatic pyramid of ash on the gallery floor and the faint scarring visible on Samael's chest and arms – thin lines appearing out the edges of his clothing. As a blood-letter, The Archivist was renowned. When he changed his identity and started painting with cattle-ists, Leanor had criticized him for attempting to deify his work. "*Samael*," she said, "*as in the archangel of death? The so-called Venom of God? For the love of – Do you always have to be so melodramatic?*"

It was Kimiko, though, who'd seen beneath the surface of his newly adopted nom de plume. The night of his first exhibition as Samael, she'd watched all evening as he drank and celebrated in a way never before seen. Arriving home that night, when asked how it went, she replied, "*I wish you weren't so scared to be you.*"

"The push-back is becoming severe," Leanor says, changing the subject.

"These people don't even know why they're protesting in the first place." Samael pauses. "Using a tool is not cultural appropriation."

Gregor looks to Leanor, who silently shakes her head, turns, and enters the gallery. The agent puts a hand to Samael's shoulder, pats three times and walks on, leaving the artist on his own.

iv.

Walking home in the brisk October air, head swimming, Samael starts to feel as if the ground is vanishing beneath his feet. He wraps his scarf tight around his neck and stuffs his hands into his pockets. Stares seconds longer than usual at the people he passes on the street, wondering if they recognize him, if they even care. He worries that he'll be forced to reinvent himself yet again. Cowards, he thinks, retracing the conversation at the Satellite. A gallery space isn't meant to be safe. Besides, it's not as if protesters had come to either of their homes; it isn't like they have anything real on the line.

Samael arrives at his West End home a short time later. Calls to Kimiko – no answer. He takes off his jacket and scarf and knocks on the closed door in the front hall. Still no response. Slowly, he opens the door.

The cramped, ten-by-ten room is an editing suite filled with filmstrips and equipment. To the right, shelves of film reels and canisters; to the left, three linen bins with long strands of celluloid pinned to clotheslines strung over top. At the centre, a desk with a projector, a film splicer, and numerous discarded strands of film.

He picks up a few loose strands, holds them to the light. He sees in each set of frames a different individual's backside from just a few metres away, tailed through city streets and into stores, off skytrains and buses and through large crowds of people.

Standing there, holding filmstrips showing women and men ducking into restrooms, on their phones engaged in private conversations, Samael feels as if the long celluloid strips suspended on clotheslines to his right were veins pulled from the bodies of Kimiko's subjects, like visual strands of DNA. He thinks of her work as being starkly envious; the way she selects her prey, without their knowledge or consent, and without showing their faces, is akin to stalking, though she rationalizes her motives as benign. "*People interest me,*" she said when they first started dating. "*But I don't always want to know them. I like to explore lives in moments; when you take away someone's individuality, when they're made faceless, you stop viewing them for their idiosyncrasies. It's then you see that*

the homeless man standing on the sidewalk, shouting at the sky,
has more in common than first realized with the businessman
who an hour earlier couldn't spare him two dollars for a bite to
eat."

Samael's thoughts are interrupted by a tinkling sound,
like glass breaking. He exits the editing suite. "Kim? Is that
you?" He moves into the kitchen. Through the sliding glass
doors he sees the shed, and a smashed window up high on
one side. Samael hurries outside. Approaching the shed, he
sees blood, bits of torn fabric caught on the jagged glass of a
barely person-sized hole.

Inside the shed, the floor mat is kicked aside, the hatch
open. Downstairs, amidst the sounds of Brahm's Symphony
No. 4, Samael hears more glass shattering, water spilling out
across the floor.

Descending into the studio, he sees a young man with a
bloody, torn-up calf hobbling from tank to tank, tipping them
over onto the concrete floor. Two of the cattle-ists have
already dissolved, their insides running out beneath their cel-
lophane-like exoskeletons.

"Hey!" Samael shouts. The young man turns. He's fair-
skinned, with short, close-cropped blond hair and full sleeve
tattoos on both arms. His columella is pierced with a large silver spike. "The fuck do you think you're doing?"

The young man glares and overturns another tank. Samael
watches helplessly as the creature inside spills onto the concrete, skitters for a few seconds before shuddering, falling
still. Continuing to stare, the young man pulls a blade from
his back pocket and stabs the creature in the head. Its body
deflates into a slick of paint, joins the other puddles sketch-
ing the edge of the raised dais on top of which the artist's latest continues to set.

"You put that note on our door," Samael says. "Who the hell do you think you are?"

"One of many," the young man says with aplomb. "Here to return what's been stolen."

Samael looks down to the painted remains. "Fucking funny way of showing it. When you return a shirt you don't like, you take it out back and piss on it first?"

"Better they die like this than on your canvas, thief."

"Thief? I paid good money for these things."

"They were never for sale. Their voice was never yours!"

"Christ, what is it with you assholes?"

The young protester tips over a fourth tank. The black and maroon body of the creature housed within ripples, water sloughing off its tentacles in rivulets. Samael crosses the room as the protester adds to the flood of colours along the floor – a technicolour disasterpiece. He stops when the protester places a hand on Kandinsky's tank.

"Don't," says Samael. "Please."

"You think it's blood you've spilt, you're mistaken. Their blood *is* their voice. You've been painting their screams."

Samael watches nervously as the protestor grips the edge of the overly full tank, preparing to tip it over. The protester grins, noting the fear in Samael's eyes, not realizing when one of Kandinsky's tentacles breaches the surface. Wraps itself around the outstretched arm – squeezes. The protester, surprised, raises his knife to the tentacle, giving Samael enough time to close the gap between them. He grabs the protester's arm. Wrestles away the knife – sends it sliding through the paint. The protester wrenches his arm free from Kandinsky, grapples with Samael. The two slide on the painted concrete, tumble to the floor. The protester crawls through the paint as if it were mud, lunges for the knife as Samael reaches behind to a small table and a tin of brushes off to one side. He retrieves a flat, one-inch brush from the tin, spins it around. As the protestor grabs hold of the knife, rises to his knees and turns, Samael dives forward, drives the pointed tip of the brush into the protester's foot, thigh, and stomach in quick succession. The young man staggers two, three steps back, and crumples onto the still-drying canvas set atop the raised dais.

Samael stands, out of breath. His entire body covered with paint, he stares at the corpse of the young man, his blood pooling beneath, swirling with the cephalopod's from the night before.

v.

The police are still there when Kimiko arrives home four hours later. She shouts her name at them, runs inside. In the kitchen, she sees Samael leaning against the counter, a towel draped across his shoulders. His shirt and pants and up his neck are heavily stained with paint. He sips tenderly from a coffee mug as two detectives, a man and a woman, question him. Her eyes travel; she sees yellow police tape cordoning off the shed, and, a few feet away, Gregor on his phone, mid-meltdown, pacing a small circle with one hand to his forehead to dab away sweat.

Samael spots Kimiko and goes to her. She drops her camera bag and they embrace.

"What happened?" she asks. "Are you all right?"

The detectives go to leave. The woman puts a hand to Samael's shoulder, says they'll be in touch. They tell Samael and Kimiko to take care as they make their way to the exit.

"Adewale," Kimiko says, "what's going on?"

"I was attacked. I'm okay," he adds, seeing her eyes widen. "A little shaken up."

"I don't—"

"There was a man waiting for me in my studio. He was killing – He tried to hurt me. We fought and…" He looks away, not wanting to finish.

Kimiko swallows. "This man, is he—"

Gregor enters before she can finish, still on his phone. "Of course I'm pissed," he shouts. "This isn't how you do business. This isn't fucking professional!" He ends the call, looking like a man who's just lost a bet. "Leanor's bumping you," he says, addressing Samael. "Says she can't deal with this right now – she doesn't need the drama."

"What the shit?" Samael steps out of Kimiko's arms. "Call her back. Tell her she can't do this – we had an agreement."

Gregor throws out his arms. "I don't know what to tell you, lad. She's not willing to bend."

Samael's eyes narrow as if realizing something he hadn't before. "She wants to fuck with me, fine. I'll make it impossible for her to turn me away."

"Whatever you're going to do, do it fast. Bubbles burst."

Kimiko waits until Gregor and the remaining officers are gone before speaking again. "Adewale, I need you to tell me everything. Are you all right? What happened to the man that attacked you?"

Samael glances at his paint-speckled hands. "He's dead. He came at me with a knife and…I was forced to defend myself."

"Oh god."

"Where have you been?"

"What?"

"I came home and you weren't here. I thought maybe something had happened."

Kimiko nods to her camera bag. "I was working."

"But you were gone so long."

Kimiko shakes her head. "It's not important." She walks to the sliding door, looks out. "Is Kandinsky—"

"He's fine. Lost a few of the newer additions, though."

Kimiko hugs herself. Samael goes to comfort her but she steps aside.

"What's wrong?" he asks.

"I don't know." She picks up her camera bag. Samael follows her to the editing suite, watches as she removes a handheld 35mm video camera from the bag and places it on the desk. She proceeds to pull out several used canisters of film for development.

"Where did you go today?" he asks, staring at the multiple canisters.

"Just…around. Listen, are you sure you're—"

"I'm fine, I just didn't know where you were. I was worried, Kim."

She laughs. "You get attacked, and it's you who's worried about me." She pauses. "I was tracking someone. It started out like any other, but…it was different this time."

"Different how?"

"I first saw her – the woman I followed – on the skytrain. She looked just like everyone else. She had long brown hair and wore a nice jacket and skirt. She looked like she was going to work, or maybe to meet someone at a bank. But when I looked down there was blood on her shoe – a red splotch on her white pumps so perfect it looked painted on. It was small, maybe the size of a quarter. I doubt anyone else would've noticed. Almost as soon as I saw it, though, she stood up and got off at the next stop. I didn't even think; I grabbed my stuff and followed her out."

"Why would you do something so risky?" Samael asks, horrified.

"It didn't feel risky at the time."

"She could have been a psychopath, Kim. A—"

"Killer? Yeah, but she just as easily might have cut her leg on something. Or maybe it was ketchup from whatever she'd had for lunch. That was the point. I didn't know, and I had to find out."

"You had to?"

"I wanted to."

"And I still don't understand what could've compelled you to—"

"I liked how it felt. The mystery, the...tension. I had no way of knowing where this person might lead me, or to what end, but it was exhilarating." She pauses. "I do what I do because it helps me to understand people, and because even a woman with blood on her shoes has to make a show of life same as the rest of us." She faces Samael. "But here you tell me, calmly, that you killed an intruder in our home, and I see clearly the flaw in my thesis."

"You think I killed that man out of spite? He was threatening Kandinsky!"

"I thought it was you who was threatened."

Samael straightens up, steels himself. "I did what I had to do."

"But don't you see? That's exactly what he was doing."

"You're taking the protesters' side now?"

"Maybe it's not about sides," Kimiko says. "It's about voice. And right now you're speaking with another's."

Samael extends his arms angelically. "This house, all that we have, is the result of my work, and now suddenly that's a problem for you."

Kimiko frowns. "Except maybe it's not so sudden. We all need to find our voice, in our own time."

"You don't know what you're talking about. I know my own voice. I'm proud of what I've done."

She walks forward, stares into his eyes as she runs her fingers up and down the textured crosshatching of his left hand. "Yours, that man's, these creatures…whatever its shade, the blood on your hands is blood all the same."

vi.

Samael wakes alone. He reaches out, but the other half of the bed is empty, covers pulled tight like they'd never been disturbed in the first place.

Blood rushes to his head as he stands. There's shouting, regrets and hurled objects clattering around in his brain. In the washroom, he splashes cold water on his face. He straightens up in front of the mirror. His body appears to have lost some of its tone; he grabs the flesh around his stomach, tugs at it as if expecting it to come away in his hands. Flexes – his scars pop and bulge, writing pinkish exclamation points across his arms and torso. Several, he notices, are different than before. He puts his index finger to what seems like a gap between two halves of a lateral incision from sternum to belly button, digs out a dried red clump of one type of paint or another.

Boxes are piled three and four high in the front hall, tops un-taped, filmmaking equipment packed with little care as to what fit where. Samael approaches the open door to the editing suite but stops mere feet from the entrance. He thinks of calling out to Kimiko, though he knows there will be no reply.

Wearing a ratty, paint-splotched T-shirt, Samael travels the short distance from the house to the shed. He tears the yellow police tape from the entryway and enters.

Descending into the studio, he switches on the iPod but doesn't listen to what plays. The floor is still damp; paint is swirled in long, sweeping arcs from a mop. The glass from the overturned tanks has been cleared away, their vacant spots along the wall an unfortunate reminder of the previous day's events. The dais at the centre of the room is empty; the canvas is in police custody, having been taken in as evidence.

The music crescendos – thick, tree branch-like tentacles press against their confines like a person streaking glass with their bare hand. Samael looks to the studio's end, where the two-metre-long body of Kandinsky presses uncomfortably against the close quarters of its aquarium. He approaches the tank, puts his hand to the glass. Again he thinks he sees Kandinsky staring back at him, its large, black eye shining in the light suspended above. The moment passes, and he realizes it is not the creature's eye but a trick of the light – a snatch of abstraction rolling across the surface of its translucent skin.

Samael turns from Kandinsky's tank. He sets the stage, unrolling and positioning a large, ten-by-ten square of canvas across the surface of the dais. He clamps the corners of the material in place and proceeds to prime it with a two-inch brush. No sooner has he finished covering the material's surface in its entirety, signing it at the centre with his thumbprint, than he returns to the aquarium containing his prize.

Standing over Kandinsky, he puts on his apron, places a daggered brush crusted with dried innards in the front pocket, and slips a black rubber glove over each hand. He reaches into the tank, attempts to lift the giant cephalopod from its home-of-sorts as if trying to pull an object through too small an opening. Kandinsky squirms against Samael's grip, lashes

out with its tentacles, which slap the water's surface in irides-
cent splashes and primary waves. The more Samael struggles
to free Kandinsky from the tank, the angrier he becomes.
Having had enough after just a few minutes, he suddenly
grips the side of the aquarium and, with a grunt, tips it over
onto the concrete. The glass shatters with a cymbal crash and
water floods the space, surrounding the raised dais as if a
moat.

The cephalopod thrashes along the ground in undulating
surrealism. Samael dashes around to the creature's backside
and uses his body weight to heave it toward the centre of the
room, up the raised platform and onto the canvas. As he
shoves and lifts what little he can, he feels Kandinsky's movements slowing, stalling. With his entire body, he manages to
roll the dying cephalopod up the lip of the dais, rippling the
still-drying gesso on the canvas. Samael hurriedly attempts to
encourage the creature to settle into the paint of its own
accord – he wiggles its tentacles, hoping for a response but
receiving nothing. He tries to move the creature into position
himself, but is unable to arrange its limp body and tentacles
with any degree of symmetry.

Exhausted and out of breath, Samael stands above the
body of Kandinsky, dead across only the bottom third of the
canvas with a wide ridge of white paint outlining its form. He
tries again to move the body but it is too heavy, leaden with
colour and pattern, having been nurtured so long.

Resigned to any outcome, Samael removes the sharpened
brush from the pocket of his apron and stabs Kandinsky in the
head. Nothing happens. He tries again and again but to no
avail; the creature's skin is too strong for the wooden spike to
pierce. Frustrated, he searches the pool of water surrounding
the dais and, slicing his palm, retrieves a blade of broken glass

in the shape of a mountain's peak and drives it as hard as he can into the top of Kandinsky's glistening head.

Instantly, the cephalopod's body bursts and a flood of paint surges out from beneath its skin. The force is strong enough that Samael is pushed right off the dais and into the water, shimmering with Kandinsky's abundant insides – like swimming through a sea of elegant viscera.

Samael fights to his feet, glances down at himself. His body is diffused with paint – a gunshot spray spreading out in dense veins of colour as if bathed in expressionism. He looks to the canvas, sees Kandinsky's remains blooming out from the bottom right-hand corner in currents of abstraction. He reaches out, lifts the leftover skin from atop the canvas, careful not to disturb the still flowing paint as it betrays all hope of symmetry, order. And as it continues to flow outward, pooling off the edge of the canvas in one direction while creeping over the midpoint and Samael's signature in the other, he notices a single, precise strand like angel's hair threading the canvas with red – blood from the slice on his palm – navigating Kandinsky's insides as it searches for a place of its own amidst the screams.

TAKE TAKE TAKE

BRAYDON BEAULIEU

I'm frozen to Tony's front step when he pulls his SUV into the driveway, his brother in the passenger seat. I've sat here long enough for the ice to melt and then refreeze against my ass. Why the hell don't we hibernate in the winter, like ladybugs? Stack ourselves one on top of the other, red and black polka-dot towers. To stay awake all December is to deny biological imperative.

Tony jumps out of the car, leaves it running, scurries over to me. He needs new shoes. Those are ready for the donation bin. Leather peeling from scuffs, seams unstitching.

"Jesus Christ, Angela. Your face. Who did this? How long have you been sitting here?"

Today I was the soccer ball.

He scoops a snowball and holds it against my lips. My face so cold I don't need to recoil, but I do anyway. "Sorry, sorry," he stammers. He pulls his hand back holding pink snow. Not white or yellow or sludge-grey. Grapefruit pink. Or bubble gum ice cream. Cherry popsicle. Strawberry Slush Puppy while watching the 73's game with the girls and shouting into the din of cawing, cackling, roaring beasts. He says, "Jesus Christ. Jesus H. Christ. Jesus, Mary and Joseph, Mary Magdalene, all the saints and martyrs and Jesus."

"That's from a movie. What movie?"

"Angela, God. You must be a popsicle. What happened? Where's your dad's car? Where's your dad?"

"I'm a cherry popsicle."

Tony's brother turns off the Land Rover and gets out, blows steam between his teeth. He looks like Tony except for the smaller nose and the glasses. And perfect teeth. Hair a bit darker, too. Rugged, but clean. Looks like he could play James Bond. Wonder if his Bond girl's been cast. What's his name again? Avery, Emilio, Jameson. No. I blink back tears that aren't there, will never be there.

"Goodness, Tony," says the brother. "Let's get her inside, get some ice on those eyes."

Ice coats the trees, the porch railing, my back pockets. And we're going inside to find more. Tony hands the bloody snowball to Avery/Emilio, who tosses it to the street. It shatters on the pavement and blossoms pink in the slush. I'd have drop-kicked it over the house on the other side. Tony wraps an arm around me but I knock back his hand and say, "Don't touch me."

"Right," he says, rooting through his keys with his antennae. The lock unclicks, his antennae flick. My coat holds in the scent of beer and pickles. Sweater speckled like a crow's egg, with dry rusts of blood.

NTS: Remind Tony to broom the frozen cobwebs from the porch gable.

Emilio/Jameson holds the door. I kick off my flats and shrug out of my coat. Always too hot at Tony's, like we've tunnelled too close to the earth's core.

"Gum?" the brother asks me.

"Whitening?"

"You know it," he says, holding out a crinkling green packet. I pop out a piece and peck it out of my palm. Mash it between my mandibles. Spit; hurts too much to chew. Tony's brother picks it up with a tissue. He wears his antennae slicked back. As though he wants to hide them. I touch mine with ginger fingers, feel an extra kink in the left one. So sore. Fuck.

Out of the kitchen buzz Tony's mutterings and ice cubes shattering from their white tray. I ease onto the couch and turn on the television. Champions League standings. Please, anyone but those hyenas of Barcelona or those fucking snakes of Real Madrid this season. Pleeeeeeeease.

"She might've just fell or something," says Avery/Jameson in the other room.

I don't catch Tony's next sentence when he mutters it, but millions of tiny vent-voices repeat it to me: "Don't be a moron, Emery."

Ah, Emery. I was close. I shove my hand between the couch cushions, looking for spare change. None, but I do find sticky Oreo crumbs and a *Trivial Pursuit* wedge. I lean over the couch arm so I can see into the kitchen. Emery's ass is fantastic.

"This is the way of the suburbs," echo the voices, bringing Tony's words to me on platters like morsels of pie, crumbs of pistachio bread and Oreos. "We do backyard barbecues and share gardening seeds and gossip under the hedgeroots and bring each other pecan pie. But everyone's still a fucking animal."

The Christmas tree beside the ottoman fills the room with forest scent. *L'arbre de Noël*, it's called in French. *Examen finale a été il y a quelques jours. Un sapin, des biscuits, du lait, Père Noël, des cadeaux, du papier d'emballage, du sang, un nez cassé, tabernac. Des fourmis* climb the tree and nestle in its needles. They will extract the sap and regurgitate it among our larvae. Emery asks, "Her dad?"

NTS: Look up "regurgitate" *en français*.

"Or her boyfriend. I'll kill him. Either one."

"Who is she? Why is she coming to you?"

"Let's make sure she's okay."

Emery crosses his legs on the loveseat. Tony curls his legs under himself on the edge of the coffee table, hands me ice wrapped in a taupe tea towel. I don't know how many times I've told him to get new linens. These things look like they're straight off the dollar store rack. It's his nature to use scraps, I guess. Decomposing shoes, 1950s tea towels, discarded newspapers.

NTS: Buy him new linens with my Naples Pizza pay-cheque, kick the old ones directly to the curb.

"Lie down and put this over your eyes," he says.

"I'm fine sitting." I hold out the pink *Trivial Pursuit* wedge. Thousands of voices whisper from the vents as I drop it into Tony's tarsal claw. I thumb the edge of my mouth, feel drying blood binding my lips together. "You're blocking the TV."

Emery clears his throat, says, "I can leave."

Tony nods. His solemnity is melodramatic, annoying as fuck. I want to paint a bloody red hourglass between my breasts and drink him dry. But that's not my nature, Brian would say. I'd drain Brian, too. Emery escapes into the bath-room. Gargling sounds and the scraping of bristles against enamel. Emery, the smile of the sun: something Tony once said.

NTS: Go home and lock the door. You idiot.

"It was Brian," I say. I want my bottom lip to quiver, my jaw to clench, or my eyes to well up and spill over. Some-thing to crack this exoskeleton. But I just watch the scores roll across the bottom of the television screen, praying for a Barcelona concession. "He's here visiting his parents. And me, I guess. Came over drunk and calling me a skank. He had a smell on him: pickles and beer and Lysol. Like he'd sprayed himself. He pushed inside and the door hit me in the mouth, here. Then he hit me. Punched me in the nose, broke it, I think. I fell against the wall. Then I grabbed the umbrella by the door – my dad's big green golf one – and speared him in the nuts with it. Fuck! Fuck Barcelona, honestly. Pack of buzzard-fuckers. He held a present for me in one hand the whole time. He'd done that thing where you curl the ribbon with scissors. The ribbon was brownish red. *Tabernac*, I think I forgot to lock my front door."

"I'm going to kill him."

I put the ugly towel of ice over my eyes. "No. Tony. He was drunk. It's his nature to fly off the handle. He's never hit me before, but he's hit so many people he should have a Guinness world record. That's why he gets all these bartend-ing jobs; he can fight. He's a damn spider. You know, those black spindly ones with the yellow splotches. Corn. Corn spi-ders. They used to spin their webs underneath the porch when we lived on Talbot Street. They taunted me. Told me one day they'd eat me whole. They had the prettiest zigzags in the centre of their webs. Like red lightning in the summer. You smell like bread and pistachios."

The coffee table creaks as Tony stands up. "Emery and I bake a different loaf from our mom's recipe cards every year." He scratches his nose, licks his mandibles. "On the twenty-third, then scatter it around her grave." He sits back down on the coffee table, stands, sits next to me, stands. "They pro-nounced her dead on the twenty-third."

"You're just attracting crows to her grave." The ice soothes my swelling skin. Better than calamine lotion. Feels swell.

"Brian came over to your house specifically to beat the hell out of you," says Tony. No question mark.

"He was drunk. And he had a present."

The voices murmur louder in the vents. They crave bloody vengeance, the taste of veins and tendons tearing between their teeth. They want to swarm Brian's face and dissect it from his skull. They want to make his eye sockets their nest.

Tony pulls at his lip and says, "Are all the ant-traps still at every entrance? The clear plastic containers of baking soda and icing sugar?"

"It's winter. I'm pretty sure the ants are hibernating in warm tunnels."

"Not the insomniacs. Or, you know, the ones scavenging other people's houses and restaurants that don't clean their floors properly."

I lock my fingers behind my head and lie back. "You and Emery can go check. This feels good, right here. Lock the door behind you."

Tony and Emery have driven over to my house to pest-proof it.

I stand in Tony's living room, surrounded by ants that pour up from the vents and surge. They rise from the ground, a black jelly of gripping teeth and wiggling legs. Coat the drapes. Flood the tile floor. The couch sags under their weight.

"Those traps," they clamour. "We couldn't get in."

My fists would be magnifying glasses.

Their antennae twitch. Legs stroke my socks. "Tony's fault. We're your sisters, for God's sake. *His* sisters. What gives?"

My fists would sear tiny holes through any exoskeleton. Leave smoking wounds to cool under blue and white icicle lights.

They swell up and mould themselves into one massive ant. The woman-size ant made of ant-size ants lays a tarsal claw on my shoulder. Which is just a shoulder. "Get rid of the baking soda and icing sugar," they sing. "No sister should be isolated from the family. We never abandon anything that's ours."

"We never abandon our own," I say. The woman-size ant dissolves and my colony swarms over me, through me, as me.

My fists would crash the sun into the wet snow, roll it across colonies and leave every sinful body sizzling and twitching in the melt.

⁓☼⁓

Brian smears The Grand Central Tavern's bartop with a rag dirtier than the stinkhole's kitchen. He doesn't turn away from the television when I walk in. Game's on: Jets and Pens. Crows caw caw caw outside, having long devoured the bits of the body of Christ that Emery and Tony scattered this afternoon. I envision the body of Brian, scattered in the same way. Flavoured with pistachio and thyme and oregano, strewn amid icy headstones. Tithing paid over Tony and Emery's mother's empty grave. Her coffin offers no oblation to tunnelling worms, millipedes, and carpenter ants.

Still mesmerised by Evgeni Malkin's stickhandling and absently wiping the bar, Brian slurs, "Wuddletbee?"

Still drunk.

Behind me, crawling over the pool table and the windows and the ketchup bottles, millions of colony-mates whisper and giggle and rub their legs together. I reply, "A stinger, please. You fucking fuckweed."

NTS: Come up with better insults.

They surge around me and over the bar, scrambling over each other to reach him. The room becomes a squirming foam of black bodies, ready to be scraped flat and served. I drop to all sixes and join the swarm. We avenge bruises as well as all our cousins this inebriated jerkoff has dissected in his studies. Claw our way up his body to his face. The pupil of one wide black eye dilates. I sink my jaws into its vitreous gel. He'd scream, but we're already tearing at his throat and licking the taste of barley and hops from his oesophagus.

A rum bottle smashes. Steel caps spill over the floor. Brian's flesh smells of golden nugget corn on the cob and pickled beer. We carry pieces of his skin, tendons, and teeth down the vents to observe under microscopes and distribute to the crows, but leave him alive and panting on the tile. His blood mixes with the spreading rum.

"My face," he sobs. Like a fucking larva. "Whaddid ya dooda my face?"

My fists would scatter the Sacrament of Brian unto the crowing masses. Caw, caw, caw.

The lightbulb above the bar flickers and goes bzzt bzzt through its blackening filament. Brian chokes and snivels. Crickets wring their hands outside the windows, warming chilly tarsi. The last of my sisters scurry down the vents.

I wipe my bloody tarsi on Brian's dirty cloth. Drop it and punt it into the bin behind the bar. Coach convinced me I could kick any item into a wastebasket within thirty metres. He told me I'm a shoo-in for the Canadian U20. I once tied Tony's sneakers together and kicked them into the back of a moving garbage truck from my open living room window and made him walk home in his socks. I told Tony, "If you think you're the saviour of the world, you won't need shoes. Jesus himself wore sandals. And no socks with them, Captain Italiano. You should grow a Jesus beard. You'd look hot."

I bend down over this weeping excuse for an entomologist and say, "Now everyone's going to know you, the guy with these papercut scars all over his face, the one who beat up his ex-girlfriend. You think we won't tell? You complain to anyone, I don't just tell my friends – I go to my father. I go to the entire fucking soccer team. You think this beating is bad? Wait till you've had fourteen. And the cops. Assault charge not going to look too good beside that grad school transcript, is it?"

"Jesus Christ, Angela. You're insane."

"Have a nice flight to Toronto, prickwick." I grab a bottle of Tequila Rose from the rack. On second thought, "fuck-weed" sounds more badass.

I answer the door in a pink bathrobe. Tony. I leave the door open and head back to the kitchen. Lean against the counter and thumb the booze's label. Call my cat, Fievel, with kissy sounds. NTS: Wash the pot of mac and cheese you just scarfed.

Tony sits on the porch. I blow him a kiss through the kitchen doorway. "Thanks for taking care of me. You and your brother."

"You took off."

I scratch a dry red spot on the side of my hand. Missed it in the shower. Tony moves to get up, but I say, "Brian's, not mine. No one else at the bar."

"That was my job, Angela."

"Don't tell me what I can and can't do. You wouldn't have, anyway."

The Tequila Rose label peels in my hands. Tony nods toward it and asks, "You want me to pour you some?"

"No. I want you to pour it down the drain."

"I can't come in until you move the baking soda and icing sugar."

I do. "I don't ever want to drink again. Not even beer. I can still smell his breath. Fucking pickles and lager and salted butter." Before he can get up from the porch and into the house, I open the bottle over the sink myself. The alcohol swirls around and down the drain, gargling like Emery in Tony's bathroom. "I wanted to kill him. I wanted to cut the face right off his skull and hang it up like a trophy, right between my dad's buck and moose. Is that weird? That probably sounds weird."

"But you didn't?"

I put the empty bottle on the counter, pull a plum from the fridge and sink my teeth into it. A stream of juice runs from the corner of my mouth to my chin. Tony reaches out to wipe, but I smack his hand away. "Don't touch me. I may not be drinking age across the border, but I'm not a fucking toddler."

Fievel meows and walks around the corner, rubs against Tony's leg. Tony crosses his arms, kisses at the cat. Fievel meows again, purrs, sits, licks the pads of his paws.

"I got the cat last week. His name is Fievel and he's Jewish."

Tony blinks. "Your cat is Jewish?"

"Yeah. That's why my dad and I put up Hanukkah lights instead of Christmas lights this year, before he left. Blue and white. For Fievel. I'm actually glad he's gone."

Tony picks the cat up, cradling him and scratching under his chin. "Your dad?"

"No. Brian. I mean, he's still in Essex. But he'll go back to Toronto and I'll never talk to him again. I have to focus on soccer this year, anyway. The women's under-twenty club is scouting me, did you know that?"

"You play soccer?"

I laugh. It hurts my lips and my ribs. "Shut up, it's a big deal."

"You've told me two hundred thousand million times. But congrats. Did you know Emery was drafted into the NHL? I joked that he'd have the nicest teeth in the league. Because, you know, he'd actually have teeth. Then he tore that knee ligament."

"Yeah, he told me. His ACL. That blows."

"When did you talk to Emery?"

"About an hour ago."

"Ah, that would've been when I was grocery shopping, then. Picked up some more baking soda, by the way. Anyway, took him too long to get laced up again, so they told him to hit the showers. Permanently. What happens if you make the team?"

I drop the plum pit and punt it into the trash can. It rattles inside against aluminum foil and shrink wrap. Fievel leaps from Tony's arms and darts to the garbage, swishing his tail. I pump my fist in the air. "I get out of this place. Spread my wings, and all that jazz. Pray like a mantis I don't pull an Emery."

Before Tony leaves, he checks the baking soda traps. The clear plastic containers are all in the right spots, all full. When he's gone, I empty them all into the trash and rinse them. I pull the baking soda out of the cupboard and drop-kick it out the back patio door, into the tarp covering the pool two houses down. Goooooooooal by Hölldobler, first of her campaign, and certainly not the last. Such a talented left winger, she's Gareth Bale with ovaries. She has no fear. She has no mercy. She has no icing sugar left. It's all in the trash. No way my sisters are ever barred from my house again. No fucking way. We never abandon our own. NTS: Need more mac and cheese, bread, butter, Oreos, pie crumbs, pistachio shells.

A DOOR
IN THE ROCK

CHADWICK GINTHER

There had been an "accident" with a troll from the mine.

It was the talk of Svarta Mining, that troll, and how it wouldn't return to any dwarf's call. Brunna Sindradóttir volunteered to try one last time, before it was destroyed, because her parents had crafted more rock trolls for the Company than all other *dvergar* together – and this rogue troll happened to be one of theirs. She'd been promised right of travel if she succeeded. She'd make the troll recognize her blood.

So far the Company had kept the Flin Flon RCMP out of their business. Locals listened to the Company. Veiled by the illusion of a jackknifed tanker trailer, was a maimed and angry rock troll, wailing over its dead handler and not allowing anyone near the body.

Brunna didn't know why they'd bothered with a cover story at all. Let the *Northern Miner* put the troll on its front page. Invite the damned CBC. Her uncle Andvari *wanted* the *dvergar* to return to the days of old, crafting legends. How could that happen when mortals turned a blind eye to what happened around them? If humans never saw magic, how would they know to seek out dwarves for weapons to fight monsters? How would they forge new legends?

How would they even know there *were* dwarves?

On the road leading to the troll, she could see the smoke-stack from the Company's smelter – taller than the Eiffel Tower – standing out from the rock like a giant's middle finger directed at her. There was nowhere in town that she *couldn't* see that stack, or its trail of smoke, venting waste from the Company's mortal and magical labours.

Flin Flon, dubbed "The City Built on Rock," was about 800 kilometres north of the provincial capital of Winnipeg. It was a border town, straddling the provinces of Manitoba and Saskatchewan in the same way it bordered the magic and mundane. Not large as cities go – six thousand souls, give or take. But it had been a perfect place for the *dvergar* to settle, carved out of the Canadian Shield as it was. And the ancient volcanic belt had been a shield indeed, in the days after Ragnarök.

They say that happened. God fought god. Monsters ate the sun and moon. Winter never ended. The dead walked. The very sky shattered. Brunna hadn't seen it, but it was recorded in Sögusalur the History Hall, that the Nine Worlds had ended. *But here we are. Still living.*

If one could call being in this tiny town living.

Her wayward troll waited near a path leading to the lake; she hoped it hadn't rambled. If it had, she'd hunt it through the residential streets, where magic was myth and dwarves were naught but a story.

Which would complicate things.

But that story was changing. Magic was returning to Midgard.

Which meant soon, humans would come to *dvergar* again. For weapons. For charms. For jewels. And they would pay, in gold or favours. Humans would always pay for glory.

Brunna wanted the time of legends to return as much as any dwarf, if not more. Her parents had talked of nothing else since she was a squalling youth. She also wanted to be long away from the tunnels, seeking adventures of her own when that happened. Once the glory seekers came, a life of crafting supplies for the stories of others would be her doom.

Brunna wanted stories of her own, not to be an afterthought in others'.

"Soon enough," she whispered, slapping the dash of her pickup.

It was an old truck, big, and ugly, but it could hold the rock troll, and the truck's covered box would help to hide it and its dead handler from prying eyes.

Brunna stopped at the roadblock, pulling alongside a steep rise of rock. She could see the overturned truck; workers in white suits and respirators. Her stomach trembled, filling her with an overwhelming desire to turn away.

She knew the feeling was false, but it was hard to convince the mind that what it saw was not there. Brunna didn't like the idea of entering blindly either. The troll would see past the illusion. It would know she was coming. She patted the trumpet case she used to transport her sword: Skeri – The Sever – could cut magic as surely as flesh. The blade had been her mother's, before Hilde had settled on the forge and given up the fighting life. With Skeri she'd carved truth from giants' lies, and fought in other campaigns she'd never shared. Comforting to have along, but if she drew Skeri now, it would destroy the illusion of the wreck utterly, and with the troll still rampaging about, that would not end well for her or the Company, troll, or town.

A grue crept up Brunna's spine as she inched her truck over the line of blood she knew painted the pavement – all *dvergar* workings required blood. It was afternoon, the autumn sun high overhead, but here, now, in this singular moment, it was twilight. The sun muted, pale, glowing like a full moon, a reflection of its usual intensity.

Her shoulders tightened, waiting for the troll to crush the hood of her truck. For a windshield to spray glass and slice her face.

She needn't have worried.

The troll was gone. So was the dead dwarf.

There was nothing on the road but a rocky arm and rusty bloodstains.

A raven pecked at the blood, lifting and then discarding a spherical pebble. A second raven landed and the two scavengers cawed imprecations and threats at one another. The birds were everywhere around town. Brunna wondered who they told their secrets to, now that Odin was dead.

She hopped out of the truck. Brunna was tall for a dwarf woman, but it was still a drop. In the chunky soles of her steel-toed boots she topped five feet, if you measured from the top of her curly red hair. And you didn't push down too hard. She straightened her maroon hoodie, the local hockey team's exploding "B" logo emblazoned in white, and tugged it down to hide the shining mail shirt she wore beneath.

The ravens hopped aside as she approached, eyeing her warily. They could fly away. *Unlike me.* They didn't stay rooted to the earth. *Just like me.*

If Brunna had possessed wings, she'd have been gone from Flin Flon already. "But that's not going to happen, is it?" she asked the ravens as she eyed the pebbles scattered from the rock troll's shattered joint.

The pebbles were spherical, like ball bearings. Thousands of them allowed the giant creature to move and shift its stones. Brunna set her trumpet case down on the road. Her boots crunched over the asphalt. She didn't call to the pebbles. Not yet. Instead, she listened. She'd wanted a rock troll of her own once, but hadn't earned the right to make one.

Binding spirit into rock with blood was serious business. Brunna hadn't taken this task because she'd wanted her freedom, or because her parents had made the troll, but because this was their *last* creation together. Her father Sindri had been a master of crafting them, his trolls were larger and stronger than any other's. Her mother Hilde's gift was instilling instinct and a semblance of thought.

Brunna hoped she could fix this broken troll – assuming she could find him. She felt another rockcaller's pull; a long-spent song, its last note lingering. She was glad she hadn't released a call of her own, it would have alerted whomever had sung this song, letting that unknown voice know to expect her.

Strange, she couldn't place the song. She'd heard all of the voices of the Company's rockcallers. All, it seemed, but this one. She would not have forgotten this wet, gurgling command. She wrinkled her nose and spat, as if that act could get the song's vile taste from her mouth. Instead of singing, she put her hand, palm up, on the asphalt, beckoning to the stony spheres. The pebbles rolled up into her palm as if following a track.

She felt their shrill keening. The troll was in pain. She hadn't known they *could* feel pain. Holding the pebbles though, she felt its wound, as if one tectonic plate were being ground under another, a shuddering tremor of hurt. The spheres circled in her palm, pulling her toward the broken arm upon the street.

Brunna put a pebble in her mouth, tasting the rock troll's trail. She felt where the troll had gone; its trajectory ran from here into the centre of town. She knew the place it was going. She knew where it had been called. She opened her trumpet case and nicked her thumb on Skeri's edge. Brunna squeezed the drops of blood over the pebbles, coating them; the stones drank the liquid like sponges.

It could come in handy, tying my blood to the troll's mortar.

She stuffed the troll's arm in a beat-up hockey equipment bag and then drew Skeri from its case, slashing it through the air. The illusion had served its purpose. It wavered, like a heat mirage, and collapsed.

In Flin Flon there was a door in the rock.

Beyond a ragged bit of orange mesh netting, and to the right of a billboard proclaiming the pleasures of McDonald's coffee, it lurked between two triangular wedges of cement and underneath wooden scaffolding bearing steps up a huge slab of granite. Graffiti stained the rock, the stairs, and the wooden boxes hiding the city's aboveground water and sewage lines.

The square wooden door had existed as long as Brunna had been alive. There were stories told by locals, and then there were the stories told by the dwarves. It was a bomb shelter left over from the Second World War. It was the abandoned early mines from when the dwarves alone worked this rock. It was a work station for Manitoba Hydro. It led to the last remnants of Niðavellir, ancestral home of the *dvergar*. The only thing dwarves and miners loved more than telling stories was embellishing them.

Dropping the hockey bag holding the troll's arm to the ground, Brunna squinted at the door. It was padlocked on the left and had a bolt that went up and into the rock. Rusted hinges, almost the length of her forearm were on the right. The door mocked her with a spray-painted profanity.

Fuck, indeed.

Brunna tried to pop the padlock, but it held fast. Unwritten on the door, but just as apparent, was the "off."

The last time Brunna had walked by, there'd been a two-by-four nailed across the door as an additional security measure. Brunna saw it, snapped in two and tangled in the orange mesh. Otherwise, the door didn't appear to be damaged, although some of the supporting scaffolding for the stairs above it was.

The door might be locked, but that lock was made of metal and she spoke its language. Brunna didn't hear or see anyone. Feeling safely alone, she spoke to the metal.

"Open," she said, coaxing it. Nothing. It was stubborn. She commanded it, and it dug in like a deer tick. She whispered, using a lover's tongue. It remained shut up tight.

She puckered her lips, ready to spit. *How had the troll even gotten in there?* The lock wouldn't budge. *It should have opened.* She remembered that strange rockcaller's song. Her rock troll wasn't missing. It'd been stolen.

More than one way to crack a lock, Brunna knew.

She spoke stone as well as steel. And she was tired of illusions and subtleties. Brunna laid her palm flat against the granite; the rocks shuddered, cracking the door jamb, and splintering the door. The metal bar screeched as it was pushed out of the stone. Brunna slid the broken padlock out of its bar and opened the door.

She hefted her bag over one arm, carrying Skeri's case in the other. Beyond the door was a room of rough-hewn stone so heavily clad by pipes and conduits it seemed the stones were dressed in serpents – as if Brunna had walked into Hel's hall itself.

Boxes and crates littered the floor. They'd been pried open and long since emptied, now guardians to broken beer and whisky bottles, spent cigarette butts, and discarded home-made water pipes.

Some local party boys must have a key.

She shut the door behind her and grimaced when it wouldn't close flush. There was no troll, and even to Brunna's sight, there was no other way out of the room.

There was a squeak, followed by a burring rumble. The troll *was* here. It had blended into the rock seamlessly. She called it, trying to drown out that other, more insistent voice, the one she didn't know. Now that she was here, and had the troll in her grasp; she didn't care who heard her. Brunna drew the pebbles out of her pocket. They rolled up her body and into her palm. She sought the tie in her blood, her parents' blood, that would allow her to wrest command of the troll.

It limped toward her, head cocked like a curious hound's, revealing a tunnel its bulk had obscured. Brunna hadn't re-membered hearing its leg had been damaged too. She stared, trying to sense any other hurts, rocking a little unsteadily, her head buzzing from the sharp throb of effort and the thrill of conflict, of testing her voice against another. The troll rocked along with her, its joints sounding like car tires on a gravel road. With a booming thud, it dropped to its knees and looked her in the eye.

Kneeling, the troll was taller than Brunna. It must've topped ten feet standing. Her parents' work was reflected in its polished quartz eyes as much as it was in her. She felt a kinship with this troll. Even in the dim light, dwarf eyes saw much. The dried, rusty stain along the troll's damaged side. A spring still weeping blood. She pocketed the pebbles, and knelt to unzip her bag. With a grunt, she hefted the troll's arm to its broken, ragged socket.

The troll let out a rumbling growl before it loosed a landslide roar. Brunna cut her left palm on her sword, hoping the mixture of blood and Skeri's magical steel might cut through whatever was agitating the troll. It pointed at itself, then Brunna, and back to itself; rocky fist cracking against slate chest. Imploring for aid. Comfort.

Rock trolls were neither once-living souls bound into stone, nor stone given life. They weren't *living* at all. Fossilized bones and a jumble of mismatched stone all mortared together with blood, given a semblance of human form, and sung awake by the will and voice of a rockcaller. Tireless. Near-invulnerable hunters. Unfathomably strong. Smart as a truck full of rocks. When they slept they looked like a pile of stones to the magic-blinded eyes of Midgard. This was what Brunna had always been told. But facing this one, feeling its pain and sadness, she felt what she'd been told was wrong. They *could* possess a semblance of life.

The living deserved names. Names were important. If her sword could have a name, so should the troll.

You are *alive, aren't you, Rocky?*

She wanted to know for certain. Focusing her will on the troll, Brunna sang to its stones; a ballad of stitching Loki's lying mouth shut. It flinched and rumbled backward, circling as if it were trying to roll into a fetal ball. She reached out a calming hand with her whispered song.

Rocky brushed her cheek with its rough, stony finger. Even that gesture, meant to be gentle, hurt. She ignored the throb in her cheek where a bruise would surely form. She held the arm to the broken joint, keeping her voice steady and she sang. She could see where it should fit together. But it wouldn't.

She felt sorry for him. And then realized with a start that she was no longer thinking of Rocky as a pile of stones, as just a *thing*. She called to the spherical pebbles, and they rolled out of her pocket, up the rock troll's body, and settled into grooves in his wounded arm. He roared, trying to backpedal when stone touched stone.

"I'm trying to fix you, you clod!"

He didn't react to the insult – but someone else did.

In the troll's moment of shock, that foreign rockcaller resumed their song. The voice sounded like the wet gurgle of blood-filled lungs.

"Maggoty child of cowards and thieves."

It sang to Rocky. The vileness of the song was overwhelming, pushing Brunna to her knees. The song didn't stop, but the singer spoke, "Kill her!"

The troll shot up like a geyser and Brunna jumped back with a startled yelp. Rocky's good arm slammed into her, hurling her into the wall. She heard a grunting pained cry from behind her before she was enveloped in a darkness too deep for even dwarven eyes.

Brunna awoke, amazed at the simple fact of her survival, head pounding and ribs throbbing. The troll was gone. A sound like an avalanche rumbled off in the distance. Rocky had run off. Again. So had the other caller. She could feel them, moving down, ever down.

She smiled though it made her wince. *You can't lose a dwarf under the earth.*

Rocky was bound to that other call, its drowned voice echoing in her ears, fouling her mind. She grimaced. But she'd found her troll, and she'd return him intact. *Alive.*

She found Skeri. A man's running shoe lay next to its case. Perhaps it belonged to whomever she'd crashed into. With the force the troll had struck Brunna, she half-expected to find a foot inside it. She hefted it cautiously, happy to be proven wrong.

Rubbing at her ribs, she winced; her chain shirt had dissipated the force of the troll's blow, turning it from crippling to inconvenient. It was good that her skull was almost as sturdy.

Why would the caller leave her? Had he tried to kill her? Had Rocky stopped him? The troll must have resisted. Both caller and troll had had every possible chance to finish her, but had not. She'd heard the voice's words: *Kill her.* If she was alive, it was the troll's doing, not that caller's. Brunna wasn't out of this fight yet.

The entrance, obvious now with Rocky gone, gaped and waited. She had to delve deeper to get out.

Down, down, down, following the call.

The pull of the earthen darkness emboldened Brunna as she felt the massive weight of the rock above her. If she'd been born among mortals, the dark underground would be overpowering. A tomb of stone, enough to drive a timid person mad. But rock was home to her, even if she wished to part ways with it for a time. She trailed her hands over the tunnel, admiring the work. A dwarf had made this place. The work was too fine for human hands.

It was strange she didn't know it. In her desire to get away from this town, she'd walked every tunnel dwarves and men had carved. At least, she'd thought she had. Listening to the rock, it was as old as any tunnels she'd ever been in. Older. Brunna felt like she could have delved into Niðavellir itself – if only the first home of the dwarves had survived Ragnarök.

Down, down, down, following the call.

This tunnel wasn't mentioned in Sögusalur. Brunna had walked the History Hall with her family, and she had read much. *Dvergur* did not keep secrets from *dvergur*. She'd always been told this.

But carved into the walls of tunnel in runic script were entries detailing new lore. Families. Histories. Names. None of which Brunna knew. But they were here, and sunk into the stone without the use of tools, in the *dvergur* fashion.

She looked at these and thought of the stories she'd been told were "lost" in the early days after Ragnarök. Stories don't get lost. They're hidden, buried, forgotten. But stories are truth, and the truth will come out. Of days when a great schism fractured the *dvergar*.

There were those who wanted to subjugate and kill humanity, those who wanted to share the toil (if not the wealth) with them, and those who, having been found, wanted to abandon the mines and start over somewhere else, somewhere even more remote, where they would be done with all of Odin's creations.

Her uncle Andvari had risen to power when men had come to the Flin Flon region before it had been given an English name. His faction wanted to use the humans, not harm them. What happened to the dissenters was never spoken of. Their names, and in some cases, their entire lines, had been gouged from Sögusalur during the conflict, and they were to be forgotten.

Odd to find their story here, and when she had Rocky in hand, she'd commit it to memory, but it was not the story she was interested in. More relevant to the moment: revenge fantasies. Scrawled more recently, the stones told her, and torturous descriptions of prospectors' ends in the city's early wilder days.

Her parents' names were on those walls. That was troubling. Uncle Andvari's name was inscribed there too. Seeing how often Andvari's name repeated, and the varying ways in which it had been defaced, changing its meaning, was more troubling. As was the repetition of the name Bláinn.

Brunna didn't know a dwarf by that name. But she had heard stories about such a dwarf. They still told stories of his death in hushed whispers in the beer halls, and how it was *ages* before the stones took him.

When she'd asked her parents, they'd said, "We do not speak of him. He is dead. And each of the Nine Worlds is better for that."

The light was faint at first, the dying glow of a distant star, but with every step, more and more fire was poured into that light.

With every step, the caller's gurgling song grew louder, madder. The light grew brighter, and warmth flooded the tunnel. Brunna broached the room where the caller waited, his back to her. A great burning oven filled the chamber with light. The caller sang, and two bladders on his back inflated and deflated like forge bellows with every wheezing word. Sweat poured down Brunna's brow. The smell of hot metal and burning coal filled her nostrils. Despite those comforting sensations, what she saw made Brunna want to retch. Those bladders were lungs, carved out of his body, and left to flap against his back. A "blood eagle" the torture was named, and it was invariably fatal; but somehow, this dwarf had survived.

This had to be Rocky's unseen caller. He appeared bent and broken at first glance, the rest of his body as ravaged as his back. More a spider crushed underfoot than a sturdy dwarf. But when he moved, it was with a speed that pained Brunna to watch: undulating, a boneless sack of flesh. She shivered to witness his tortured limbs scurrying about his workshop from one arcane item to another.

Snapping her gaze from the rockcaller, she scanned the chamber for her true quarry. Rocky stood impassive, arm reattached, on the other side of the work table. On the table itself a young human male – barely an adult – was bound.

"You thought you'd killed me. All of you. Bláinn the Bold did not die, even when you made him Bláinn the Bloody, Bláinn Blood-Eagle. Bláinn will not die. His hate keeps him alive."

Brunna buried a gasp in her hand. The stories were true. She begged the rocks not to reveal her, and found stillness in their touch, and strength in their enveloping presence.

"Please, mister. I didn't..." the boy stopped, as if trying to fathom what the creature was implying. "I didn't do anything."

"Your ancestors, then. And the ancestors of your woman."

"What woman? Oh, Jesus, I stole the key. I just wanted to smoke up. This isn't fair."

The creature gestured at its ruined body. "*Fair*? Is this fair? What you did to me?"

"I didn't – I'm sorry."

"Sorry? I will teach you sorry. Order your lackeys to give me the blood eagle and then wait for me to die? And as I welcomed Hel's release, even as Sword-Sleep came for me, you healed me, so more of your puppets could do the same? Have you *any* concept what I have suffered?"

"N-no."

"You will." The creature's voice went from dark to light. Growl to sing-song. "You will."

The dead handler of the rock troll was here also. His body, already going to rot, leaned against a table in the centre of the room; the corpse's face was turned to look at her, a neat hole in its forehead staring like a third eye. But another body had more of her attention, and given his constant sobbing, Bláinn Blood-Eagle's as well.

Brunna may have only known Bláinn's name from stories, and those tales were but tin to the steel of this horror, but she'd seen the boy strapped to the table. She knew him from around town. He'd smiled brightly as Freyr's golden boar when he asked to buy her a beer. Now his wide eyes hunted escape, not romance. His must have been the cry she'd heard before Rocky had knocked her out.

There were oddities in jars, and the walls engraved with charts of creatures' anatomy. Brunna saw locals the newspaper had reported dead in a recent wildfire, not burned, but still very, very dead.

The boy's gaze locked in on where Brunna hid, and he wailed, "Help me."

Brunna ducked down as Bláinn spun, following the boy's eyeline, and hoped she hadn't been seen.

"Please," the boy cried and that single pleading word seemed to echo for an eternity.

"Enough of that," Bláinn wheezed.

When the wails finally stopped, Brunna worried the boy had been silenced by death. She chanced a furtive peek and saw an iron bit crammed into the boy's mouth. It stuck out like a railroad spike waiting to be hammered.

Light reflected in the boy's tears, which ran freely from red-rimmed eyes down cheeks to spatter on the table.

Oozing around the boy, the once-dwarf inserted needles into his prisoner's arteries. The rubber tubing attached to the ends began dripping blood *pitter pat, pitter pat* into a large flat vessel positioned underneath the table.

Rocky stood, impassive and uncaring as the scene unfolded, restrained by bloody runes drawn upon his every stone. Brunna wasn't certain she *could* free him, or that she could command him now, even if she won the troll his freedom.

But she called anyway.

STILL ALIVE, he answered, using words, which surprised her. *STILL HURT.*

"You would try to take my work from me?" Bláinn asked, lungs puffing up in indignation.

Brunna froze.

"You weren't supposed to be here. You shouldn't have followed."

Brunna didn't answer, but did wonder to herself, *Why not?*

"I expected you to bring them down to me. Summon the Company. Oh I would have loved to do to them what they did to me."

The Company did this to him? He had to be wrong.

Wrong, wrong, wrong, her thought echoed, picked up by the caller's song, mocking her.

"I felt you wandering my halls. You thought you could hide your song from me? I know everything, living or dead under the earth."

She hadn't been sure at first if Bláinn had been bluffing, but when he'd named her... Brunna stepped out to face him, Skeri drawn. *"You don't know me."*

"Yessssss," he whispered, drawing out the word, like a cartoon serpent. Scuttling over the table, and the boy, the once-dwarf said, "Oh yes, I do, Brunna Sindradóttir. I know your entire cursed family."

"Uncle Andvari wouldn't have given that order."

"Such a bright girl you are. Like a ruby in the sun." He paused. And in the waiting, Brunna saw the truth.

Bláinn charged her. Brunna raised her sword and winced. There was no time for pain. Only the craft.

She hacked at him but his boneless body had no resistance, nothing to cut into. When she slashed, his flesh folded around her blade. She tried stabbing, but his boneless movements were hard to predict. Brunna hit nothing but air.

"Your uncle, your *Company*—" he spat out that last word "—you think they know better? Crafting weapons? Making humans into weapons? Humanity is *wood*. Coal. Fuel to be spent in the forge. I will craft my own weapon. When I need blood for a working, *I will take it*. I will make the mortals fear the night again. Only when they know fear, terror – monsters. Then they will pay for the tools to triumph. And if the world needs monsters to be great – *I* will forge those monsters. Once-Dwarf. Bláinn Blood-Eagle. Not Bláinn the Bold. Never again, Bláinn the Bold. I will show them *bold*. I will show them *monsters*."

She kicked at him. His leg wrapped around her ankle. Brunna grabbed at Bláinn's wrist with her free hand and looped the boneless appendage around her arm, dragging him closer and closer.

Close enough to stab.

"That's a damned cart full of slag," Brunna said, sliding Skeri into the once-dwarf. His rubbery skin was hard to pierce. "I read your twisted History Hall. *You* were a monster before this happened to you."

He hissed, as if a forge spark had landed upon his arm, and nothing more.

Through clenched teeth, Brunna said, "And if my uncle hurt you, you *deserved* it."

Bláinn choked out a wet laugh and wriggled free of her, biting and scratching. "We all deserve it."

Brunna reached out to Rocky, hoping the troll could help her. Stone scratched over stone as his head turned to regard her. Bláinn had Rocky penned with a ring of blood. Bláinn recognized her plan, and his lungs pumped against his back as he resumed his song, holding the troll still. Brunna needed to get closer so Skeri could cut through Bláinn's wards, through his call, and release Rocky.

She stabbed at Bláinn – a feint – and when he shifted away, she dove, her blade crossing the plane of the protective ward, severing the enchantment. Rocky's eyes enveloped his head as the runes painted on his stones flared and burned away. Rocky rumbled forward and Bláinn howled. Rocky was free. Free to choose whom to serve. To help. To hurt. Or to run. She called to the troll, reached out to her blood and the connection that bound them. Her blood was in his very bones now, just like that of her parents.

Rocky's newly repaired arm grabbed Brunna by the throat, his other snatched a wriggling Bláinn. Bláinn's command, "Kill," burned, hot and loud. By comparison, Brunna's request, "Please," seemed almost silent.

Bláinn's touch, and toxic blood coursed through Rocky's repaired arm as it strangled Brunna, as rockcaller duelled rockcaller to see whose song was superior. Her eyes dimmed as she rooted out Bláinn's influence.

Crafters put something of themselves into their work when they created. A bit of heart, a bit of soul – whatever, *however*, a skald might describe it. And Brunna's parents' souls were there in Rocky. Her mother and father had made this rock troll as surely as they'd made Brunna. Brunna rooted it out. Blood leaked from his mortar and the arm fell away from the socket, its grasp still tight on Brunna's throat.

Brunna couldn't hear Bláinn's surprised cry through the pounding of her ears, but she felt the air rush from the room, as if his flapping lungs had blown it away.

Brunna pried Rocky's arm free of her throat and sang the same song her mother had sung to her in nights past, and Bláinn's blood poured from Rocky's arm. It went still.

The rock troll turned to Bláinn, head tilting as he held the dwarf tightly.

Bláinn rasped out, "No."

Brunna shook her head. "Goodbye, Bláinn Blood-Eagle."

Rocky made the only choice he could.

Bláinn resisted, his legs wrapping around Brunna's, hugging tightly even as his fingers pried at Rocky's hands. She sawed at his rubbery body until he let go of her.

Bláinn may have looked boneless, but judging from the cracking as the rock troll wrung him out, there were still some hard points in his eel-like body. His lungs inflated rapidly, filling until they burst, spilling what seemed to be every drop of blood in his body. The rockcaller's final song was a wheezing gurgle as Rocky dropped him to the stone, and then ground him underfoot.

Brunna turned aside, not needing to see Bláinn's end. There was nothing she could do for the troll's dead handler, but at the least she could get the boy out of here before he woke to a different nightmare.

She cooed at the troll to pick up the dead dwarf.

Gently, gently, now.

Rocky hefted the corpse as if he were holding delicately blown glass.

Brunna freed the boy from his restraints and Bláinn's instruments, and considerably less carefully, hoisted him over her shoulder. His fingers and toes practically dragged on the stone while she walked back to Rocky's side.

She held out her hand to the rock troll, who took it, enveloping her palm in his giant stone mitt. "Let's get you home," she said, flashing the rock troll a broad smile and wiping away a sooty rune image. "You look terrible."

Rocky made a pleased little trill, a sound like shale snapping between her fingers, and fell in behind her.

Whether anyone in the Company would believe her story, Brunna didn't know and she didn't care. There was nothing left of Bláinn Blood-Eagle to show. His story was over.

Hers had begun.

BLACK THORNS AND UNICORNS

REBECCA SCHAEFFER

Umeko jerked backward as the coffee splattered across the front of her shirt. She winced in anticipation of the inevitable burn, but ended up shuddering as the cold, liquid-soaked shirt stuck against her skin and raised goosebumps.

"I'm so sorry," said the stranger standing in front of her, hands stretched out as if he could still catch the coffee cup that was now rolling across the floor.

Umeko shrugged, grabbing a napkin. "It's fine. The coffee wasn't hot."

The stranger grabbed several napkins and started wiping the book she'd been reading at the table, trying to dry it. Umeko ineffectively dabbed at her shirt with the napkins. She sighed, checking the time. Her flight would be boarding any minute.

"Would you mind watching my suitcase while I clean this up in the washroom?" she asked the stranger.

"Of course," he responded, his own coffee forgotten on the table.

Umeko grabbed her purse and went to the washroom. Her reflection in the mirror told her it was worse than she'd initially thought. Coffee stains covered most of the front of her white button-up business shirt like the inkblots used at psych exams. This one looked like a disembodied hand poking a loaf of bread.

Sighing, she stripped her shirt off and used paper towels and warm water to wash the coffee smell from her own skin while she soaked the shirt in the sink. She opened her purse and pulled out a pink T-shirt in a plastic bag. It was supposed to be a souvenir for her little sister, who, at sixteen, still held on to her love of unicorns with a fierce passion. The cartoonish little horse had a rainbow horn shooting little sparkles.

Umeko pulled the shirt on and promised herself she'd wash it before she gave it to her sister. Yuka would understand.

Ignoring her overly pink reflection in the mirror, she wrung out her business shirt and stuffed it in the plastic bag that had been holding Yuka's. She tied the plastic handles shut, shoved it in her purse, and hoped it wouldn't leak.

When she came out, her plane was already boarding. The large TV screens by the gate had news stories running across the screen. Apparently another tour boat going to the Bermuda Triangle to see the giant sea monster had been eaten by said sea monster. Umeko rolled her eyes, unsurprised.

The stranger was sitting at her table, drinking a new coffee and waiting. He glanced up as she approached.

"You a fan of unicorns?" he asked.

Umeko shook her head. "My sister."

The man smiled. He had blue eyes and brown hair that seemed determined to flop in front of his face no matter how he tried to push it back. Umeko estimated that he was her age, maybe a little older. His jeans and T-shirt made him look like a college student. Or just someone who liked to travel comfortably.

"You look a lot younger than I thought," he said.

Umeko pulled the long handle from her carry-on bag and swung it out from under the table. "Everyone says that. It's like, the default thing people say to Asians."

He laughed, waving his hands in denial. "No, I mean, you looked so professional before, I figured you must be a businesswoman."

Umeko shrugged. "I just finished an internship."

"Doing?"

"IT." Umeko looked toward the dwindling line of people boarding her plane. She wondered if there'd be room in the overhead compartment for her bag.

"I'm sorry, I didn't mean to keep you. And sorry about the coffee." The man rose and held out his hand for her to shake. "It was nice talking to you."

Umeko swung her purse back so it wouldn't slam into him when she shook his hand. "Likewise. Don't worry about the coffee."

When she touched his hand, she almost gasped in pain. There was a horrible sensation, like someone had cast a fishing line and the hook had caught on her heart. It tugged insistently, and she winced.

The man leaned in close, voice concerned. "Are you all right?"

"Fine." Umeko put a hand to her chest, instinct telling her to apply pressure to the wound, even though there wasn't one.

She gave the man a tight smile and made her way over to the plane. She never saw the faint smile that played across his face as she left.

She tried to read on the flight, but was distracted by the faint tugging of the fishhook in her heart. It didn't hurt nearly as much now, but it was still there, determined. She wondered if she should go to a doctor when she got home.

Waiting around for her checked bag, she saw the man again. Their eyes met, and he gave her a bright smile and came over.

"Hi again."

"Hi." Umeko gave him a polite smile

"I didn't realize we were on the same flight until I saw you run up to the boarding gate." His voice was light.

"I see." Umeko turned her attention to the baggage going round and round on the dispenser.

He laughed, scratching his nose in embarrassment. "I'm sorry. This is probably really awkward. You don't even know my name."

"Ah, no, it's fine—"

Before Umeko had finished, he was holding his hand out. "Can we start again? My name's Kenneth."

"Umeko." She took his hand.

"Japanese?" he asked as they shook.

She nodded. "My mother is. My father's from Vancouver."

"Neat." He smiled. "I guess this is home then?"

She nodded. "Yes. And you?"

"I'm from Albuquerque originally," he laughed. "I'm studying at UBC these days."

"Me too." Umeko saw her luggage and went to take it from the belt. Kenneth beat her to it, pulling it off with ease. "Thanks."

"No worries." He gave her a disarming grin.

"What do you study?" she asked.

"Folklore." He winked. "Ghoulies and ghosties and long-leggedy beasties."

She laughed despite herself. Folklore was the politically correct way of saying he studied "unnaturals." The political activists insisted that calling them unnaturals was wrong, since they were natural. Just not necessarily natural in this world, if you believed the alternate-world theorists. The scientists were still fighting about that, just like they fought whenever they discovered a new species of "non-human sentient being" or another recessive gene that popped up in humans, making them fall into the "unnatural" category.

Umeko never paid any attention to it. Half the things people claimed existed didn't, and the other half usually kept a low profile. Estimates of the worldwide population of all the "unnaturals" – all species included – never ranged over a few thousand. Chances were, she'd live her whole life and never meet one.

Her pants vibrated and she pulled her cell phone out. A text from her sister telling her that she couldn't come to the airport, so please take the train from YVR to Broadway station.

"You have a ride?" He pulled his own suitcase from the belt.

Umeko shook her head. "Train."

He grinned. "Me too."

It wasn't until later, lying on her bed at home, after dinner with her family, that she realized there was a second fishhook in her heart.

Umeko met Kenneth for coffee on campus a few days later. He wanted to make up for the one he'd spilled on her.

Kenneth was early but Umeko was earlier. All through their conversation, the hooks in her chest tugged and tugged, pulling her toward Kenneth.

It was during a particularly strong tug – when Kenneth laughed at something, hair falling in front of his face – that Umeko wondered if the fishhooks might be a sign of a crush.

Umeko had always been a little behind the development curve. She read books and watched movies, so in theory she knew how relationships were supposed to go and what people were supposed to feel. She just hadn't really felt it herself. Having just turned twenty and never been out on a date, she wondered if this might be what it felt like.

She wasn't really sure how you were supposed to know if you liked someone, but she figured since she was actually thinking about it, that might be the case here. She decided to go with it.

So when they finished their coffee and Umeko rose to leave for class, she didn't resist when Kenneth took her hand and leaned forward shyly, almost tentatively, to press a light kiss to her lips.

When the third fishhook sank into her chest with enough pain to make her scream so loud she felt like she would never speak again, she knew this wasn't love.

The pain was gone.

Umeko opened her eyes and was surprised to find there was sky above her. It was the vague colourless grey that was too dull and bored to be white, but didn't want to expend the effort to be ominously black. It was just grey.

Where was the coffee shop? How did she end up outside? Her mind conjured up the questions, but she felt numb, almost disinterested in the answers, the sort of strange dream mentality where she just accepted things, no matter how unnatural.

She was standing on a path. The dirt might actually be brown, but the weird lighting made it seem grey, too. Her skin, her clothes, everything looked grey in the light.

The path was lined with tall black rose bushes, except there were no roses, only thorns. They didn't look solid, more like the formless black of rose bush shadows than actual rose bushes.

"Hello, Umeko." Kenneth was standing behind her. She turned around and blinked, confused because he was all in colour. "Walk with me a bit?"

She hesitated a moment before walking with him, mind fuzzy, like she hadn't quite woken up. As they walked, the thorns on the rose bushes seemed to snake out and cut Umeko's arms. She flinched away from each scrape, fighting the sensation that the road was narrowing.

"Have you ever wondered why unicorns only approach virgins?" he asked.

The black thorns were tearing at her now. She winced with each step, fighting their spiky claws. "Not really. Unicorns don't exist."

Even as she said it, she was thinking of all the other kinds of folklore creatures that people said hadn't existed but turned out to be real. And all the unnaturals that were nothing like their folktale counterparts.

He smiled at her, but it wasn't the good-natured smile she was used to. This one was condescending. "I'm a unicorn."

Umeko stopped and stared at him. While she stood frozen, the black thorns seized the opportunity to entwine themselves around her body, rooting her in place. She was overcome with the strangest, most inappropriate sensation to laugh. She felt like he was going to follow that sentence with, "and the horn's not on my head."

Thousands of tiny little cuts covered Umeko's body. Rivulets of blood clung to her skin in a way that reminded her of the coffee he'd spilt on her when they first met.

Snapping out of her sense of unreality, she began to struggle against the thorns, swinging her arms and twisting her body to try and escape. But the thorns were everywhere and every time she moved they dug in deeper.

"Why?" Umeko snapped her mouth shut when a vine of thorns tried to crawl down her throat. Turning her face away from the encroaching vines, she continued, "Why do unicorns only come to virgins?"

"Because virgins are usually young and not yet comfortable in their own bodies. And that means their souls are easier to pull out." Kenneth's smile was wide, wider than humanly possible, and his teeth were all black thorns.

Umeko gasped when one of the thorns sunk into her side so deeply that her body began to tingle in the strange mix of pain and numbness that came when you knew you'd hurt yourself *bad*. Her strength slipped away and she would have fallen if the vines hadn't held her so tight that she couldn't even move, never mind fall. "But why do you want their souls?"

He spread his hands. The thorns were blocking part of her vision now, so his whole figure seemed criss-crossed with black lines. "To eat of course."

Umeko would have responded, but the thorns had clamped like a vice around her, and she couldn't seem to get any air. She gasped for breath and a thorny vine finally clawed its way down her throat.

The last thing she saw was her own black hair spilling across the thorn branches, dripping with blood.

Yuka sat beside Kenneth in the hospital waiting room. He'd followed after the ambulance in a taxi, and met her family at the hospital. He'd taken the liberty of going through her phone and calling them. It was too late by the time they got there. Umeko had passed away en route to the hospital.

Yuka wore the pink shirt with unicorns that her sister had brought home as a souvenir. Her hands were clenched in her lap, and her eyes were squished shut to prevent the tears from slipping out.

Kenneth put his hand on hers. "I'm so sorry for your loss."

The pain of her sister's death stabbed Yuka in the chest, causing her to double over in racking sobs.

It felt like a fishhook in her heart.

ANTONY'S ARBORETUM

RENÉE SAROJINI SAKLIKAR

Once, when Time held its sway, a Canadian city grew into Northern and within its sphere, both ken and kind, there was found that giant of a man, Antony. His hands spanned easily into two neighbouring districts and some locals said the hands of Antony might be a bridge over the river, when it broke ice, later come the May. Antony's full name was longer than was ever custom to speak. In his name, as given to him by his poor dear mother, two days before she died, were the names of every settler ever arrived into the city. Raised lonesome by his gruff father, Antony ran wild with his boy-cousins, and of those cousins, the one he hated most was John. From the time the two boys fell into the river – cold were its waters, deep and even then filled with effluent – from that time, woven and wended, when John offered nary a twig to Antony, hatred stored its roots into Antony as if an acorn. And willed by Antony, how that acorn grew!

Cousin John grew up to be the sort of man who would filch more land than might bear a mine. Cousin John learned how to commandeer more waters than might harbour a fish farm. Cousin John grew into the ownership of mills so plentiful that when one blew off its own smokestack, injuring dozens of men, Cousin John in his counting house, looked up from his desk, and with a half-smile, signed many a voucher to help those men and their families: from the Mill-Store, many a provision, and lots of credit. The city built a plaque at the site, commending Cousin John for his good care of the men. At the ceremony, there was Cousin John, resplendent in a blue wool coat, his pockets stuffed with more vouchers. All his long-term thoughts helped Cousin John well into Regulatory, where he schooled in the ways of land, its accumulation. If we were able to time-travel, back into this Northern city, and arrive at Regulators' Hall, there in a room panelled in cedar, we'd find, on a Wednesday afternoon, Cousin John smoking a pipe, seated at a table strewn with land deeds and at his elbow, a Collect of Redactors, them with their high collars stuck straight. Every man in the room sure to give Cousin John a nod. Every man sure to look the other way at the time of filching: that would be three tracts from Antony, them with the best timber, the highest stumpage fees. Every man sure to slant-smile, when, worst of all, Cousin John stole from Antony, the girl named, Naomi. Naomi was known far and wide as Naomi the Black Haired. Now, you may know the many stories of Naomi and you may wish to have her deeds cited here in this tale. Understand, though, the stories of Naomi are as if a nest of wasps and sting so sharp and swollen that today it is best if they lie dormant. Even to this day, all over the city, loudspeakers mounted pole-high share the daily motto: *Believing Makes You True.*

Although some held Naomi's inheritance as middling, those who ticketed in Knowing whispered that Naomi's father dealt in diamonds, that there were residing in her house what was known at that time as closet-servants. (Now, information on the indenture of closet-servants will be excised from this story by order of the Redactor. We may as well interrupt the path of narrative, whose flow carries within its surface, the names unspoken, those strewn highway to highway, that stretch of blacktop, frost heaved, that runs out from the city limits.)

So deep did Antony dream of Naomi, so fixed were his imaginings: his desire grew about him as if a castle, that not one mote of light reached him, the light that would shine over Cousin John's many manoeuvers to bring Naomi the Black Haired within reach. And reach her he did! Cousin John, him with his wily ways, his winking eye, his easy grin, he found Naomi, he brought her into an understanding of herself. It were his height that did it, the slant of his jaw (strong, not huge and misshapen like Antony's); it were about that ratio, broad shoulder to narrow waist; it were the way Time slowed, when, next to Naomi, Cousin John would place his thumb on her wrist, would stare into her eyes. Crafty Cousin John: he with his easy ways, smart enough to ask Naomi The Black Haired to dances at Regulators' Hall, to stand leeward out back, long after the dances ended, him with his hand-rolled cigarettes, he'd blow smoke into her hair. Not one elder were present to hear the sighs of Naomi touched by Cousin John. Some say she wrote nightly of her trysts with him: the colour of his eyes, his hair, the feel of his taut skin, the way his hand crushed her own. Of the journal of Naomi the Black Haired, not even all the Collect of Redactors would ever find—

With Cousin John, Naomi birthed three sons. Two to work in the mill, one to farm the fish. A girl was born and died. Cousin John and Naomi never spoke of this stillborn girl. In fact, Naomi spoke not even to her best friend, Sara, who at night would creep away from the clothes shop, where all of Naomi's family worked. Now, it were the custom of Naomi's family to bring to succour those girls who might have met hard times and this is how Sara the Orphan first crossed Threshold into the home of Naomi's family. Sara, her bright red hair in curls, sang herself into chores about the house: in the kitchen over a pot of stew, in the quilting room over fabric squares, at night, emptying the chamber pots. Sara would warm the bed of Antony's father, Ronald. All this was known in the town. Always there were that which swirled, eddies of story, around Cousin John, around the family of his wife Naomi, around the goings-on of Antony's father, Ronald. And with all the swirling, Antony grew and grew. Antony grew his jaw, jutted and steep. Antony grew his limbs, his hands and feet.

Father Ronald was an engineer. He built the mines that ran the town. He built the mills that fed the town and housed it. Antony's father and all his miners drilled and dug into the earth. Antony's father said, "There's no drill like a sharp bit." He said this nights when at table, across the long sweep of linen, where sat his long-jawed, shoulder-hunched only son, Antony, who said not a word. At night, Father Ronald spoke of bitumen, iron, and gold to himself, after the girl Sara left his bed.

In those days the custom of Father Ronald was to sit afternoons when time sat also, in icicles, in the grey of February. With him, Cousin John, who laughed every time Father Ronald said the word "drill." We can no longer imagine the depth of this laughter, no more than can we imagine a miner laughing his coal-black dusty fate away. Yet Cousin John would dig his lungs deep and laugh a miner's laugh, his eyes on Father Ronald's face. There the two of them sat.

They spoke together, there at that table, all the ins and outs of agreements, the workings of mill, mine, and fish farm. Cousin John sat at table, his eyes on Father Ronald's face.

Antony grew and grew. His frame bony and ungainly, Antony stooped from a great height, the better to look at things on the ground. Antony gardened, there under the Northern light. Hothouse flowers gazed at him gentle under his geo-dome, the Observatory, made hand over hand, made cedar and Douglas fir, made green ceiling glass. Outside there was the great flourishing, a grove of trees, Antony's Arboretum. All the trees that might grow North. All the plants that underlay the trees – Douglas, Spruce, Hemlock. Also, the growth of shrubs and berries. Heather and crowberry. Antony learned how to Bring In, how to root into container, to graft and to breed. Hardhack from the swamps, sagebrush from the dry and salal from the coast with Indian plum.

These were what Antony called his Outside Passion.

Inside, under glass, Antony spent hours devising a heating-hydration system that brought warm moist air to breathe on all his plants. The names of these foreign plants, housed in his Observatory, were as precious to Antony as all the timber cut and tied and sent on barges down the river outside the city limits. Antony made potions from his plants, creams and lotions stored in jars. He made so many salves and ointments that he had to dig into the earth of the grounds of the Arboretum great storage cellars. The water that fed the trees in Antony's Arboretum, and that were the mainstay of his Observatory system, came from the well dug into the estate, owned by Father Ronald. The well dropped into the family all manner of disputes. These were rarely spoken, and a very curious sort of person, a person perhaps not welcome within the confines of this story, might well call up the Book of the Redactor, or wander back into Regulators' Hall, or, on a dare, drift down Main Street to the Barracks of the Militia, there to find in those places that weight of Not Speaking, and to shoulder the weight, and then to move on—

As fame of Antony's Arboretum and Observatory grew, men would bring their sons and daughters (the mothers stayed mostly at home). Young women came to see Old Giant Jaw, as Antony was sometimes called. Now, many of these women visited in order to gawk and stare; some to mock and scorn. Antony paid no heed. Again he was deep into dreaming, and his dreaming kept him strong in interest, gathering plants, learning their names, building and making, that rhythm that allowed him to embrace the vision: Arboretum.

One fine August Sunday, the day before the largest moon of the year, a young woman visited Antony's Arboretum. After close inspection of its many trees, she entered the Observatory. When she smiled, her habit showed a chin tucked to one side. This woman's name was Susan, brought to visit by her elder brother. He was known everywhere in the North as Prester, and some of you will have heard his crop of stories. Why, inside Regulators' Hall, you might have seen those bound black books, tucked away behind the Rolls of Land Accumulated. That's where many of Prester's story-ideas first found impetus. They have no business inside this one!

Prester could not stand the sight of Susan. Her frizzy grey hair and drooping breasts embarrassed him. How could a woman not yet thirty look so old thought Prester, when he let such thoughts inside his busy calculator brain. Himself was but twenty.

Mindful of his mother's urging that he, the youngest son, best help out his sister, Prester ushered Susan into Antony's Observatory. Prester, for weeks before the visit, dreamed dreams about which he spoke to no one, wherein he saw under moonlight, Antony's famous Gingko tree. After dreams of this tree, Prester would feel himself full and straining. Prester would rub his close-shorn skull. Prester would avoid touching—

At the Arboretum, Prester soon saw the ancient Gingko. All the whisperings of his dreams would soon find their hold under that outspread canopy. Prester knew at once, without anyone saying a thing, that at night, as close to the midnight hour as possible, young men under Antony's Gingko tree would find much fortune and also pretty girls. Sometimes, too, pretty boys. Under the Gingko tree things were bound to happen. And they did and all over the town, not one word was spoken. Well, at least not on the surface of the talk that accumulated like leaves in a gutter, between shop and mine, between mill and fish farm, and down the rafts on the river's swift current, and out far away, to the tides.

Once inside the Observatory, away from her brother Prester, happiness found Susan. Both her hands were a touch away from Antony's plants and he liked that. Antony liked the way Susan's head tilted up to him. Antony liked the way Susan's lips – at first thin and parched – grew fuller every week. Inside the Observatory, Antony would glance at Susan's lips, parted open, and she listening, to the names of things. Inside Antony, there sat always a long list of names and in Susan's presence, out the names came, for orchids, for the wild flowers plucked by Antony and carted inside the Observatory, where, in pots and jars, they also grew fuller, more lush and vibrant. Oh, Susan on a Sunday inside the Observatory! That was joy. That was as Antony wished for things to be.

Antony created flower-rituals, cuttings tied ribbon-wise, especially for Susan to hold. Soon, long lineups of folks from all the surrounding districts visited Antony's Arboretum. *Sunday's Show,* Father Ronald came to call the procession of people who stood and waited hours to be let inside. Cousin John took to selling tickets. Inside the Mansion made magnificent by Father Ronald, down in his basement study hewn from North Country rock, Father Ronald had two closet-servants embroidering a banner that hung post to post, for the monthly Guild of Miners meetings: *Many Men Making Money Makes the North Great,* said the banner, its threads in red, white and black.

The young men who visited slowly abandoned the Arboretum in favour of what became known as Susan's Corner, that place by the orchids – tall white bog flowers, Denseflower Rein, *Spiranthes diluvialis* – where girls would flock to stand by Susan. She only had eyes for the plants, although she spoke friendly-like to Antony. The girls stared at Antony's chin, his huge drooping shoulders. The young men stared at the girls. They looked at Susan, too. Around this time, gold was found on the estates. Antony's father was very rich indeed.

One afternoon, deep inside his Observatory, filled to the brim with every kind of plant imaginable, a fantastic fantasy of green, Antony heard the roar of Father Ronald's truck, come home early from the mines. At last, thought Antony, fervent to talk to his father about a new invention. In haste, Antony overturned a vessel full of seedlings. They fell out of their little pots, their spindly stems soon trampled. Antony did not notice at the time – he was too busy explaining to Father Ronald about a new germination process for the purest and most emerald green of ferns, an Irish moss, lacey as an old handkerchief, which, if rubbed and held a certain way, would sprout microscopic gold coins, bankable at the Great Northern Bank.

Once in from the Observatory and upstairs in Father Ronald's home Antony indulged in a great delight: he would affix batches of this Irish moss to his chin, where the moss beard anchored onto his great mound of skin. Antony called, "Father, Father," and raced his huge limbs down the staircase of their now palatial home.

Across the marble parquet, Antony lunged toward his father. Father Ronald took one look at Antony's moss green beard, and groaned. Father Ronald called his son a freak. "You and your appendage," cried Father Ronald, and gestured to his son's chin. "You're diseased!"

Antony turned down the corners of his mouth, hulked away, and decided not to tell Father Ronald about the new germination process with its yield of tiny gold coins.

Years later, after Ronald was long dead, the invention for the germination of seeds out of air and a bit of damp, nothing more, would be patented and bring to the family even more fortune. The time of riches on riches is always with us, of course. Never mind, though. We have our stories.

The following Sunday, there was Susan. Inside the Observatory, week after week, Susan's cheeks grew rosy instead of sallow. Susan's frizzy hair, with streaks of grey, grew lush and glinted chestnut brown, her droopy breasts plumped. Tiny drops of moisture collected in a halo around her head, clung to her hair, the top of her lip. A jewel she was, strolling about the Observatory, with Antony at her side, her small smooth hand resting inside Antony's huge paw: small to large, that were a ratio that Antony adored. He loved that Susan's hands, once red and raw, were now smooth as flax in the sun, for Antony had made Susan a potion for soothing into each groove, on thumb, on palm. Susan exclaimed to Antony, how his garden under glass brought her to happiness. Her

smile touched past his chin and entered his eyes – the
colour of flat river mud, Susan noticed. News of Susan's
blossoming spread across the region. The town took note.
Mothers were distracted, piqued by the interest of their
already betrothed sons, who flocked to Antony's Arboretum,
who lined up to get inside the Observatory. All to catch a
glimpse of Susan.

Soon, when touring the Arboretum, young men of the
landed class trailed behind Susan and Antony. Neither Susan
nor Antony would ever know that Ronald wrote letters to the
sons of the Town Fathers, urging them to pay a visit, *to see the
sights*, he said. Soon, Susan had a row of suitors, all vying for
her hand. Antony's Observatory became a place where mothers could match up their daughters – after all, there was only
one Susan, and so many of the young men grew bored by
plants.

Such was the Observatory-overflow, that once again the
Ginkgo tree became a special and favoured spot. Especially
when the moon shone full and bright. Stories spread, rumours
started, gained fire like wild weed, then petered out. In the
end, not much was said, at least not officially.

Sunday at the Arboretum was now a respected thing, with
the landed fathers meeting Ronald on the verandah of his
Mansion. There was the gold, the mills, the mine, the fish
farm, and the river. Mothers paraded their daughters, who
could not help but notice that the more time they spent on a
Sunday inside Antony's Observatory, the smoother their skin,
the fuller their lips. At night, before Monday's workday
started, many of the girls would dream of sleeping under the
Gingko tree. And, the next week, there were also one or two,
seen out the corner of a father's eye, fleeing with head held
down, skirts clutched.

One Sunday when the moon was but a pale rinse of white in a light blue sky in the middle of summer, a fine strapping man introduced himself to Susan. He was none other than Cousin John, Antony's hated cousin. Cousin John loomed into his rich man's height. How happy he beamed, his smile full of intemperate thoughts, his own self recently divorced from Naomi, for reasons undisclosed. He put his clean well-proportioned face close to Susan, he said nothing of her age, he impressed her with his knowledge of plants, spoke well to Antony, smiled even while all the time Antony glowered. It must be said: Antony behaved bad and then went thumping about.

When walking about the Observatory, for the first time that Antony could remember his Susan failed to put her hand inside his own. No more small to large! How Antony's huge chin ached to quiver and yet did not.

"How well you look today, Susan," said Cousin John. Indeed, on that day, she looked ten years younger than her age, which was past a certain marker. Her breasts strained against her already too-tight bodice. John noted how shapely her thighs, how her skin glowed. Susan smiled at Cousin John. She turned to Antony who had disappeared somewhere between rows of hydrangeas in pots. Cousin John spoke knowingly of the names of plants. How she liked the tone of his voice. The trail of other men soon grew thin. There was, of course, too much talk. Or, there was too much talk without enough intent. Or, intent took to ways not charitable. Everywhere in this Northern Canadian city, things held fast to surface, where on the streets of Main Town, people stuck to their own streams, one group within another. No one thought to merge, no one tipped their hats.

The next Monday evening, Antony's assistant, Jane, found a couple trysting under the Gingko tree. On a Monday! That had never happened before. Their bodies glistened under the fronds of branches, on their limbs the impress of scalloped leaves. The next Tuesday, Cousin John wrote to Antony's father, Ronald. A meeting was held to determine assets, the extraction of land and minerals. By that Sunday, very early in the morning, it was settled: Susan would marry Cousin John.

At the terrible news, Antony smashed every pot in his Observatory, and the hands that made the walls, the shelves, each glass and good thing, tore everything asunder. He flung himself under the Gingko tree and surveyed his Arboretum. So great a hatred burned within his heart, it were a poison, spread to his hands, fiery enough to scorch the ground which buckled, rumbled and quaked in tremors. No one noticed.

By the time of the weekly arrivals, a mysterious fire burned to a crisp every acre of Antony's Arboretum. Except for the Gingko tree. The Mansion also remained intact, thanks to Father Ronald's armed militia, which, although they laid nary a finger on Antony, prevented him from doing any damage to his father's house.

For weeks Antony sat, slept, dreamed under the Gingko tree. He fired Jane. Some nights, if a cold Northern moon would dare to show her round-ivory-shining-She-Face, Antony would lay his great height full length down on the ground, hand between his thighs, and fall asleep, dreaming no, not of Susan, who once she left Antony's Arboretum, would eventually shrivel, her hair again frizzy, her skin leathering. So, what were the nature of Antony's dreams? Even this story, with all its wiles and ways cannot find a way into Antony's dreaming.

Susan's inheritance entwined with Cousin John's land holdings and the marriage stayed on. Cousin John brought back Susan's brother, Prester. Together, Cousin John and Prester developed a series of tree farms devoted exclusively to *Moon Growth Gingko Trees,* patent pending. Prester, adaptive to gadgets, would accumulate success in later years, long after this story entered The Age. *It were enough,* Prester was heard to say, on afternoons in the city, *that one time in Antony's Arboretum.* To this day, every motel off the Rentalsman Highway will hold rooms where, in a drawer, bedside, you will find a storybook. Each storybook will be in fragments. These fragments will include mention of Cousin John and his wife Susan. Once, upon the Before-time, lived Cousin John and his Susan. He rarely visited her rooms. She took up philanthropy, her days measured in driving village to village doing good works.

Once, upon another time, lived Huge-Chin Antony also known as Giant Antony, who dreamed of water: gushing wells, heavy rivers. Antony located to an abandoned public school. The walls of this school, like all public schools, suffered from years of a neglect so severe, that the buildings were studied worldwide. Their walls oozed with moisture and no amount of retrograde fixtures or remedies staunched their pools of wet sighing water. As we now know, this condition is world famous as the Schools Walls Disease and, should you be any kind of an Aware Person, all the research and literature on Schools Walls Disease sits in binders and warehouses. About this dreaded Disease, none of the young minded much, for as soon as they were able, down they would go into the mines, or to work the mills, or to sail boats on the river. And the least smart would work summer after summer at the fish farms. After basic writing and reading, the girls took to the homes of their suitors.

Without Antony's Arboretum Sundays, trysts squeezed together in haylofts, in cars parked outside the churches wherein the righteous brought to altar the greenest ferns, those whose spores shed tiny-like, little gold coins. And with the girls there was the baking and the sewing; with the boys, the trapping, and learning how to shoot a gun. Everyone managed. There was the getting by. Everyone knew enough to sing anthems. Northern and free. And, that old implacable enemy, Time – well, as you might imagine – passed.

Alone in the school, Giant Antony cleaned rooms and hallways as if driven by soul-banshees, them that sing with the Northern lights. Some mornings, Father Ronald visited Antony, the more to argue about money. And at night, the stars which we know are really faraway suns, looked down and laughed their silvery laugh, heard only by the greenest ferns, the smallest pots of things, stored on shelves, under windowsills.

Busy altering Time, who would set Susan in a fine mansion built special for her by Cousin John. Were a stranger to visit, he'd see her breasts flat, her grey hair frizzled. Now, we know strangers do visit in and out of stories such as these, having, perhaps, first stopped off at Regulators' Hall or, if by chance, waylaid a musket carrier out by the Militia Barracks. Of these persons, Susan in her mansion, would say nothing. Instead, Susan would sit at her mighty oak desk shipped in from the East, the special bill of lading paid in cash by Cousin John.

Day after day, Susan wrote letters to Giant Antony. Now, you might wonder about the inner contents of these letters and if you were tiny enough, tiny as the smallest fern-born golden coin, your micro-eye might rest in the margin of a letter penned by Susan who wrote, "*Dearest Antony, Desire surprises.*

That longing for the touch of a giant hand on my own small wrist, the pressure of bone to bone – Well. Susan would write much more, but she, conscious of the micro-eye of tiny watching things, learned to devise a coded script, undecipherable. And no manner of prying into Susan's letters, bequeathed after her eventual death, by Cousin John to the Collect of Redactors has yet yielded the key to unlock Susan's encrypted letters to Antony. What we do know is that by sled, by horse carriage, by pedlar's cart, Giant Antony sent Susan ferns.

Susan would finger these plants; would lift them out of jars and tins, to discern a scent which any one of us might know as earth-smell, were we to bend toward the tiny fronds. The ferns arrived most times when Cousin John and Father Ronald ventured to the far North, to hunt, and to dig, deeper for ore.

One Sunday in late spring, when Susan walked into her drawing room, she surveyed a fern, fingertips to the underside of green.

The next night, the fern's reach extended from oak desk onto the carpet and the next night, at midnight, Susan repotted the plant. Within weeks the fern was almost ceiling height. With the help of a handy-man (named Albert, whose story was sent long ago to the Redactor and never seen since), Susan hauled enough earth in to settle the giant fern into its new holder. How green it was, and soft its fronds. Susan dismissed Albert and gave him extra for a holiday. That afternoon, Susan shut the door to her office. Susan removed her dress and petticoat, and lay in her slip under the giant fern. The tips of its fronds brushed against her skin. Time caressed Susan, minute by minute, and passed, and the fern grew and held Susan's gaze, until she were naked, marble-limbed. And if we were there on the carpet with her, would we too, see the spores on the underside of the fern, protuberant and glistening? *Life withholds its secrets*, Susan said aloud to the empty room.

⁓ᴵ⁓
⁓ᴵ⁓

And Time, that great wheel, that purveyor of light in the sky, passed into and over thresholds, forward and back. All over the North, at the desk of every known Redactor, in the board rooms within Regulators' Hall, and down in the Barracks of the Militia, everyone spoke of the mansion built by Cousin John. Not one speaker said anything about Susan.

There was the office with the huge oak desk, brought in special from the East. There was the fern sent to Susan from Antony of the Giant Chin, as he was then known. There were all the public schools, empty as dry husks from a beech tree. Outside the river burbled like a child let out after a day inside.

Life is a knowing wink, said Time on its wheel, up, up, to the wild-eyed moon. The fern inside the room was known to have said to Susan: *Life will get the better of you.* Susan refused to acknowledge that she now owned a talking plant. Susan picked herself off the carpet. Hands trembling, Susan put her clothes back on. Susan sat with a sigh at her mighty oak desk. In the weeks to come, Susan would write again to Giant-Chin Antony. Susan would urge him to begin, again, the Arboretum.

At night, the stars! The stars! There is Time's wheel, turning, turning, true North, bought-out, rented, mined and dug. There in the too-proud Mansion, deep in the basement, Father Ronald is known to have sat, head bent to a microscope shipped in special, where under glass, tiny gold coins glistened, plentiful enough to burden those green fronds, glorious and counting—

THE RUGARU

DELANI VALIN

In Métis legends, there is a creature known as the Rugaru. The name is a Michif word derived from the French loup-garou, meaning werewolf.

Sandra got on the bus, inserting her magnetic monthly pass in the fare box and then pulling it out. She thanked the driver without looking up.

She liked to sit near the back, so that if someone elderly or with a disability got on, she wouldn't need to draw attention to herself by getting up and grabbing all of her bags to give up her seat. It was also easier to be inconspicuous while exiting the bus if she chose a seat near the back door.

Sandra made herself small in her seat, piling her purse and her backpack into her lap. A large man took the seat beside her. He grunted as he sat and dangled one leg into the aisle to give Sandra more room. She appreciated this. She wondered whether the man was trying to be inconspicuous, too.

The bus pulled away from the curb and began its jerky journey to the Downtown Eastside. It was a trip Sandra had made many times, but she still recognized a slight flutter in the left of her ribcage. She planted her feet firmly and visualized rooting herself into the ground, like her therapist had taught her to do. Grounding, it's called.

She heard a noisy, looping beat from someone's headphones, and this reminded her of her son, whom she hoped was currently sitting in class.

She chewed her fingernails as the bus crossed over the bridge from Burnaby. The buildings here were increasingly old, crumbling and deteriorating. Makeshift curtains made from sheets and blankets hung in the windows. On the sidewalks, she saw more than one person push a shopping cart full of bags and bottles. The bus was pulling close to Main Street. Sandra pulled the yellow cord and the "stop requested" sign lit up in the front of the bus.

"Excuse me," Sandra muttered to the man beside her. She shifted slightly to show him that she intended to get off.

He stood in the aisle and she squeezed by him to wait near the door. She could feel the eyes of the other passengers, but she refused to meet them. It was easier to keep her head down, easier to be inconspicuous that way.

An old Chinese woman and a university student waited beside Sandra. She led them off the bus, and they both rushed passed her once on the sidewalk.

Sandra hesitated. She could have gotten off a few stops later, but she needed this walk to collect herself. She always needed this walk, this time beforehand.

Like most legends that are orally passed down, stories featuring the Rugaru vary widely. While some accounts have the Rugaru resembling Wendigos from Ojibwe and Saulteaux stories, others give the Rugaru characteristics more in common with the werewolves of contemporary pop culture. Generally, the Rugaru is described as having large hairy ears, sharp teeth, and cold black eyes. But even this is disputed, as the Rugaru can take on many different forms.

It didn't frighten Sandra to walk down East Hastings Street. In fact, she felt strangely at home here, surrounded by people who avoided eye contact as much as she did. Maybe this was because she had spent a lot of time here in her youth. The street was familiar to her. No, she wasn't scared of the street and its reputation or inhabitants or history. What made Sandra's stomach tighten was her not knowing how her mother would receive her. It had been nearly a month since her last visit, and it had ended badly.

So she focused on the pavement, counting the discarded cigarette butts as she walked.

"Hi ma'am," a man called out to her. He was on crutches, and had only one leg. He wore an old blue windbreaker and a pair of torn jeans, knotted below his absent knee.

"Hello," Sandra said, nodding.

"Do you have any change?" he asked her.

Sandra didn't. But she had known she would be asked, and so she brought along packs of cookies as consolation.

"I'm sorry," she said. "I just have this." And she handed him a packet.

"Thanks," the man told her.

The main difference between the Rugaru and the werewolf, however, is that unlike with werewolves, a person does not need to sustain a bite from one to transform. In the case of the Rugaru, one simply needs to see one. This is enough to become one.

Sandra spotted her mother sitting on the same blanket she'd sat on for years. It was an old store-bought quilt with fiddleheads and stripes. The batting inside was clumped to the corners of the blanket, leaving the middle thin and vulnerable to tearing. Sandra's mother was looking at her hands, examining her tanned, wrinkled skin. Sandra often found her mother in this position; it was as if she were reading her fortune over and over.

"Hi, Ma!" Sandra said, standing at the edge of her quilt.

Her mother looked up and blinked.

"It's me," Sandra continued. "I just came to bring you some food, and some little shampoo bottles – that soap that you like."

"I know," her mother said. "But I told you not to come back."

Sandra brushed this off and knelt down beside her mother. She pulled her mom into a one-armed hug, which her mother did not return.

"I just wanted to give you some things," Sandra told her. "It's no big deal."

"It's not safe here," her mother insisted.

"If anything, Ma, it's not safe for *you*. You're an old lady now. Old ladies don't belong in the street!"

Sandra's mother waved a hand at her dismissively.

"So have you been to the doctor lately?" Sandra asked.

Her mother squinted. "You ask so many questions."

"Fine," Sandra sighed. "I'll just give this to you, then."

She unzipped her backpack and produced a large ziplock bag filled with a toothbrush, clean underwear, socks, and bottles of shampoo, soap, and toothpaste.

"And here's the one with the food," Sandra said.

She pulled out another bag, this one filled with homemade cookies and bannock, packets of peanut butter and jam, and jars of baby food.

"What are those?" her mother asked.

"I got you custard, apple, banana, and pear flavours. I thought you might like them for dessert, and they'll be easy on your teeth."

This made her mother smile, a smile showing yellowed teeth and receding gums.

"That's kind of you," she said. "But I don't eat. Give them to Mason instead."

"Mason's sixteen! He wouldn't be caught dead with baby food!"

"Sixteen, already?" Her mother shook her head.

"Yeah," Sandra said. "And what do you mean, you don't eat? Everybody eats, Ma."

"I got used to being empty, I think," her mother said.

Sandra crossed her legs on her mother's greying blanket.

"Don't get too comfortable," her mother warned. "You have to go."

"I don't get you," Sandra told her. "You don't let me help you find a place to live, and I can't visit you here. You never want to come over – and you haven't seen Mason in years. Do you hate us, Ma?"

"Of course not," her mother said. "I don't expect you to understand."

Sandra shook her head and looked around her. There were people trading money for clothing and other goods that Sandra knew were illegal. There were some younger people, not much older than Mason, who drank out of bottles tucked away in brown paper bags. There were people in wheelchairs, and elderly people like her mother. Every so often, an argument would break out, and there would be shouting. Then there were people who passed by, on their way to some other place. They seemed to exist on another plane, not seeing anyone, just staring straight ahead. Sandra supposed she must look like that, too, especially with how hard she tried not to be seen.

"God, you're stubborn, Ma," she said.

"Watch your language, miss."

Sandra rolled her eyes at this. The fighting and the yelling from the people surrounding them was filled with expletives, but she knew better than to argue with her mother about this.

"Thank you for the bags," her mother told her. "But I don't want to get any more of them."

"Don't be silly," Sandra said. "How else would you get any of this?"

"I'm warning you right now, Sandra: this is the last time you'll find me here."

"What do you mean?"

"We're *both* stubborn." Her mother took Sandra's face into her hands. "I don't want to leave, but I also don't want you to come back here. It's too dangerous."

"But nothing bad's ever happened to me down here," Sandra said. "Actually, sometimes I feel safer here."

Her mother dropped her hands, and her face darkened.

"There are more dangerous things than being mugged," she said.

"Like what?" Sandra asked.

But her mother shook her head.

"Don't come back," she said. "I won't be here."

Sandra sighed and zipped up her backpack. She stood and shouldered her pack, looking down at the small, frail woman sitting crossed-legged on the old quilt.

"I just wish you would let me help you."

"I know," her mother said. "But it's not worth your safety. Remember the stories I used to tell you when you were little?"

"Sure."

"Sometimes people tell stories to make the world easier to understand."

"Yeah, like saying the sun is a god, or something," Sandra said.

"Yes, and some stories are told to keep people safe," her mother told her.

"Like the boogeyman?" Sandra asked. "To make kids go to bed on time?"

"Exactly. The boogeyman might not be how we describe it, but the purpose is to keep children safe in bed."

Sandra pursed her lips.

"So what are you trying to say?" she asked.

"I'm saying that when we are grown up, we need to recognize the monsters from our stories and use the advice we were given as children."

"But there are no monsters here, Ma," Sandra said, gesturing around her. "These are people."

"We are not monsters, Sandra. But we *know* the monsters. And if you come here, unprotected, you're in danger. There's a reason you feel comfortable here, and it's not good."

"But I'm a grown woman, with a job and a kid. And a home," Sandra protested. "And I would give that to you, too, if you let me."

"It could happen to you, like it happened to me. You're lucky it hasn't. You've survived too many encounters with the Rugaru, Sandra. It's time to stay away now, before you see it and it's too late."

Sandra dusted off her knees. She bit her lips, trying to find an argument, but found none.

"I love you, Sandra," her mother told her.

"You too," Sandra said.

She said goodbye, and walked past the people greeting her with outstretched hands, looking for something Sandra no longer had to give. She made her way back to the bus stop, to the back of the bus where she couldn't be seen. And back to her apartment with Mason, who would soon be getting home safe from school. She hoped.

WHERE ROOTS AND RIVERS RUN AS VEINS

DOMINIK PARISIEN

Here there are no historical associations, no legendary tales of those that came before us. Fancy would starve for lack of marvellous food to keep her alive in the backwoods. We have neither fay nor fairy, ghost nor bogle, satyr nor wood-nymph; our very forests disdain to shelter dryad or hamadryad. No naiad haunts the rushy margin of our lakes, or hallows with her presence our forest-rills. No Druid claims our oaks...

Catharine Parr Traill, from The Backwoods of Canada, 1836.

Dear Annie,

How pleasant it must be for you in Montreal, to live on an island where it is so easy to forget that you are surrounded by rivers. Here it feels as though all is running water. Such noise. Even the voices of your thrice-damned French neighbours were not so grating.

The inhabitants of this place are of a disquieting disposition, Annie. The people are stunted, rough in appearance – they are weathered, resilient, but dull-witted and move as beasts do, with single-minded purpose like the golems of rabbinical tradition. In contrast, others – no doubt new arrivals like myself – appear perfectly smooth as though they have washed up like polished stones from the rivers. This is a paradoxical place – the overwhelming sense is of the crispness of youth intertwined with terrible age. My own room smells of fresh-cut pine, but the furniture is ancient and everything creaks.

On the subject of the new, Grant has begun calling me his Little Birch Tree. I feel he means this affectionately, but I find it is rarely said with kindness. It is because I am so pale and thin. I would not be so elsewhere, I am certain. The trip was long and arduous, but there is more involved than that – Peterborough does not agree with me. Grant knows this, and still he insists we stay. I cannot believe this place is conducive to his health either. At night I lie awake next to Grant and I can scarcely hear him breathe. There are times I place my hand on his chest just to remind myself he lives. He never stirs at my touch like he did back in Exeter. Perhaps I have already become too light in this place.

Winston's health has taken a turn for the worse, and there is little doubt Grant will soon be the sole proprietor of the general store. I feel as though I ought to be sad for Grant, but I cannot help but resent his brother for forcing us to move here. It is no fault of his own, of course – if anything his misfortune may alleviate the financial strain Grant and I have suffered these past few years. Still, were Winston not of ill health, Grant and I might have continued to eke out our meagre, if tolerable, living back in Exeter. A difficult prospect, but a familiar one, at least.

Please do not judge me for my apparent coldness, sister – it is terribly petty, I know, but Grant himself almost seems unmoved by Winston's condition, and I know so little of the man. Grant keeps him confined to his room, and he will not allow me to see him, for fear his illness will strike me. It is difficult to care for a stranger, even one whose house you inhabit.

But the store does profit, and Grant seems happier than he has been. I feel that can only serve to strengthen us.

Your loving sister,

Abigail

P.S. Grant told me of an incident at one of the lumber mills today. Apparently, some plots of land that workers claimed to have cleared were completely intact, not a twig displaced. I know the lives of lumbermen are often short, that their work is treacherous, and that, every day, men are swallowed up by the woods and the rivers. And yet. There are fewer and fewer honest folk in the world. I wish you would visit.

Dear Annie,

Despite the insectile swarms and the interminable saw-songs and river whispers, these backwoods do offer one peculiar marvel, a woman of singular quality who had a queer influence on our youth: Catharine Parr Traill. Do you recall those nights we lay awake reading *The Young Emigrants*, how those idealistic sketches fashioned our early fascination with the Canadas? Grant informed me that she is its author, a fact known to a few here. And stranger still – few books have ever occasioned the bitter disappointment that *The Backwoods of Canada* did with the cruel reality and terrible hardships the author described. That is also one of Catharine's. Oh, Annie, I had never been so conflicted in meeting someone in my life.

Catharine, it turns out, is a long-time friend of Winston's, and his illness has been particularly difficult on her. I hardly knew what to make of her at first. Yesterday this strange little woman came knocking at our door, and after some heated words with Grant, she left just as suddenly. He later told me whom she was and asked that I meet with her at her home, to bring her news of Winston. *Tell her the man is frail, and his countenance could not bear the taxing company of others at this time,* Grant said. Imagine, Annie, facing such a woman as Catharine, responsible for some of my wildest and most terrible dreams of this landscape, armed only with such scant information.

Ah, you must be the wife of that brutish fellow, she said by way of greeting when I arrived at her door. *It is one of the peculiarities of nature that such a dear as Winston should be kin with a man of his disposition. Come in, come in.*

She was, of course, quite cross with Grant when I informed her of the impossibility of seeing Winston at this time. As you can imagine, we did not make the best of impressions upon each other. Still, I cannot begrudge her her frustration in this regard, what with Winston being her friend. Grant was also not as courteous as he might have been, which has tended to be his manner since we arrived here.

Truthfully, I half expected her to turn me out of her home, but instead she served me a very good tea and we spoke.

Have you been married long? she asked. I suspected she was only making polite conversation and I welcomed it. I had interacted with so few people since we arrived here, and I was most eager for it.

Four years, I said. We lived in Exeter, behind the shop my husband ran for an acquaintance.

There must have been something to my tone for next she asked, *And if I may be so bold, how receptive was your family to this union?*

At first I feared this life of penury has wracked me so that even a stranger can read the want there, but then I noticed a discerning gleam to her eye, which ought not to come as a surprise, given her writing.

Forgive me if I am too forward, my dear. One naturally develops a certain rough manner here in the bush. I ask only because I know the look – I myself am in a match looked upon unfavourably by much of my family. As you are no doubt aware, following one's heart can lead to certain, shall we say, challenges.

I nodded, thinking of mine and Grant's financial woes before his work here in Peterborough, of Mama and Papa's many unkind words at his expense, of the pitiable sums they provided us before our departure. I fear they were quite content to have us out of their sights.

But I am most fortunate. Thomas is a good man, she said. A good man, but from what Grant has told me, it is Catharine herself who supports their family with her writing.

Grant is also a good man, I told her. He moved us across the ocean when he learned of his brother's illness. Now he cares for the man's business, putting every ounce of his energy in it. Because he must if we are to live, I might have added, but what good would that have accomplished? It might have led to questions about the dismal state of our affairs in Exeter, at the shop, and I had no intention of sharing such miserable details with a woman like Catharine.

Yes, well. Remember to make your own path in things as well. When I frowned she asked, *Do you have family, here in the Canadas?*

I told her about you, Annie, of how you and your husband welcomed Grant and I into your house upon our arrival in the New World, before our trek to Peterborough.

That is good to hear. My sister, Susanna, has been a staunch supporter of my marriage. Her husband is a good friend of my husband's, and we are fortunate to have them near us. I hope that, come what may, your sister can be a similar pillar in your life.

We then spoke at length of your home of Montreal, that beacon of light in this terrible Canadian landscape. Catharine is a strange woman. She would rather the natural desolation of open fields or green forests and raging rivers than be in the bosom of a metropolis. One can commune with nature there in the many parks and still enjoy the comforts of civilization, I told her. But she would hear none of it.

Her disregard for the city is all a front. No one can truly love the pregnant emptiness of the bush, no matter their words. When Catharine speaks of this place her blue eyes are animated, yes, but mostly cold it seems to me, and the voice is that of the author, and not of the woman Catharine. Of that I am almost certain.

I told her the author of *The Backwoods of Canada* had many a dire warning to those who would seek to tame the Canadian landscape and make it their own, but she shrugged away my criticism. *Of course I wrote of hardship. You will find that in great supply here. I also wrote of the many beauties, and how hardships borne with perseverance, hope, and faith may bear fruit.*

I have learned that she frequently has newly arrived women at her home, and that many come to see the author when they learn her identity. Myself, I care more to know my neighbour, and make a true friend.

Yours,

Abigail

Dear Annie,

I have been thinking of Montreal, how there must be a great dark lake within Mount Royal, at the heart of the mountain, beneath the roots of all the trees. I imagine it is quiet there, peaceful. Peterborough has no heart; it is all veins and arteries pumping furiously, enough to drive one mad.

Grant says the Aboriginals who live near here are all mad, that they speak to animals and think that lightning is a bird. Catherine was quite displeased with Grant when I told her that today. She appears better inclined now toward these people than in her earlier writings. She handed me a few chapters from her new book and told me to have Grant read them. Grant will not, of course. Here he has no time for books, and he no longer makes attempts at poetry.

I see so little of Grant. At times I worry he is purposely avoiding me. His days are divided between the store and conversing – at times dicing or even drinking – by fires and makeshift tents on the shore with the lumbermen and the raftsmen. He has even returned with scrapes and bruises from confrontations. What little time he has left is mine to grasp at. Some days he snarls at me at meal times, then consumes his meals with crude abandon. This place has made him rude and rough, Annie. It is the tavern all over again, only worse. All the ways he buries his many disappointments, amplified by this terrible landscape and these crude people.

I feel someday he may simply be joined to a raftsmen's barge like a felled pine and disappear down the Otonabee River.

This is not how I imagined my life – my marriage – would be, spending my days in this land of green and blue, listening to the wrenching coughs of a dying man. But then, when have we ever recaptured the aura of those blessed days before our elopement, before that shameful return home to Mama and Papa and the move to that dank room behind Mr. Whitehall's pathetic store.

No.

I will leave off here for now, I do not like the turn of my thoughts.

Yours,

Abigail

PS: I want you to know, I give thanks to the Almighty each day for your presence here in the Canadas. Though you are far – so very far, dear Annie – I take some small comfort in knowing that the roots underfoot may extend underground, entwine with others all the way to you. That the rivers here, maddening as they are, may at least flow out to those surrounding you in ways never possible when I resided across the ocean.

PPS: There appears to have been a second incident at the lumber mill over another uncleared plot of land. Some workers claimed to have done the work, had sent the wood downriver by raftsmen, but when the land was checked all the trees were there. Accusations of theft were bandied about by other workers, which led to fisticuffs. I do wish Grant would take us away from this bush full of scoundrels and thieves.

Annie,

I have a confession to make, dear sister. I was quite startled at first by Grant's new name for me, his *Little Birch Tree*. For you see, there is a tree in my head. A white tree, a birch tree, with many trunks growing from the same base. I know this tree, even better than the back of my hand. I do not care for my hands, especially now that they are so pale. But the tree, when I close my eyes the tree is there, perfectly formed. I know each line in its papery bark. When a leaf falls, I know which branch it came from.

You remember the great stone in the forest near Mama and Papa's in Exeter, the one so covered in moss it looked more a grassy hill than a rock? I know you will recall I brought you there when I was ten to look for the white shawl you gifted me. I never did lose that shawl. It was the birch tree I meant for you to see. I had come upon it earlier that day, quite by chance, as one can only come upon things of great portent. I held the trunk to my bosom, ran my cheek across the bark, put a leaf or three in my mouth to taste my dream. My ear to the tree's base, I heard the sap flowing through it, like the sound of rushing water. I remained in that blissful state for such a time, breathing with the tree. But I needed you to share in that, to prove how a dream can be made manifest, though I knew you would doubt. Thus, armed with the sub- terfuge of the shawl I left, though it was with great reluctance.

You were so furious when I arrived home. You had thought me lost, and you were certain you would be blamed for my disappearance. But you were so kind when you saw my feigned distress, and together we rushed into the woods to retrieve my "lost" shawl. You cannot imagine my shock, sister, at the tree's absence. Or, perhaps you can, since my despon- dency then was not feigned in the least. *It is only a shawl,* you told me as I wept. But no, it was the tree, my tree, and there was no way to make you understand what its disappearance meant. After we searched the forest in vain, you carried me home on your back while I wailed. Oh, how I blamed you for the absence of my tree, Annie. I wrapped my arms so tight around your neck while you carried me, and still you bore your burden without complaint.

That night I cut my white shawl with scissors in my room, and buried the ribbons in the backyard. Reading this, you may think it was for spite. But, dear sister, in truth it was so you would not find it and think me false. Absurd as that is, at the time I could not think to act otherwise.

I am sorry and I love you,

Abigail

Dear Annie,

I have been to the post office today. Still you do not write. You are cruel to deprive me of your letters. Have I angered you with my talk of the tree and the shawl? Have Mama and Papa written and finally turned you against Grant, and by extension, me? I know you and he did not always see eye to eye during our visit, but, please, do not forsake me as Mama and Papa have. I still hold hope they will learn to love Grant in time, but you I cannot bear to lose, not even for a moment.

But perhaps I am being unkind. It may be the French have rejected the union of the Canadas after all, that rebels have been seizing the mail? They were well-behaved when I visited you, but one can never know with the French. I pray that is not the case, I do not wish for another rebellion. Especially with you so very far away.

Catherine's husband, a veteran, believes peace will be lasting, both in Upper and Lower Canada – I must remember to call these the Province of Canada now – but I have my doubts. Much as I love Montreal, I do wish you would move somewhere the French could not overwhelm you. Something like Toronto. Here would be best though – I cannot trust a town that had that rebel, William Lyon Mackenzie, for a mayor.

I continue to visit Catharine, and she is lovely, but she does not have the ear of a sister. She also remains inquisitive regarding Winston, and I fear she is growing irritated with me for my lack of information in his regard.

Your worried sister,

Abigail

PS. Yet another incident at the lumber mill. One man was stabbed and the culprit has not been apprehended. We were told Peterborough was a welcoming community, the thriving lumber trade a cornerstone of its dedication to good, civilized living, and king and country. What lies these Canadians tell. I asked Grant for more details – I know he has been with the lumbermen again – but he would tell me nothing.

Annie,

We have had torrential rains, and the rush of water is deafening. It fills my head so. I hear it flowing in my very veins. Yesterday I went to Grant at the store, even though he does not like me visiting him at work, and I am told I was quite insensate, screaming for quiet. Grant had his assistant carry me home and put me to bed. Robert is his name. On our way home, he told me that all of Peterborough is in turmoil! They have closed down a lumber mill, and there is talk of closing others. The lumbermen are rioting. It is terribly bad for business, according to Robert, all these unemployed men. Grant has been quite preoccupied with it all apparently, though he shared none of his concerns with me.

Robert says his brother has been to one of the work sites. He said the site, a good plot of cleared land, was overrun with trees! I felt myself become faint at that, and when Robert reached for me his skin was rough as bark. Upon closer examination I saw the fingers slowly elongate, take on the consistency of oak branches. Poor Robert looked positively unfazed by his unnatural affliction. Fortunately, the transformation ceased and reversed quickly. I fear for his well-being. What sort of hold does this place possess over its people? Is this also the nature of the terrible illness affecting Winston?

I cannot help but think of my tree. I am a little birch myself. My dreams have set root in the earth and are feeding off the horrid waters here. Annie, my dreams are bringing forth the trees!

Later.

I am relieved I did not send you my letter upon writing it. I was feverish, delirious from lack of sleep. I enclose it for your perusal, but you may rest assured I am much improved, though the rivers remain distracting in their intensity.

The local doctor has recommended a rest cure in the nearby drumlins, but Grant refused. He cannot leave the store, especially now with the turmoil with the lumbermen, he cannot leave Winston, and he will not allow me to be sent away from him. I am to remain inside. I have begged him to take me on his evening walks at least, but he refuses. In moments such as these I cannot fathom how this Grant and the Grant I married are the same man for whom I soiled my reputation. But then, on nights when I lie in bed and silently curse his name a thousand-fold as he enters the room, he tiptoes to my bedside, drawn like some uncanny spell, and bends to kiss my forehead, my closed eyelids, the bridge of my nose. On those nights he does not always hold me as he sleeps, but when he does, oh, then it is hard to imagine the past is not here with us, somehow superimposed on this strange present.

Catharine visited again. She believes good company will do me wonders in ways a rest cure never would. Though I must have looked disconsolate for she took me in confidence.

She is growing wary of the backwoods. I knew it. Even she cannot endure it, Annie. The Traills have previously moved within the area, and she means to do so again, soon. Perhaps far away. I am not surprised – a woman of her insight cannot fail to recognize the power of this peculiar place on the mind.

I also inquired about that situation in the village, but Catharine refused to enlighten me. *I scarcely know what to make of that myself. I have met a few lumbermen and raftsmen, and those I spoke with were kind, honest fellows. This business with them affects us all. But you cannot burden yourself with such matters. You must rest.*

I heard her knock at Winston's door quite insistently. She was even so bold as to call his name and fiddle with the door-knob, but it was locked.

Catharine has kindly promised to visit me when time permits. I believe she may do so in the hopes of seeing Winston, but her motivations do not truly concern me so long as she is here. The only regular conversations in this house are the creaking floorboards responding to Winston's raking coughs. Write me, Annie, dearest. Break your incomprehensible silence.

Your pleading sister,

Abigail

Annie,

Please forgive this barely legible scrawl. Writing is proving difficult.

I followed Grant on his walk tonight, once he closed the store. That is not the way of a dutiful wife, I know. In other things I have been a good wife to him, I believe, but I am allowed my moments of weakness, just as he is.

Grant went to the forest, as I knew he was wont to do. I followed close behind, the canopy of leaves weighing oppressively on me. It was dark, but the moon shone bright.

Annie.

Once he was far enough from the village, Grant broke off branches, whipped them on the trunks of trees like he was flogging them, shouting Mama and Papa's names. Sometimes he shouted mine, or even Winston's. When the branch broke he ripped another and started anew. I watched him trample dirt and leaves, scour the forest until he made it to a new clearing by the river. There he palmed small stones and cast them into the water, screaming, *Dammit*. The stones pierced the surface, and every time I flinched as they disappeared in the white rapids. Grant did this over and over, until he tired and sat by the shore. After a time, he wept, loud racking sobs. I took shelter in a bush some distance behind him, under the shadow of the trees, and watched the rise and fall of his shoulders.

This man is my husband, I thought, watching him. We know so little of this world, Annie. Men and women like Catharine write of their experience, take meticulous notes of their surroundings, but I do not think we ever really know anything, or anyone, until moments such as these. Watching Grant, for a moment I saw him as Catharine – who has never known the version of Grant I carry – must see him, only as a frustrated, fragile man in want of a simple life, a wealthy wife, and he has neither. I saw how those lacks had not quite broken, but twisted him, certainly.

With all his rage, I wondered if he loved me still. I trust he did back in England, when we had no concern other than that we should be wed, even with Mama and Papa disapproving of our union. It would have been easy then, with my promises of their eventual support. Which would not make that love any less pure, only simpler.

But that was him, and this is him now. What was I, here, at the other end of the world, a disgraced wife, daughter, sister, struggling in the bush? In my mind, Annie, I was anyone but Abigail. This frightful uncertainty, it could not be me. Whatever I was, I thought then I would be that with Grant, or I was nothing.

I made to walk out to Grant, but before I could reach him a figure dressed in tattered clothing ambled out of the forest from a path opposite me. The man's gait was awkward, stumbling, and he hummed off-key one of the songs popular with the lumbermen. I knew him for a drunken lumberman, and immediately I feared for his safety – I have never known Grant to harm another, but his unprecedented display of violence in the forest worried me. Grant took little notice of the man. In fact, the tone-deaf song seemed to soothe him, and I too found myself lulled by the man's fumbling melody.

The lumberman took position on a stump behind Grant. It was an odd sort of companionship, the three of us there by the river and the forest, each seemingly ignorant of the other, but one I decided was likely not unprecedented. I knew lumbermen and raftsmen frequently camped out on the shore, here and all along the Otonabee, and it was unlikely all of them sought company, despite their proximity. We remained in that peaceful state for a time, until the lumberman rose from the stump. I thought he had to have been whittling a piece of wood and cut himself – I caught sight of blood on his palm, which the man wiped on the stump. The sight filled me with dread – what if the drunkard meant to harm Grant? He was probably armed after all. I rushed out of the forest to warn Grant as the tree sprang up.

There is no other way to describe it, Annie. The stump where the man sat expanded upward, bursting great branches in all directions. The tree obscured my sight of the moon, seemed to reach toward the stars as though it would nest one in a nook like a robin's egg.

When I looked down, the man beckoned me over. Still he was humming. His fingers were long, almost taloned together. Strangely, it was not a frightful hand. I walked over. Up close, I saw his head was covered not with hair but a multitude of vines, that his ragged clothes were leaves held together with mud. The face was indeed that of a man, if a man could be carved from ancient bark, with the beard on his chin the greenish-brown of lichen. He was of this place in ways we would never be.

I found myself humming along.

The man placed a hand on the tree and held the other out to me. I took it. His touch filled me with such longing, Annie. Like I was made of seeds, and he was the dirt and the sky and the rain, simultaneously in and around me, drawing me out and up. Through him I felt the tree coursing through my veins, the life of it a blinding light warming me from the inside. I felt Grant seated by the water, the roots beneath him telegraphing his pulse. He seemed so small, but significant. I could not let the moment pass as it had in Exeter, when you and I failed to recover my birch tree. I needed him to witness, to commune with this strangeness and with me. I needed to make it true.

I called out to Grant.

That made the man cease to hum, made his jaw shift left to right with the low rumble of a landslide. His mouth full of mica glinted in the moonlight.

A few feet away, Grant shook off his lethargy. I cannot imagine the sight we made, the green man and the tree and I all entwined. Grant's face contorted into hideous rage at the sight, and he picked up a stone and cast it at the green man, striking him on the temple. I cannot tell what came next. I believe I screamed. Grant may have delivered more blows. Perhaps he thought he was protecting me, or it may have been something darker, more animal in nature. I only know he grabbed hold of me, dragged me away. The forest around us still seemed lit, more effervescent than the streets of Montreal. I meant to stop, to get back to the green man, but the landscape was dizzying. Everything shone, until it didn't. The contrast was terrifying. I felt myself a child again, back in Exeter, being carried away from a dream I knew to be real.

We fled in silence. In the centre of the village there was a commotion, perhaps lumbermen squaring off with residents, perhaps with each other. Violent lights shone off windows. Somewhere there was smoke. We avoided the area and made it home. Inside, Grant paced the floor, refusing to look at me. He mumbled to himself.

Winston. The store. The responsibility of it all is crushing me.

That cannot account for it, Grant, I said, finally.

What do you know of the time and effort I spend to keep us well? he said, more to the room than to me. *If your family had dowered you properly, if they supported us as they should have, then we would never have had to move to this Godforsaken place. And now we are here.*

This is not about us, Grant.

It is about us, Abby. It is only ever about us.

But the green man, I said. He must have called to us. Or we called him.

What do I care of some green man? You are like Winston, driven to delusion by this land. Too weak for it. Infected by it. It slips into your bones. Dammit, I am too weak for it. This is not our place. We should not be here. There is nothing here but our failure.

His indifference I could bear, his distance, but not his cruelty. I burst out crying, covered my face with my hands.

What is that? Abigail, what is that? He grabbed my right hand, held it out, and dropped it almost instantly.

Annie, my fingers were – are – not pale but white and rough, the ridges of my knuckles split and greyish-black where the green man touched me. My skin, it is almost peeling, papery.

Abigail! He screamed over and over while I examined my hand. Grant's face held such disgust. Not at the hand itself, I think, but at the fact that it belonged to his wife.

In the next room Winston's coughing worsened until the floorboards groaned and seemed to give way under his weight. Grant left and found Winston collapsed beside the bed, crawling toward the door.

A doctor was called for – for Winston, not I. Grant waited for him by the door while I penned this. I heard them discussing about draughts to keep Winston immobilized. The man is not long for this world.

Next day

Annie,

I have been to see Winston.

Grant left for work today without a word, and without locking Winston's door. Perhaps out of distraction – we do not know the state of the store after last night's riots – or because my safety no longer preoccupies him. It may have been shame that kept him secretive, or a feeling of terrible impotence regarding his brother's state, and after last night that may no longer matter. It is of little concern in the end.

I am ashamed I never tried to visit Winston before. Catherine has often told me of his kindness, his good humour, and I learned more of him from Catherine than I ever did from Grant. The plump storeowner I had seen only in a painting back in Exeter lay there, replaced by a whipcord-thin man with layers of flesh folding over itself.

He was breathing raggedly, but he opened his eyes when I entered the room. His pupils were hazel, I noticed, and the veins around them red and sharp as scars. He looked dazed, no doubt from a draught prescribed by the doctor.

I placed my misshapen hand on his forehead without thinking. The moistness there was not unpleasant, and my fingers seemed to drink it in.

Winston smiled, mumbled under his breath. I bent to listen, but he shook his head, kept shaking it until I backed away. When I did, he opened his mouth.

His tongue, I saw, had shrivelled, turned the rough brown of black walnut bark. When he spoke, the words were the rattling of branches rubbing against one another. I rubbed my wooden fingers together in response, and a similar sound filled the room. Winston nodded, and for a moment, it was as though we knew each other.

He expired shortly thereafter.

I sat by his bedside for a terribly long time. Eventually I lifted the covers, saw his legs had turned to stumps, with roots edging out of every part. It is strange, to mourn a stranger who would have been kin, not by blood but by nature.

Later

I have been sitting here, smelling new-cut pine, listening to the slow-creep of bark in my blood. Thinking of what to write you. What will Grant say, when he returns? Whatever it is, it will not matter. I can see my fate with him.

He will keep me here, locked away like poor Winston, because he cannot understand. For Grant, it would be another failure to give me what I will ask for. He must have felt much the same with his brother – they have been apart so long – I trust he thought letting go would be abandoning the man, not delivering him.

As you can no doubt tell, Annie, I do not believe Grant to be a vicious man, only overwhelmed, twisted by his bitter disappointments. But I have been wrong before. There is a roughness to him that seems more at home in the bush than he realizes. Though, if I am to be truthful, that is not my concern now. I have been a daughter, I have been a wife, and I have been a sister, which has brought me great joy, but I have rarely been myself.

I will go to Catharine. She must be told about Winston, and she has been good to me. Surely she will think up some suitable lie for Grant should he come looking. Who is to say, perhaps she will write a curious sketch of all this someday. Somehow, though, I doubt she will accept the truth of it.

Then I will leave for the forest, to find my place amongst the creatures and the trees. Where a part of me has always been. Unlike Catharine I have never truly cared for the wild. I do not care for it still. But I care for my tree. I touched something in Exeter, all those years ago, the day I cut my white shawl. Here, I think I can become it. Visit me someday, sister. You of all people will know me as a birch tree.

Yours, always, your loving,

Abigail

THE HAIRY MAN

ALEXANDRA CAMILLE RENWICK

The Hairy Man showed me his pénis today at the castle and though my maman would not have approved I looked with Great Interest and when he pushed his matted brownish hair back over his man-thing and covered it up again he waited and I knew it was hoped I would return the Favour. I did not.

Then X̱a finally turned up and threw rocks at the Hairy Man until he ran away. I have decided the Hairy Man is really more of a Hairy Boy or he would not have been so easily frightened. At fourteen X̱a is not very Large or Imposing. Not even to myself, who is by all accounts Scrawny and Unfeminine, and though younger stands a head taller than my friend when barefoot.

You should not let that gogit hang around, X̱a tells me after the Hairy Manboy runs away.

You are not the Boss of Me, I say to him. And also, *What is a gogit?*

Gogit is a stinky nasty monster, X̱a says. *They always lurk at the edges of our village and try to steal food scraps from our communal midden.*

But why do you care? I ask him. *If you threw it away, why do you care if gogits eat your trash?*

He makes that face he makes when I'm being Particularly Annoying. *It's just gogit,* he says, *or the gogit, but not gogits;*

they're all alike enough to be the same nasty creature, all hairy and stinky.

I don't tell him the Hairy Manboy was not stinky. Also, I don't tell him about the manboy's soft little pénis under his matted red-brown fur, pale and defenseless. Instead I hold out my hand and say, *Let's go ghost-hunting.* He takes my hand and as we climb together up the rubble hill toward the fire-ruined shell of Craigdarroch Castle I sense everything between us is Forgiven.

X̱a is my best friend, but I keep thinking about the Hairy Man. Keep thinking about him that afternoon as we look for dead little girl ghosts, poking through rain-moulded wallpaper and the ruined sticks of charred and rotting furniture that was Oldy-Old even in the beforetimes, before the plagues and fires swept the Island and wiped away the world. Keep thinking about him even after I'm safe home in Fernwood Village, tucked under maman's warmest quilt, as she and my père talk in the next room about trading with the new Haida settlement in James Bay where X̱a's family lives. Maman is too worried to eat any fish caught there because of the beforetimes Dirty Bomb, but père argues that is Old News and the Least of Our Troubles and he'd One Hundred Percent rather trade with the Haida than Those Bitches on the mainland. It's here maman shushes him for his Language and Volume because what about the child. I'm not much of a child anymore, but knowing my parents lost others before me, I humour them in maintaining this Minor Fiction.

Opening my eyes wide, I smile big so he knows I'm not asleep when my père peeks in past the cracked-open door. *Sorry if I woke you, Kitten,* he says. *You didn't,* I say, and, *Come tell me a story.* It's been a long time since I've asked for a story, and though I'm surely too old for bedtime stories by

Conventional Wisdom (of which there seems to be plenty in our village), I can see my père is pleased to be asked.

He comes and sits on edge of my bed. His weight pulls the quilt tight over me, binding my arms underneath against my body the way I like it. I indulge in imagining myself an Ancient Mummy in her Wrappings, or a beforetimes Ghost Girl suffocating in her Satin Coffin, or something equally delicious from any number of my père's excellent stories about all the poor sad lovely monsters and their Tragic Fates.

When I was your age, père begins, *I used to detour on my way home from school so I could pass by Craigdarroch Castle and try for a glimpse of the shadowy lady in black and the pale flitting apparition of a little girl peering down from the upper windows, who everyone knew had been dead a hundred years –*

Père, I interrupt, *that's a Very Good Story, but could you tell me a different one tonight?*

I like it when my père's eyebrows shoot up. He's much older than maman, older than most other fathers in Fernwood. His eyebrows are like two wiry white caterpillars thinking of becoming moths. *What would you like to hear about?* he asks. *Airplanes? Tutankhamun? The Internet?*

Tell me about the gogit, I say.

Eyebrows flocking together, père says, *I don't know that one.*

Gogit is a large hairy man, I explain. *He walks like this…* I sit up straight and tug my arms free from the covers so I can hunch over and swing them from my shoulders as though attached by puppet strings. *His feet are very big. Like this.* I hold my hands much farther apart than if I was measuring even my père's foot, which is big and hairy but not nearly so big and hairy as the Hairy Manboy's.

Ahh, he says. *You're talking about sasquatch.*

Who? My eyelids feel heavy. I rub them with my fists like the little girl père still sees.

Not who; what. His voice is low and mellow. Soothing. *Long before I was your age, folktales described the sasquatch as a mythological creature living deep in the woods, a huge terrifying beast covered with long filthy hair, with feet like Haida canoes...*

I fall asleep to his words as he tells me about the gogit, but nothing he describes is much like the Manboy I met, with his dark shaggy mane and his little pink crotch and his sad brown eyes like a beautiful hungry seal's.

Morning is my favourite time of day. There's a fleeting Moment before the sun rises over the ocean when the sky is Forever Blue and almost everything on the Island is still asleep. Maman and I sometimes wrap ourselves in quilts and sit on our back porch and watch the sky pinken between black branches. But this particular morning I find her standing inside the back-door screen. She puts a finger to her lips when I approach. She stands as still as when hummingbirds come for the sweet sugared water she leaves them even in snow, quiet as when she watches a mother deer and fawn pick their way through our wild mint with sharp dainty steps. She points. I look. At the edge of our garden, past the winter beans and neat-trimmed lavender stalks and budding pumpkins, sits the gogit.

I don't know if it's my gogit, but he looks to be the same size as the one I met yesterday. He has the same hunched posture where he crouches balanced on the split-log fence that runs along the back edge of our family garden and keeps at bay the Brambles and Tangled Trees that choke the uninhabited houses surrounding ours. Père has of course told me a million stories about all the people who lived in all these houses when he was growing up, but only about School and Saturday Market and Soccer Practice, never about the sickness and fear and neighbours shooting each other over canned peas or because they hoped to prevent their own families from catching the diseases so many were dying from.

A tug on aman's sleeve gets her to lean close enough for me to whisper, *Maman, he looks hungry. Can we give him something to eat?*

She slips away from the screen and I listen to her rummage behind me as I watch the gogit watch me back. I imagine my face is a blur to him, obscured by wire mesh as his is obscured by cowlicked tufts of hair. Maman returns with a cloth bundle my Nose and rumbling Morning-Stomach tell me is cold roast squash and sweet crumbly bread from last night's supper. Though she always warns me to be wary of Random Men and their man-things, she and I appreciate in each other the qualities of Fearlessness and, above all, Compassion. In the blue dawn stillness the gogit is very obviously Young, and looks more Vulnerable even than when he exposed himself to me. I unhook the screen door and push it open. Maman grips my hand tight, and together we step into the Forever Blue air of the garden.

Slow as cold honey, maman and I ease over rounded yellow pumpkins and past blueberry bushes already disrobed by fall. We pause at the rosemary border, spikes tinting the air between us and the gogit with sharp green scent. This close the Manboy's eyes are even larger than I'd thought. His lips are pink and bare in his hairy face, which is flatter than my own rounded cheeks. The lashes above his enormous eyes are a lush black, so different from the reddish down over his chin, the longer, thicker hair covering his head, the matted tangles between his legs and on his forearms. Mirroring our cautious motions, he reaches to take the food. Still slow, he peels back the cloth, then holds it to us in a gesture of Unmistakable Invitation to Share.

I break free a small corner of maman's rich honey bread, break it again in half and pass one to her. We three chew and munch companionably in Silence as the sky streaks lavender, then canary. When the Sun crests over the humped black winter brambles, the gogit slips back into the dense woody growth, leaving us with a neat-folded cloth empty even of crumbs, and the memory of a final careful gesture of open hand held palm inward, fingertips toward lips, then dropping in what we easily understood to be a Sign of Thanks.

A strange Hollow Fullness sits in the centre of my chest, a winded elation similar to what one feels reaching the top of a steep rocky ocean cliffside: exhilaration tinged by the knowledge one might yet Fall, one's footing give way to send one crashing to Waves and Ruin.

As maman and I return to the kitchen to make our Morning Tea, I contemplate with no small Satisfaction that the gogit had not been even remotely stinky. X̱a is not always right about everything after all.

That afternoon at the castle, X̱a is in what my maman would call a State of High Excitement. His father and some other men have discovered a gogit den in the dense northern woods near Elk Lake. They plan to burn it down.

My ribs are suddenly clamping too tight onto my lungs.

I clutch my friend's hand. *I have to go home, speak to my père*, I tell him. *Now.*

Sometimes I find it charming when he pouts, but not today. *I thought we were going to look for the little dead girl*, he says.

Thoughts of Violence at Elk Lake Woods make cold prickles stab the base of my spine. I'm itching to shout at him that ghosts aren't real. What has seemed a pleasing Pastime, an Adventure, suddenly feels childish. I want to scream. I want to tell X̱a I only poke and muddle through these moulding ruins all day to Spend Time with him, to hold his hand while we clamber over rubble, to grasp him close in Emulation of Fright at Imagined Sightings of apparitions and spirits. I want to tell him it's okay the Hairy Manboy showed me his sweet little pénis and to Not Worry I might have liked it better or thought it more Handsome than his because I didn't, despite looking on that tender organ with Great Interest in the moment. All this seems it would take an awful long time to explain and so I choose the quickest shortcut I can think of: I kiss him hard on the mouth.

We run the whole way back to my house, dodging lichen-covered branches, leaping over asphalt buckled by fire and rain and years. The inhabited shopfronts along Fort Street glow warm and inviting in an afternoon turned cold and wet, the way it can on the Island without Warning or Preamble. We find père in his woodshop beside the house. He looks up from his workbench with surprise to see us in his open doorway, drenched and breathless. X̱a as always goes abruptly silent in my père's presence, but nods in mute support to my panted words as they tumble from me, about the gogit in the woods to the north, and how his father plans to burn them out.

Père looks down at the piece clamped in his lathe. A spindle, I know, for a new cradle ordered by a neighbour. It's a beautiful piece of wood. All my père's pieces are beautiful. At last he says to me, *Is this why you were asking about sasquatch last night?*

He's not like either of you describe him! I say. *He's not stinky. And he's not a monster. He's polite. He likes honey bread. And his eyes are very sad. Ask maman, she'll tell you I'm right. Ask her!*

Both X̲a and my père are watching me with flat expressions. It's a Subtle and Unwelcome feeling to be the odd one out in a group of three. Something occurs to me with what maman would call a Flash of Insight and I buckle at the knees, clutch for balance. It's as if rock I've always taken for Solid has crumbled under my feet, those footholds on the steep cliffside giving way, those crashing waves below...

You knew, I say. *You knew about burning down the Elk Lake Woods.*

Père picks up a small brush and begins whisking away bright curls of wood from his spindle. *Fernwood Council and the Haida Elders have agreed it's best for everyone. But I didn't associate your sasquatch with—*

You can't! I don't want to hear more. *He likes honey bread!*

When père looks up from his spindle again I see how unhappy my unhappiness makes him. His eyes are almost as sad as those of the Hairy Manboy. *Kitten, remember when I told you stories about mutation? About genetic aberrations, about radiation from the west? About unknown weaknesses compromising the gene pool?*

Like with X̲a before, I want to scream. Want to shout and yell, as though it's the only way my words will be heard. Instead I wrap my arms around my middle, hugging myself, squeezing across my chest to make my heart stop hurting so much. I say, *So what if the gogit isn't exactly like you or me? So what?*

So, most think it's safest for the health and longevity of our community not to encourage proliferation of obvious genetic abnormalities…

In my imaginings I see the mass of men who will gather, coming together from X̱a's village and mine. I picture the clubs and spears, the guns and axes they'll carry with them to the edge of the forest. Almost, I can smell the torches, the noxious burning pitch they make which ignites even in drizzle, even in sleet. My stomach heaves at the sensation of tumbling, crashing. Falling. Waves and Ruin.

Unable to listen to more I turn and stagger from the workshop toward the house. X̱a runs after me, catches at my hand where it swings with the angry flailing sway of my arms. *Go home*, I tell him, shaking free from his grip. *Go be with the other men*. My tone must ring with the authority of Righteous Fury, because he stops following. I feel his Injured Gaze on the back of my neck even after I disappear into our house and slam the door behind me.

Sagging, I slide to the floor, the door the only thing holding my spine straight. I scrub my burning eyes with angry fists and try to think. Dry clothes, warm scarf, rainproof hood and jacket, good hiking boots: this is what I need.

Dressing in speed and stealth is difficult when one's Breath aches in one's Chest with that old Hollow Fullness. Having intended to slip out through the garden and avoid my père's view from his workshop, I'm startled to find maman waiting at the back door. She's wearing a warm scarf, a rainproof hood and jacket, and her good hiking boots.

Spoke to your father, she tells me, sliding a rainproof pack over my anger-stiff shoulder. Scents of warm honey bread waft up, fresh from her covered outdoor ovens. *I wrapped a couple extra loaves for you to take, as a gift for when you get there to warn them*, she says. *One for us too, of course. It's a three-hour trek in this weather, and the road between here and Elk Lake isn't so great. We're bound to get hungry.*

This time, I let my eyes sting. Wordless with Gratitude, I grasp her close. The rain pounds its light tattoo on our back porch, batting down wide squash leaves in the garden, rattling the dead sticks of spent summertime perennials. Maman's hair smells like ground wheat and rosemary in the cool moist air. I'm startled to notice we're practically the same height, she and I – when did that happen?

I draw back and lift my hand to my chin, palm flat inside, fingertips toward lips. I let my hand drop away. *Thank you,* I'm telling her, *Thank you.*

VETALA

RATI MEHROTRA

The night I was to leave Delhi for Toronto, my grandmother told me I was making a big mistake.

"The *vetala* is going to follow you," she said, as I stuffed my clothes higgledy-piggledy into the shiny new suitcase I had bought for my shiny new life. "Think of how lonely it will be."

I slammed down the lid of my suitcase. "There are demons everywhere," I said. "Even Toronto."

My grandmother sniffed. "Not *our* kind."

"How would you know?" I countered. "You hardly ever leave home."

She looked at me out of her sharp, blackbird eyes. "And you hardly ever stay here. What are you looking for, Pooja?"

"A good job," I said flatly. We had been over this many times in the last four months, ever since I'd gotten an offer to work for Recreated Realms, the biggest Timescape company in Canada. "Money. Peace. Security." *Freedom.*

"None of which you will find until you stop running away," said my grandmother.

I didn't reply. We didn't talk about the past, but it sat between us, clacking its teeth and rubbing its stomach.

"What about Amar?" said my grandmother at last. "Nice young man like that won't wait for you forever."

I made a show of rolling my eyes, although the mention of his name still brought a lump to my throat. Now, I regretted having brought my ex-colleague home and introducing him to my grandmother. As if the demon wasn't enough. "We're through. I told you that weeks ago. Let it go, Nani."

She subsided into a quiet grumbling that lasted until my taxi arrived – early, so she was forced to race through the *tika*, the ceremonial goodbye in front of the small kitchen shrine.

Later, at the IGI airport, I opened my suitcase and removed every item I had packed. It took over twenty minutes and people glared, but I found the three things my grandmother had sneaked in when I wasn't looking: a pocketbook Hindi translation of the *Bhagavad Gita*, a sachet of ashes – my mother's – and a small, red-painted stone. I closed my eyes and counted my breaths until I had vanquished my desire to scream. The stone, of course, was where the spirit of the *vetala* dwelt.

I stuffed the book and the sachet back in the suitcase along with everything else. The stone I flushed down a toilet. A gesture, nothing more, but it made me feel better, as if I truly had the possibility of making a fresh start in a new country. As if physical dislocation could dislodge the demon I was haunted by.

Toronto froze and bewildered me. I didn't know where to *start* in that city, how to breathe in the -20° C air, how to navigate the driverless buses and taxis. Luckily, Recreated Realms had a guest suite in its headquarters, a sixty-storey tower at Yonge and King. I stayed there the two weeks it took me to find my footing, and a cheap studio in Parkdale.

Lisa, my boss, introduced me to the different teams – Design, HR, Marketing, Defence. People from all over the world, picked for their talent, their brilliance. And now I was one of them. I shook hands and smiled until my jaw ached.

"Not that you'll remember everyone's names right away," said Lisa brightly, "and you'll be in Deep-Net most of the time. Still, it's useful to know that Gemma makes the best scones and Jorge the best sangria. Pick your poison." Everyone laughed and I joined in.

Later, I got my password to Deep-Net, the super-computer that ran the simulations of the Design team. I immersed myself in the familiar landscape of coding, already building my first prototype, a Roman bathhouse. For a few blissful hours, engrossed in my work, I forgot all about the *vetala*.

Then at lunchtime I opened my box, and found the red-painted stone sitting on top of a sandwich. I gagged and threw it, box and all, into the wastepaper basket below my desk. I logged back into Deep-Net and tried to continue work, but the stone kept dancing in front of my eyes, taunting. I gave up after a couple of hours and went home, only to find it waiting for me on my pillow. I hurled it out of the window, feeling sick, knowing it would turn up again. Knowing I would have to face the *vetala*, sooner or later. Knowing that nothing had changed.

I meet the *vetala* in one of the recreated realms I have helped design.

An old man sits on the beach, repairing a fishing net. Gulls screech overhead and children chase them away. Triangular fish flakes stacked with cod punctuate the beach like exclamation marks. The sky is a deep blue, the harbour dotted with colourful boats. The simulation is perfect: a Newfoundland coastal village of the 1960s, before the cod fishery collapsed and oil spills devastated the marine ecological reserves.

I walk down the beach, inhaling the tangy sea air, feeling the wind on my skin like a living thing. It's one of my favourite realms; I come here again and again, on some pretext or the other. Fine-tuning it for Marketing, I tell Lisa. Perhaps today I will climb the lighthouse and see a humpback whale.

But something is different about the realm today. Something I do not remember coding. *The old man.* My heart sinks. I squat opposite him. "You aren't real," I tell him. "Not here."

"The unreal never is, the real never is not," he quotes the *Gita*, and smiles before continuing his work.

This is not a coded response. This is not the simulation of an old fisherman. I push my fingers into the rough sand, letting the gravel scratch my skin. I am a child again and it is that terrible week my mother died and I met the *vetala* for the first time. I couldn't cry – I didn't quite believe she wasn't coming back – and everyone else was at the funeral. So I lay in bed with my face turned to the wall until the *vetala* appeared. He told me – he *showed* me – how my mother's body was burning on the pyre, flesh blackening and falling away to free her spirit. Then I understood, and I screamed and wept until a neighbour came hurrying upstairs to shush me.

"I didn't kill her," I tell him, although he knows that already.

"I never said you did," he says. "Would you like to see her again?"

"No," I say, although I want to, very much. The *vetala* cannot bring anyone back from the dead, can only put on their skin. I wonder what my mother would look like now, if she were still alive. If she would be an older version of me.

"You have to stop following me," I say. "Why are you here?"

"Fixing my net. Why are *you* here?" He throws out the net and I notice his weathered old hands. Hands that are on *back-wards*, palms facing front, knuckles behind.

I stand, but there's nothing to stand on. The light has leeched out of the world. I can see through it, the flawed code I myself have written – rats ravaging the fish flakes, the old man with the wild hair and too-long teeth, entrails entwined in his arms like a garland.

I turn and flee through the door that has followed me down the beach.

A month after I left her, my grandmother tripped up the stairs in her tall, narrow house and broke her hand. My cousins took her to the hospital. I called her cell when I heard the news.

"I keep telling you to move into a flat, but you never listen," I said.

"Why should I move? This is the house my father built, the house where your grandfather died." Her voice sounded thin and weak, despite her words. "This is where I'll die too. You'd better be mentally prepared for my funeral."

"You've been saying that to me for the last fifteen years," I pointed out.

"Well, this time I really mean it," she said. "Come back before it's too late."

"I'll be home for Diwali," I said. "Do me a favour and hang on until then. I need to return the stone to your shrine."

"Oh, *you* have the stone?" she said, all innocent. "I won-dered where it had gone. I guessed, of course. You were always his favourite." When I didn't respond, she said, "How's the new job? Is everything fine?"

"Of course," I lied. "You should rest now. I'll call again in a few days."

I didn't tell her the *vetala* had infected my work, necessitating hours of clean-up. She'd just have told me to come back home. As if going home would solve anything.

I couldn't get rid of the stone. I kept throwing it away, and it kept turning up: in my purse, in the kettle, inside my shoe. At last I'd caved in and put it on the windowsill of my apartment.

I sat by the window, watching the snow fall soft and relentless over Queen Street, until there was nothing but a world of white, a world of ghosts. And I wondered if my grandmother was right, if the *vetala* was as lonely as I.

My second meeting with the *vetala* occurred in real-space. It was March and the evening was grey and cold. People buttoned up in winter coats strode past, their faces bent against the driving wind. I sat in a Tim Hortons opposite my office building, nursing a cup of cooling coffee, delaying the moment of departure when I must get up and confront myself.

A slim, dark-haired man slid into the seat opposite me. "Hello, Pooja. May I join you?"

I frowned. He seemed familiar, with his boyish smile and that lilting accent. Brown-skinned, but not South Asian like me.

"Jorge, from Marketing," he said. "I work in the same building as you – just a different floor."

I attempted a smile. I was in no mood to socialize. "I remember, yes. Jorge who makes the best sangria. Have you been working late today?"

"No later than you," he said. "I'm going to grab a coffee. Can I get you anything?"

"No, thank you," I said. "Actually, I was just about to leave."

"Please wait," he said, "we have so much to talk about." He reached out and touched my wrist. His touch was cold, colder than ice. I shivered and stared at his hands. Hands that were on *backwards*. I tried to draw back, but he encircled my wrist. Fear and desire warred within me. His eyes were hypnotic; I could forget myself in them, at least for a while. I was dissolving, unable to think or move, trapped by his gaze.

"I can be whatever you want me to be," he said softly. "Not like that silly boy you left behind. Why fight it?"

Because I'm alive and you're not. I pushed the chair back and got to my feet, dragging my hand away from him. The spell broke. "Leave me alone," I said. "I don't need you anymore."

"You will always need me," he said. "Who else is there?"

Grief does not have a colour. It does not have a name, a language, or a nationality. But it has texture – the smell of ash, the taste of tears. As I walked away from the *vetala*, I remembered the dead. My grandfather, pushing me on a swing in the threadbare park opposite our house. My mother, pounding dough for *chappatis* in the kitchen, wiping sweat from her brow. My father, a shadow lurking behind her, faceless because I had never seen him, did not know what he looked like. I remembered the dead and I wondered – did they remember me too?

"You should read a bit of the *Gita* every day," my grandmother said. "It gives nice perspective."

I snorted. "What, the bit about Krishna persuading Arjuna to kill his cousins and teachers, because what does it matter anyway, they'll all be reborn eight million times?"

"That's not how it is!" snapped my grandmother, her annoyance coming through clearly even at a distance of eleven thousand kilometres. "Krishna is telling Arjuna to do his duty as a warrior in the battlefield of Kurukshetra, and reminding him that the spirit is untouchable. Don't distort the *Gita*'s meaning like all those foreign scholars do. Try to understand the essence of it. Read just one *shloka* at a time. Guaranteed to give peace of mind."

"I thought I wouldn't get any peace until I stop running away?" I said.

A pause. Then: "You won't. But I can't help hoping. You're my special grandchild, aren't you? The one the *vetala* chose." *The unlucky one*, she did not say.

"Don't worry about me," I said. "How's the hand?"

Our conversation veered to physiotherapy. I did not tell my grandmother that I *was* reading the *Gita*, the same lines every day, as if they could somehow permeate my soul:

For to the one that is born death is certain, and certain is birth to the one that has died, therefore you should not grieve over that which is unavoidable.

I am testing Design's newest creation, the last run of the *Canadian* between Toronto and Vancouver. I love train journeys, and what better way to explore this vast country than to traverse it east to west through forests, mountains, and prairies?

I wish the *Canadian* still ran, out there in the real world. There was a time when it had a daily run. The service was reduced to five days a week, then twice, and then just once. In the summer of 2021, it ran its last. Train aficionados have been clamouring for years for a simulation. Recreated Realms will make good money off this one.

I press my face to the window, and catch a glimpse of a black bear clambering up a spruce tree. We pass through lakes and forests untouched by the fire and disease that have ravaged Northern Ontario in recent years. I allow myself to relax. I have not seen the *vetala* in weeks, have been very careful with my coding. Not even Defence can find any loopholes in my work.

Twenty miles short of Hornepayne – a railroad town that no longer exists – a South Asian couple catches my eye. The man faces the window; the woman is bent over a book. Something about the tilt of her head, the arch of her neck, draws me, and I sit down on the empty seat opposite them.

"Enjoying the ride?" I ask with a smile.

The woman looks up and my heart lurches in recognition. *My mother. That's my mother.* Looking just the same as I remember – hair tied back in a knot, large, luminous eyes, forehead knit in an expression caught between surprise and worry: *what are you doing here?*

Although I have told the *vetala* that I didn't kill her, it was my fault she died. It was because of me that she went looking for him, the man who had been given a restraining order, forbidden to go near us. Because I hankered for a father. Because I didn't know what he was like, was too small to remember the alcohol-fueled rage, the savage beatings. Perhaps my mother thought the years had mellowed him down, that he wanted a daughter as much as I wanted a father.

And because I know what will happen next, I rise from the seat, thinking of the door just behind me, the escape to realspace, to my drab little office with the empty desk and blank walls and the safe hum of voices down the corridor.

But my mother catches hold of my arm. "Stay with me," she pleads, and I hesitate, and then it's already too late.

The man twists away from the window and smashes his fist into my mother's face.

"No!" I try to scream, to move, but my limbs are too heavy. I'm drowning in air thick as a swamp. I cannot breathe. Again and again he hits her, until her face is reduced to bleeding pulp. Until the jaw is broken, sharp splints driven upward into her brain.

"Stop!" My arms break free and I punch the man, raining blows on his head, his shoulders, the empty mask of a face. It's like hitting a rag doll. Like punching sawdust. He goes limp against the seat, head lolling. Still I don't stop, until he is reduced to a pile of dust on the seat. I straighten up, gasping and sobbing, and look at the seat where my mother lies sprawled.

But my mother is gone. Not even her bloodstains remain. The train car is empty but for myself and the *vetala*, who has materialized opposite me in his most fearsome form: grey-skinned and wild-haired, naked but for a loincloth around his waist. His arms are smeared with ash; his nails extend like the talons of a raptor from hands that are on backwards.

I take a deep, shaking breath and wipe my face. "A low trick, even by your standards," I say, forcing calmness in my voice. "Don't *ever* do that again."

The *vetala's* smile widens, showing elongated canines. "But you pounded him to dust," he says. "I thought that would give you some satisfaction."

I want to hit him, to slap that smug grin off his face. But it won't change anything. It won't stop his cruel games. I turn and leave.

I took the rest of the day off and called my grandmother. It was midnight in Delhi, and she'd just gone to bed. "Is everything all right?" she asked at once.

"Tell me about the *vetala*," I said. "How can I get rid of it?"

"Get rid of it!" she said, indignant. "The stone has been in the family for generations. It *protects* us."

"It didn't protect Mama, did it?" I shouted. "It let him kill her!" I had done the unthinkable. I had given voice to the unspeakable. I clenched the phone, waiting for her response.

There was silence for so long I thought the connection had broken.

When my grandmother finally spoke, her voice was flat and cold. "The *vetala* cannot protect us from others. Only from ourselves."

I disconnected the call, and discovered I was crying. What had I hoped for? Some magic mantra to make the demon vanish? Some deep wisdom to take away my pain?

I went to the windowsill and picked up the red-painted stone. I gripped it in my palm, imagining the spirit leeching out of it. "What do you want," I asked, "to leave me alone? Should I go back to India and marry Amar? Should I sleep with a *firang*? Throw myself off the office building? What. Will. It. Take?" And with each word of the last sentence, I smashed the stone down on my palm, until the skin broke and blood seeped out, a line of red pain in a world of grey.

Unbidden, a *shloka* from the *Gita* touched my mind. *Feelings of heat and cold, pleasure and pain, have a beginning and an end. They do not last forever. These, O Arjuna, learn to endure.*

And I wondered how the warrior Arjuna had endured it, the death of those he loved at his own, guilt-ridden hands.

It is my latest creation, and my best. I have spent over a fortnight working on it, day and night, have let no one else see the codes or test its integrity. Lisa thinks I'm recreating Victoria in its heyday of the 1990s, before the seas rose, submerging the southern end of Vancouver Island.

What I have built, she has never seen.

When testing day arrives, I am jittery with nerves and caffeine. My head is pounding and my hands shake. Will it work?

It has to. I have poured my soul into this one. I have given it everything I am and more. My pain, my fear, my guilt, my longing. Everything I remember of my mother, the circumstances of her death, and the child I once was.

I step inside, and the world transforms. Funeral pyres throw gouts of flame into a purple sky. The air is thick with ash, hot with smoke. The ground is littered with bones. It is a *Shamshan Ghat*, a cremation ground. The one place my demon cannot resist, cannot manipulate. Here the outer layers of our earthly selves are burned away until only the truth remains. Here I will confront him in his own skin.

I sit cross-legged on the ground to wait. Hours pass – or perhaps they do not, and the passage of time is an illusion, like everything else. I breathe in the ash, and practise what I will say to the *vetala*, the words of banishment I have made up and recited in front of the mirror every night until I can almost believe they are real. In the absence of any external wisdom, I must make my own.

Smoke congeals into a shape in front of me. The *vetala* is coming. I am ready for him, I think. I have the words, and I have the courage to speak them.

The smoke clears, and shock courses through me. It is not the *vetala*. It is a small child with a bob cut and a shy smile. She wears a dirty blue dress I can vaguely remember, and clutches a one-eyed doll in her hand – a hand that is on *forward*. She raises her other hand and says, "Hello, *didi*."

I do not answer; I cannot. It is too much to bear and I want, at that moment, to be gone from here. To leave the child trapped in this hellish place which is, after all, of her own making.

She hesitates and tries again. "Sorry, maybe I should not call you *didi*. You are not my sister. But you are older than me and I thought it would be more respectful."

I find my voice. "You're *me*. Me before Mama died."

"You look a lot like her," she says. "But Mama was prettier."

"Until he beat her face in?" I say, knowing I am being cruel, almost relishing it.

But the child does not flinch. "You're still here, aren't you? And Mama lives in you. Always has, always will."

Tears prick my eyes. "Who are you, really? Who's the *vetala*?"

She pushes the hair off her forehead, impatient. "The *vetala* is just a...*thing*. We animated him with our pain."

"How do I banish him?" I ask.

"I think you know," she says, and smiles.

I shake my head. "I can't let go of the pain, if that's what you mean."

"Who said anything about letting go?" She puts down her doll and reaches for me. I wrap my arms around her thin body, holding tight.

"Don't leave," I whisper.

"Never," she says. "Didn't I tell you? I am always with you."

And she slips away, the phantom girl, before I can ask her more, leaving the one-eyed doll in my arms.

When I return to real-space, the realm is gone, the codes extinguished from Deep-Net. And although I run recovery late into the night, I find no trace of the *Shamshan Ghat* where I met the *vetala* in my own skin.

I called my grandmother to tell her I was coming home. It had been a while since we'd spoken and she was careful with me, perhaps remembering how I'd disconnected the phone last time, all upset. But my news broke her reserve.

"You're coming back for good?" she said, delighted.

"For a while," I said. "My company wants to open an office in Delhi, and they picked me for the six-month pilot."

"Amar will be so happy," she said. "And the *vetala* too. I'm sure he wants to come back. Being in foreign parts is so depleting."

I made a non-committal noise. I didn't tell her I hadn't seen the *vetala* in several weeks. I had rendered it harmless when I embraced myself. I was more than my pain, but pain would always be a part of me. And maybe that was all right.

I still kept the stone on my windowsill, but it stayed put in one place. I knew that if I threw it now, I'd never find it again. Perhaps that is why I did not throw it.

That summer, before I flew back to Delhi, we had a team retreat in Whitehorse. We took one of the last surviving trains of Northern Canada, a restored steam locomotive, over the narrow gauge White Pass and Yukon Route.

I took the stone with me, carefully tucked into my purse. I had no fear of it now, and it seemed churlish to leave it behind when I would be returning it to my grandmother so soon. I also had the sachet of my mother's ashes and the pocketbook *Gita*. Three things that defined me, that were inextricably entwined. Arjuna had the wily Krishna to guide him in the battlefield of Kurukshetra. I had only had the *vetala*.

Maybe, in the end, it was enough.

I sat between Gemma and Lisa, letting their chatter wash over me, basking in its ordinariness. The train cut between cliffs and began to climb. Snow-capped peaks surrounded us; to our left stretched a dark green slope, dotted with spruce and pine. The train entered a long tunnel; conversations petered out, muted in the dark, as if the dark was sacred.

A hand closed over mine, ice-cold to the touch. I did not flinch; I let him hold me. And then, as light appeared at the end of the tunnel, I whispered, "Goodbye."

His hand slipped away, and we emerged into the bright light of the afternoon sun.

THE OUTSIDE MONSTER

COREY REDEKOP

There's a monster outside.

Terry shifts his gaze in Nomi's direction. The little girl is sitting atop a kitchen chair she managed to drag into the den. Her forehead is pressed up against the bay window, warm breath fogging the glass beneath her nose. From where Terry sits, his daughter's reflection looks to be sporting a goatee made of steam.

What's that?

Nomi turns, leaving the fog beard to dissipate behind her. There's a monster, Daddy. Out there.

Monster, huh? She nods, solemn, as utterly unfeigned as he knows only a six-year-old girl can be. Is it going to cause trouble, kiddo?

Don't know. Maybe.

What kind of monster?

She lowers her voice, pitched (Terry presumes) so that only the two of them may hear of her discovery. An outside monster.

Terry pushes himself up from the couch, leaving the movie he has been only half paying attention to anyway to continue on without him. He squats next to Nomi, feeling his muscles renew their list of complaints, and peers into the night.

No monsters. Only more of the snow that has transformed the house from cozy domicile to wintry prison.

It's been – Terry silently tallies it up – forty-plus hours now, with no near end in the forecast. Terry's no novice when it comes to dealing with snow (dear old Daddy McCleary made goddamn sure of that), but even with north of three decades' experience battling winter storms, he's never faced one this relentless. His every move to keep his driveway clear has been effortlessly thwarted by a blizzard so powerfully obstinate he's beginning to take it personally. It's like the weather has declared a vendetta against him.

A once-in-a-lifetime climate event, the news moron proclaimed when it began, his tone suggesting he'd rather be announcing wrestling matches. The dreaded *El Niño* going head-to-head against the great northern Chinook. A battle of titans, with the Atlantic provinces caught in the middle.

It's a superstorm, the idiot called it. A monster.

So Terry supposes Nomi's kind of right.

Hmm. He squints, playing the game. Outside monster, huh?

Uh-huh.

Those're the worst.

I know.

Terry loves his daughter's flights of fancy, how she absolutely commits to her fantasies. He'd swear she's telling the truth if he didn't know she has a history of discovering similar creatures in her closet, bed and, one memorable night, sock drawer. She must get her creativity from her mother; Terry's ancestry consists of absurdly pedestrian thinkers, people for whom the possible existence of life beyond the township's limits is at best hypothetical.

Not for the first time Terry is deeply grateful for his wife's influence. She manages to bring out the best in their daughter – and in himself. Without Alyx to keep him steady, Terry often worries he'll end up an angry clone of his father, berating his daughter at the slightest provocation.

Thank Christ Dad never had a daughter, Terry thinks. The man had barely grasped the rudiments of raising a son on his own, but a daughter? Terry doesn't like to think about it.

Don't see anything.

Nomi points, tapping her fingertip against the window. It's out there. *Tap tap tap.* Right there.

What's it look like?

Can't tell. It's big, though. Really big. She's barely talking, the words more mouthed than spoken, as if the slightest change in volume might warn the beast it's being spied on. It's invisible.

So how are you seeing it then.

She huffs at this, impatient with her father's doltishness. I can't see the monster, Daddy. I can see the snow moving around it.

Huh. Makes sense. He looks out again, debating whether there's time to make one more blower run tonight, and damned if he doesn't see…something. A glimpse of movement by the neighbour's fence. A shudder of snow curling in over itself, thickening the air for a brief instant, just long enough for Terry's brain to subconsciously connect the dots.

He rubs at his eyes; Christ I must be tired. It's just the storm. The way it's furiously scouring the city, slamming up against walls and channelling through back alleys, it makes the snow in any given area behave erratically. This, plus his utter exhaustion, means Nomi could suggest there's a parade of dancing sasquatch in the front yard and he'd probably see it too.

He watches the snow shimmy about by the fence. So what if there's no real monster? If it's real for Nomi, even for an instant, why can't it be real for Terry? It'd do him some good to stretch his imagination a bit, if only because his own father would never have conceived of doing so.

Is that it? he says, motioning with his chin. Near the fence there?

She shakes her head. No, it's moving now. It's over by the car.

Ah. He looks at the Everest of powder that entombs the hatchback.

It's standing right there. By the front. Her eyes are bulging as she tracks the creature. Alyx thinks the girl's going to be an actress when she grows up, and Terry can't argue with that. Nomi throws herself into her roles.

He scratches at the stubble on his chin. Wait. Wouldn't there be tracks, then?

Daddy. She stretches the word out, quiet no longer, stuffing its vowels with her annoyance. It walks on top of the snow. She marches two of her fingers across the glass to demonstrate. See. Just like this.

So, not a very heavy monster then.

Nope.

Is it still there?

Uh-huh. It's sitting on top now.

What, on top of all that snow? Way up there?

It's pretty big, Daddy.

But light.

It's a magic outside monster.

Must be. Guess I'd better check it out. Terry stands, again surprised at how loudly his body argues for stillness. Can't have a monster sitting on our car.

Nomi nods. It might steal it.

Exactly. Then where would we be?

Oh. Her eyes widen. I wouldn't be able to go to school tomorrow.

Hmm. He stops to consider this, watching her face as he deliberately walks into her trap. What do you think we should we do then?

Nomi furrows her brow in pretend thought. We should leave it alone, she decides.

Ah, but if it steals the car, you'll miss school.

Maybe. You'd miss work too.

Wouldn't that be bad?

Not really.

Terry snorts, and Nomi laughs at her cleverness.

You just want to skip school.

Yeah.

You had me going there.

Yeah. She's laughing harder, tickled by her cunning. It's too infectious for him not to chime in. He's still chuckling as he heads to the mudroom and starts pulling on his gear.

He stops laughing when he slips his coat on. The clothes are still damp, unpleasantly so, clammy. He's cleared the driveway of snow four times now, twice yesterday, twice today. The weatherman predicts no end to the blizzard until at least tomorrow.

He could leave it for morning. But if he hadn't been clearing the driveway in stages – the way his father forced him to do it – by tomorrow he'd be dealing with five feet, easy. Smarter to do it in manageable stages. Better to face four or five stretches of doable effort rather than one Herculean task.

But goddamn does he hate Canada right now. And the weatherman.

Mostly the weatherman.

Oh, bullshit.

As Terry zips up, the usual disparaging phrases amble through his head, imprinted as they are since childhood onto his psyche.

Bullshit on your complaints.

One of his father's favourite go-to responses. A choice piece of wisdom employed as argument against his shiftless son's pitiful attempts to get out of chores.

Bullshit on your complaints, boy. You're just lazy.

As always when life forces Terry to do something he doesn't particularly enjoy, right now it feels like the old man is standing directly behind him. Derisively adjudicating Terry's every action. He finds himself instinctively biting back a retort, just like when he was a kid. Wanting to tell the old man to eff off, fearing the consequences should he actually gather the nerve to do it.

Which he did, once. He pissed red for a week.

Terry's face flushes, feeling the man's fists work their way through his body. I'm thirty-nine, he thinks, and I'm intimidated by a memory.

Don't go, Daddy. A pair of small arms encircles Terry's right leg. Nomi's pressing herself against him. Her bunny pajamas are soaking up the pool of water that surrounds his boots.

Gotta do it, Nom. Can't let the monster steal our car. Next it'll want our television.

It can't come in, Daddy. It's an outside monster, 'member?

Either way, better not take chances. He pulls on a pair of mitts and tugs his balaclava over his head. It covers most of his face, leaving only the eyes free. He screws up his eyes, trying to look menacing for her. *Think I'm tough enough to fight an outside monster?*

She squeezes tighter, pressing her cheek into his thigh. *Don't go.* There's a catch in her throat, and Terry is shocked to see Nomi is near tears.

Hey, hey. He crouches down and gathers her in his arms. *What's wrong?*

She sniffles. *I think the monster is hungry.*

Why do you think so?

She points at the door. *I can hear it outside.*

That's just the storm.

No, that's its stomach. It's growling, Daddy.

He listens as the wind caresses the house, pushing at the wood. The walls of the mudroom groan, and Terry feels the hair rise on his arms.

Goddamn if that doesn't sound like cries of an empty belly.

He shakes his head. He's so beat he's freaking himself out. Maybe he should just call it a night.

Typical, Terrance.

Terry hugs Nomi tighter. Sometimes, holding his daughter, it's the only thing that shuts Dad up.

Hey, Nom, you know there's not really a monster out there, right? You were just playing with Daddy.

I saw it.

There's nothing out there, Nomi.

There's a monster out there.

He grits his teeth, suddenly mad, wanting to tell her, *Quit it! Grow up!* He breathes through his nose, ordering himself to calm.

He's just tired.

You're just lazy, his father spits.

Terry gives Nomi one more squeeze, then looks her in the eyes. Honey, I know you're having fun, but you can some-times take things too far. Do you know what I mean?

She nods, mute.

There's no monster outside.

But...

Nomi. There's no monster outside.

There's no monster.

You were fooling around, that's all.

I was fooling you.

That's my girl. He pokes at her tears with his mittened hand. So no more tears, okay? It scares Daddy when you cry.

I'm sorry.

I know. It's okay. It's just been a long day. He sighs. There's just so much snow.

Yeah.

Yeah.

You gonna clean the driveway?

Well, since I'm already dressed to fight the monster, figure I should.

Can I come out and help?

He shakes his head no, shuddering. She's about the same age Terry was when his father started heaping chores onto his thin shoulders. The day he treats his daughter like his father treated him is the day his father wins. Something Terry's not about to let happen.

I could protect you.

I got this, hon. He rubs her head, his mitten pushing snaps of static through her waves of brown and blonde. I think it's too late now, almost your bedtime. Besides, I think you're too scared to go outside.

I'm not scared.

You look it. He lifts her, lets Nomi look at her reflection in the glass of the screen door. See that? Your hair is standing up. Nomi the Fraidy-cat, that's you.

Daddy! The word squirms with irritation, but she's smiling, and Terry feels the weight on his shoulders lift a little. You did that. You made my hair stand up.

Yup, I did, Fraidy-cat. Cause I'm magic too. So that outside monster, see, if it's there, it knows not to mess with me. Too tough and too magic.

He lowers her to the floor, careful to land her on a dry spot. Go on, get inside, you're getting wet. Mom's gonna get mad at both of us.

Nomi's eyes roll up, another trait of her mother's. Ooh. That'd be bad.

Yup. Tell you what, you can watch me from the window. Give me warning if that monster of yours makes a move. Nomi nods and heads inside, leaving the mudroom door open and tracking wet down the hall. Tell Mommy I'm going out again, okay?

Mom! She hollers it up the stairs. Dad's going outside again!

Don't yell in the house! her mother howls back.

You're yelling, too!

Stop yelling, I said!

You're still yelling!

Terry closes the door after her, grinning beneath his mask. Nomi may have Alyx's looks, brains, and imagination, but her voice, that's all McCleary. In a battle between wits and noise, Nomi'll win out every time.

He opens the door to the outside and is hit with a shock of air that numbs his eyes. His smile flips itself into a tight scowl. All traces of the day's work have been filled in, smoothed over, and erased from existence.

You gonna cry about it, Terrance, or are you gonna get to work?

Knock if off. I'm going.

He shuts the door behind him and stands on the stoop for a moment, letting himself re-acclimatize. He's startled at the contrast between the warmth and amiable noise he's just left and the stark nullity before him. The world is nothing but white-noise wind and a dearth of colour. It feels as if he has moved beyond reality and entered an absence.

He walks down the steps into the gathering snow, sinking up to his knees. Not too bad, he says aloud, willing himself to believe it. The snow is light. Shouldn't take long.

Just gotta keep on keepin' on top of it.

He clomps to the shed, swings the doors open. He hadn't bother to lock it after the last time, because any fool crazy enough to try and steal old lawn furniture and rusty yard tools and cans of used motor oil in this blizzard is welcome to it.

The blower sits there, coated with remnants of that afternoon's efforts. He struggles to squeeze past it in the small enclosure, gets himself behind its handles, pushes it out. He can't hear anything at all out here, in the whiteout. There's only wind, groaning through the achromatic streets, underscored by the unsettlingly heavy hush of falling snow.

Wait, there's something else, a faint mechanical roar, coming from up the street. A neighbour's blower. He's cheered by this: Terry's not the only lonely soul fighting the good fight tonight.

He holds down the throttle bar, pulls the starter cord.

Again.

Again.

Terry checks the gas, tops it up, gives the cord another tug. No go. Lets it rest, tries again, pulls until his shoulder burns. Feels himself warm beneath his clothes, the frustration heating his blood. He plugs in the blower's electric starter, the never-fail last resort. He hates using it, knows his reasons are ridiculous, but Terry knows his father would think less of him for not starting it manually.

Not a click.

He curses a frosted ring into the wool of his balaclava. Glad Nomi's inside, can't hear his complaints. She'd learn a lot of new words.

Terry thinks it out. Blower's dead. Snow's still falling. Come morning he'll be greeted with at least two more feet of this shit.

If the monster blizzard has stopped.

Which, right now, feels like an impossibility.

He tells himself, go back inside. Deal with this later. Nomi's school will probably be cancelled tomorrow anyway. No rush to finish. Borrow a neighbour's blower if you have to.

But he'll still be left with all this snow. Jeering at him.

Just like dear old Dad.

Fuck it.

Terry grabs a shovel near the wall. You can't ever let the snow win, he says. Another in Dad's endless parade of clichés, delivered with intonations of disapproval that insinuated his son was a washout, a weak link in what was up until his godforsaken birth a mighty chain of manly men.

Terry trudges down the driveway, wading through thick. He breaks the beam of the motion detector and the security light above the driveway clicks on, guiding his way.

He'll take it easy, he promises himself. Only dig around the van and down to the street. Such obvious practicality would drive his father into fits, but who cares? The old man isn't around anymore to shame his son into killing himself.

The blizzard's not letting up, the flakes thick as goose feathers. The other side of the street has vanished. The rumble of his neighbour's blower is gone, swallowed whole by the storm. If it was ever really there.

He turns to the house. Nomi's set in position, poised at the window. He raises a hand, gets a tiny thumbs-up in return.

Should have dragged her out. Do her some good, teach her what real work is.

I'm so thankful she never met you, Dad.

Figures you'd have a girl.

Gimme a fucking break already.

Like father, like daughter.

You're lucky you're not here, old man.

Like you could ever stop me.

Not listening to you anymore.

Slide the shovel in.

Lift.

Toss contents over shoulder.

Repeat. Repeat. Repeat.

Soon, Terry's seeing the driveway beneath his feet. The snow is as light as he'd hoped, there's a cleared concrete track around the minivan now, and he's much closer to the street. The progress heartens him, even though he's drained. Fifteen minutes in and already he needs a break.

He leans against the drift camouflaging his car, panting a little. His breathing is rough. Not used to this much effort. Need to hit the gym, do some free weights.

Owning a blower, Terry realizes, has made him soft. He also realizes that his father would take this as proof that his son always takes the easiest route.

The insight feels worse than the ache in his back and the whine in his shoulders.

It suddenly goes dark, casting the driveway into murk, spooking him. Terry waves his arms until the sensor catches his movements and switches the light back on. He pulls his balaclava away from his mouth for some air. Takes in a lungful, gasps, coughs, hard enough to weaken his knees. The inhalation had been mostly flakes.

I'm drowning in my driveway, he thinks. It's so absurd an idea his hacks alternate with pained laughter. Wouldn't his father have loved that? His shirker son, so unfit for manual labour he suffocates to death on snowflakes. The most bizarre *I told you so* ever. The thought makes him laugh harder, weakening him until he has to drop to one knee and lean on his shovel for support.

Eventually the coughs subside, leaving Terry lightheaded, his body a mass of shaking muscles, his throat scraped raw. He wonders if Nomi saw his fit. Would she be frightened? Maybe he should head back in, make sure she's okay.

Gonna quit?

Even over the wailing of the storm, Terry hears his father's blistering contempt. It's like the man is lurking there, right behind the snow, just outside his reach.

Haunting him.

Preying on his weakling little boy.

Had enough?

Goddammit, Dad, leave me alone for once why don't you.

Terry stands, picks up the shovel. It feels twenty pounds heavier.

Gonna go inside?
Nope.
Slide. Lift. Toss.
Go cry to Mommy?
Never knew her.
Slide. Lift. Toss.
Crying won't make it easier.
Like you'd know.
Slide. Lift. Toss.

Sweat dribbles into Terry's eyes. He drags a mitten across the balaclava's eyeholes. His lashes are scabbed with frost. He blinks, dislodges the ice. Fancies he can hear tiny crystalline boulders tumbling down. An avalanche over his face.

Snow's worse now. Wind's picking up. Fucking weather-man.

Glancing up, Terry can barely see the bay window through the squalls of silver white that gust in every direction. Nomi's sitting there still, her face smooshed up against the glass, watching intently for...

Right, the monster. He had almost forgotten. It's near the car. Where he is now. He looks around for any sign of crea-ture, playing up the search for his audience. He frantically sweeps his arms back and forth in front of him as if trying to bump into the invisible threat, knowing he looks ridiculous but hoping his goofy pantomime brings a smile to Nomi's face.

There's nothing around him to bump into, of course. Nothing but snow, battering his face.

What else was he expecting?

He looks back to the window. His daughter's a faded blur now, a pale smudge behind the storm. He can't tell if his playacting is being appreciated. He can't even be sure it's

Nomi anymore. He's looking at a silhouette through television static.

He waves. No response from the shape.

No, it's moving. Or is it only the snow, fooling him again? Either way, it looks to Terry like the silhouette's head is bobbing about a bit. Tracking something.

Nomi's not watching her father at all, Terry thinks. She's following her monster again.

The outside monster. The invisible creature stalking Daddy in the static.

Terry scans the stretch between himself and the shadow. Just in case something's really there.

There's nothing there, idiot.

Leave it.

You're acting like a little girl.

He does feel slightly imbecilic. There's nothing to see. He knows there's nothing out here. Just Terry and his daughter's silhouette.

He raises his hand again. The silhouette mirrors his wave.

The storm is heavier now; an almost solid wall of dirty ivory surrounds him. It's only him and the shape now.

Terry thinks; would he even know if something was out here? Stalking him?

He's aware of tightness in his chest. He's nervous.

Goddamn, stop weirding yourself out.

He waves to Nomi again, but the storm must be too thick, her shadow remains still. Flakes gambol about his head in eldritch spirals, upsetting his equilibrium. They begin to push, hammering insistently from one side, then another, until he has to plant his feet to stabilize himself.

He gets the impression that he's being boxed in.

Cornered.

Trapped by a monster (*I think it's hungry*) that would be right on top of him before he'd even see it.

The shape is still there, lit dimly from behind, safely inside the house. Or is it? It looks too solid to be that far away. It must be the storm, warping his sense of distance, but Terry's suddenly convinced, if he reaches out into the blizzard his fingers will come up against something coarse and muscular.

Something watching him. Patient. Waiting for him to lower his guard.

A monster, Terrance? That's your excuse?

The light vanishes again, plunging Terry into gloom, evaporating the silhouette. He shouts this time, swearing as he motions to trigger the sensor. He's rattled, almost panicked, shocked to realize he's been staring into nothingness (*not nothing I'm staring at the shape it's right there*) for minutes now. The silhouette is back where it should be, in the house, of course it's inside, it's Nomi, why would she be out here? He's seen this in movies; actors pretending to lose their sense of time and space, becoming lost in a blizzard mere feet from camp. He never honestly believed it was possible, but now the reality of such an event hits him. He's weirdly afraid of what it might mean.

He thumps the side of his head with his fist. You've been daydreaming, Terry. It's all this goddamn snow, whirling about. It hypnotized you. The cold is numbing your senses, that's all. You're tired. Need a good night's sleep.

Sleep is for babies.

He looks down. The concrete beneath his feet has vanished. Already his meagre efforts are being obliterated.

Motherfucking...

Again.

Slide. Lift. Toss. Slide. Lift. Toss. Slide. Lift. Toss.

I never once let a driveway go uncleared, his father yells from somewhere out in the netherworld. That much was true; like everything else in his life, he approached shovelling snow like a battle he intended to win. Him and his useless offspring, freezing themselves numb, risking frostbite. No rest allowed until they'd scooped an oasis of concrete from a frozen desert.

Not that Dad is around any longer to fight the weather.

The snow, it finally beat him. Forced the old man to his knees.

Terry watched it happen. He's never told anyone. He leaned on his shovel and idly watched the man crumble. Listened to him moan. Went inside and called for an ambulance only when he felt compelled to do so.

It took a long time.

Mr. McCleary, forced to his knees by the snow.

Then pushed onto his back.

Then shoved into his coffin, interred in the earth, and wholly forgotten. Such was his impact on the world beyond himself and his son.

It was why Terry bought the blower to begin with. He'd purchased it at Alyx's insistence, making noises about how unnecessary it was, blowing off her worries about his health but secretly delighted at this rebellion against his father.

Any excuse to not put in an honest day's work.

Jesus wept, Dad...

Slide. Lift. Toss. Slide.Lift.Toss. SlideLiftToss. Terry's breathing is ragged. SlideLiftToss. His temples begin to pulse. Hot blood sluices through his arteries in waves, keeping tempo with the shovel.

SlideLiftToss.

Gotta find the right rhythm.

The light blinks out. He waves, but the gloom persists. The ferocity of the storm had fooled the sensor into thinking him vanished. The streetlamps are only glimmers. Might be 40 feet away, or 40 miles.

There's only himself and the shape now. Nomi's silhouette, floating, its position unaffected by the wind.

SlideLiftToss.

Never put off until tomorrow what you can do today, Dad directs from behind the blizzard's curtain.

Slide.Lift.Toss.

Nothing good ever came of a lax attitude toward life.

Slide. Lift. Toss.

(*I can see the snow moving around it*)

Slide.

He leans on his shovel, lets his head droop. He waits for the throbbing in his forehead to subside.

If you have time to lean...

Cold blows past his balaclava, down his neck, melts against his skin. Feels good. He opens his coat to the wind, letting the chill revive him.

You killed your mother, you know.

(*I can't see the monster*)

You don't know what monsters are, Nomi.

Slide. Lift. Toss.

Tore her insides out, you did.

(*it's really big*)

Yes it is, hon.

Slide. Lift. Toss.

I'm glad she never lived to see what a disappointment you turned out to be.

(*the monster's hungry*)

I'll protect you.

Slide.Lift.Toss.

Terry can't see past the end of the shovel now.

You're letting the snow win!

It just won't stop, Dad.

SlideLiftToss.

Again.

SlideLiftToss.

(*it's growling, Daddy*)

SlideHeaveToss.

His arms are lead.

SlideHeaveThrow.

His back screams in disapproval.

DigHeaveThrow.

A few seconds respite. Just to catch his breath. Just enough time to envisage the weatherman's smug asshole face.

Sorry, folks, didn't see this thing coming. My bad.

DigHoistThrow.

Every plunge cleaves the weatherman's skull.

DigHoistThrow.

Right along the line of that arrogant weatherman smirk.

GougeHoistHurl.

Fuck fuck fuck you fuck you fuck fuck fuck

GougeHoistHurl.

Gouge.Hoist.Hurl.

Gouge. Hoist. Hurl.

Gouge.

Hoist.

A tremor ripples through his body.

(*it's hungry*)

Hoist.

You never could finish a job.

The shovel slips from his grasp, vanishing beneath the snow.

...aw goddammit

Terry tries to bend over. He's mildly confused when he can't. His body is stiffening.

...out of shape

You've always been weak.

...can't argue that

(*there's a monster outside*)

His arms dangle loose. The tips of his mittens brush vainly against the surface of the snow, the shovel beyond their grasp.

...finish...goddamn driveway

He tugs at his balaclava, it's too tight. It takes an eternity to pull it over his head.

...goddamn

Terry's coat feels too close. No, can't be that, it's open. But there's pressure around his chest.

Pain is in your mind, boy.

...so are you, Dad

Doesn't hurt that much. Should be able to work through it. Feels like a hug.

Maybe it's Nomi's monster. Come over to keep Terry warm. Awful nice of the big fella.

...again

He pushes his body forward, squeezing in his stomach, trying to bend a few more inches.

Something's pressing at his eyes from behind. They're about to burst.

...pick up...where's shovel...

A little hard work never hurt anyone.

His knees buckle.

...should probably take a break...

The silhouette. Maybe it could help. Terry reaches toward it. Dimly, he wonders how it is he can see it in the dark.

Terry crumples into himself. His head falls back into soft.

...feels nice...

Excuses, excuses.

     ...can't stay...

(*hungry*)

    ...Nomi's gonna miss school...

If you lifted with your legs, you wouldn't tire so easily.

Terry looks up at where the sky should be. The world is gone. All that's left is white against black, and vice versa.

...time...   ...get up...

Snow collects on his face.

You can be lazy when you're dead.

...oh shut up

Ice crystals fill his sockets. He can't be bothered to blink them away. Too much of a nuisance.

   ...what did she say...   ...outside...

He's becoming one more drift among thousands.

Terry notices he's not cold anymore.

There's a movement, in his periphery, beyond the veil. The shape, the silhouette. It lingers in the corner of his eye.

    ...something there?

Small piles of snow gathered atop its hunched shoulders.

...that's how she saw it...

You really do disappoint me, Terrance.

...oh, it's you...

...of course it's you...

You never amounted to anything.

   ...at least I tried...

There's a roaring in his ears.

…monster…in the snow…hungry again…

…should've listened…so sorry…

(*I can protect you*)

…s'okay, hon…I got this…

Terry surrenders to the monsters.

AS WORLDS COLLIDE

STEPHEN MICHELL

I was married in the summer after I completed my Master's degree, six months after the *Great Merge*, as the newspapers had decided to call it. Our wedding day was hot. It was held outside at the university – as was Lily's girlhood dream – in the old quad among the locust trees that formed a canopy like a cathedral framed by the high grey stone, the gargoyles gazing down at us as we spoke our vows. I don't know how much it cost – Lily had said, "I want to have it at the university, and my parents are going to help," – and that was enough for me to know. My parents offered to help as well, but as far as I could tell the whole thing was much more than covered. There was seating for a hundred people, and a large gazebo, and a string quartet. I thought it all to be a bit cliché, a little girl's pristine fantasy finally come to life. But it was exactly as Lily wanted, and she was radiantly happy. I was sweating in my suit, even in the shade of the trees. It was hot. My father was in the front row, also sweating, heavy drops beading down his brow. But he nodded firmly and winked, a gesture that told me to hold my course. I braved the heat. I loved Lily, and after we both said, "I do," I stopped sweating, realizing that it had been my nerves and not the heat, which had been running my pores. And then the sun passed over the stone walls and the evening was much cooler, and there was chilled champagne and a band and dancing. Lily and I danced together. She looked up at me, and I looked back at her, and nothing else mattered then.

None of us were thinking at all about the Great Merge. It is surprising how even the most unbelievably astounding things can become "old news" given the right amount of time and media attention. It was common to hear students around campus sigh at the mention of the Great Merge, in a similar fashion as though someone were humming an overplayed song from the radio. Nevertheless, a few heads did turn with surprise when the first satyr crept into the shaded quad and joined the wedding party.

My mother cried outright, as did a few others, and my father stood stalk still, utterly baffled. Lily's parents were mortified, I'm sure, but they looked to Lily, and when, after a moment's bewilderment, she smiled, everyone seemed to relax and take the satyr's presence in stride. Still, our parents, aunts and uncles – Lily's little grandmother Marcy – were unnerved, to say the least. The older generations have had more difficulty understanding the whole situation. But who can blame them, really?

Before long, there were six satyrs among us. They are odd little creatures, pleasant and polite, always bowing and averting their eyes, but also sniffing and roaming in the manner of cattle. The first of them crept forward slowly, bowing and exalting us with raised arms, and keeping a fair distance. It was all too much, almost embarrassing, being treated, as we were by the satyrs, as gods, but there was little we could do to desist them. As they became more comfortable, a confident swagger emerged. They started to wink at the bridesmaids (and at Lily's dog Casper), and their appetite was ravenous.

They seemed like young bachelor party frat-boys – classic wedding crashers. But they were charming. They knew how to smile, and their entreaties seemed so genuine that it was not long before Lily went and offered them all glasses of champagne. It was now a proper wedding.

The satyrs laughed a great deal, which is a startling sight, but extremely heartwarming to hear, and, of course, they loved dancing and they drank plenty champagne. Near the end of the night most of them had retired to the darker corners of the quad and proceeded to "pet" one another. Lily had gasped and said, "Don't look, Evan," and she laughed. "Oh, my God, that's hilarious." Yes, it really was. I put my arm around Lily's waist and softly breathed, "Oh, my," into her ear. She laughed and pushed me away. And that was our wedding. That was the reality of the Great Merge, the early reality. A year and two months later, Lily and I were a regular married couple, and the whole world was talking about the *Shrines*.

We cleaned up together after dinner. I washed the dishes and Lily dried them, leaving the cutlery in the rack. Then we made iced coffee and sat in the backyard and Lily did the morning's crossword.

Our home was a grand lot, owned by Lily's parents, but purchased, Lily always reminded me, for us. We lived outside Midland, Ontario, a forty-minute car ride to the town, to the old drive-in theatre (actually it had shut down), and the grocery store. The area was quiet and green, with a dozen trees for every person, and the air was fresh and restorative. Unlike Toronto, where all was grey and the feeling of stagnation and collapse was pervasive, the country gave me hope. To be immersed in greenery, the ever-constant noise of birds and frogs, the occasional howl, the complete stillness of morning, and the reverence of nature at midnight that dawns almost silent, was rejuvenating, to say the least. Lily had procured, after months of hopeful anticipation, a teaching position at Huron Park Public School in Midland, grades three and four. She loved it, though the work was tiring, and emotionally draining, and she was usually in need of a glass of wine after four o'clock, then another as she plunged into piles of adorably incorrect spelling tests. I was continuing my studies at the university, working ever toward my Ph.D, but most of my research could be done at home through online journals. I seldom went down to campus unless my supervisor requested it. Sometimes we Skyped.

The university had become a rather frantic environment. Many departments, but especially Mythology – and the related History and Literature – had gained a new prominence ever since the Great Merge. I was researching a joint thesis in Mythology and Classical Sociology. My supervisor, Professor Alec Galbran, was the talk of the campus. Wrinkled, squat and round, he fit the cast flawlessly for a lunatic academic. He believed all of it. *If the creatures of mythology have come through into our world, then the gods must have as well.* He would rake his hair back and take off his glasses, then put them back on. *And with the global emergence of the Shrines – the Shrines!* He was getting either closer to losing his mind completely or possibly finding it.

On the occasions that I visited campus, there was often much laughter in the grad house of Professor Galbran, and then much furrowing of the brows and nodding if he walked through the door. None of us could ever admit (it was just too absurd), but we all hoped he was right. And we wanted to be there with him when he proved it.

But it was all a grand confusion. The world's initial question had been *how*? How in all the realms of possibility had an ecosystem of creatures, previously believed to only exist in myth, suddenly emerged in the wild? More recently, especially at the university, the question had become *why*, stirring up speculation of a mystical nature, giving rise to a new investment in an Astrology department, and garnering the ceaseless attention of the media. The campus was a sea of cameras and amateur reporters wanting the inside scoop to post on their blogs. It was chaos, to try and wonder *why*.

The evening was hot in the backyard. Every evening seemed to be getting hotter, even as leaves fell and winter approached. But that was old news. Lily and I drank our iced coffee and relaxed. Lily yawned from behind her crossword. Her students were always most unruly on Friday, sensing the lawlessness of the weekend, I suppose. She was tired from it. I looked at her, hoping she might turn to me so we could communicate, as we often did, without words, easily with only subtle intimations of our eyes. But she was caught in some clue. I looked up at the sky. It had become a bit of a constant habit, for me and for many people. Supposedly, it was now possible, though improbable, to look up into the night sky and see a winged stallion fly overhead, or as the headlines called it: Pegasus. They said the stallions only flew at night, but some high-minded thinkers posited the animals might possess a unique ability to camouflage under sunlight. Either way, I had never seen one.

Lily claimed to have seen what she believed was one, several months previous while up north around Lake Superior with her girlfriends. They had seen *something* fly over their fire at night. Or rather, as Lily claimed, it had galloped over them. I had seen only the television coverage. It was laughable, really, but if Lily could believe it then I guess I could too. Enough, at least, to wonder.

She had believed it all right from the start. I suppose I loved that about her, as much as it made me doubt her sanity. That willingness in her to accept. She called me right after the news story aired – the footage that stopped the world. A winged stallion, huge, marble white, had landed on a highway in Germany. I remember watching the CBC, gathered close in the Media Commons room at the library, crowded shoulder to shoulder, all of us staring at the television screen, watching what looked like the mythological Pegasus trotting along a backed-up expressway. Then, causing a stir of shrieks and shouts, the stallion vaulted into the air and flew. I rushed out of there, needing air, dizzy. My cell phone was ringing. That was the real start of it.

The rest just happened one day, or at least that's how it felt. I was focused on completing my Master's, and hardly noticed the sudden proliferation of wild animals, goats and deer and wolves, even eagles, that were being spotted in towns and cities all over the world. They say it was the precursor to the emergence of creatures – satyrs, nymphs, harpies, and the more elusive ones, like gorgons and centaurs. I remember studying late one night at the library and a friend of mine called me to her computer to show me a YouTube video uploaded from Hong Kong. It was a poorly shot, handycam recording of a dark underground tunnel. The person holding the camera kept looking down and recording their feet, which was irritating. But they were waiting to see something. And halfway through they stopped and stood still, and then a great bulky shape ran through the shot. It looked like a huge, half-naked man. But it had horns. The video was called *The Minotaur is REAL!!!!!* They said it lived under the shrine in Hong Kong. I watched the video again a dozen or so times and I had trouble sleeping for about a week.

It was the Shrines that were starting to bother me. The feeling was ominous, terrifying yet astounding, certainly otherworldly. I kept wondering what the hell they were. So I did some research.

The first Shrine appeared in Canada, in northern Alberta near Fort McMurray. The second was spotted off the coast of Brazil in the South Atlantic Ocean. Then in China, in downtown Hong Kong, and a final Shrine was discovered in Siberia. Each one was different, but all were colossal, mystifying, and ultimately humbling, leading some people to believe that the pyramids in Egypt and in Middle America were also Shrines, built long ago. Professor Galbran contested the validity of that claim. The main problem, he argued, was that Shrines were not built. They arose. Alberta had a Shrine within a day, with great force and violence to the wilderness; Hong Kong's Shrine tore apart the streets and buildings of the downtown core, using the very material in which they were situated; the Siberian Shrine is one thousand feet tall, an edifice of ice and snow and rock; the South Atlantic Shrine is a constant vortex of water, raised up into a flowing funnel atop the surface of the ocean. Early researchers attempted to enter the vortex but their vessel was obliterated. The human race was humbled. It was irrefutable that something far greater than our science, our art, our mind, truly existed.

Lily yawned again and put down the paper. The evening was getting on, but we still had about an hour before sunset. I was not tired. The coffee had roused me.

"Let's go for a walk," I said.

She rolled her head to look at me. "If you like."

Our house was not far from a small nameless lake with a path along its bank leading up through the hills to the forest. I often woke earlier and went for a run around the lake. The water was shaded and mostly covered in algae, but sometimes after a good wind there were spots that we could swim. The track of land was public, and the pathways through the forest was open, a fine area for people to take their dogs.

Lily and I put on pants and long-sleeved shirts to fend against the mosquitoes, and then walked down the road to the lake. We had recently purchased proper running and hiking shoes. I wore mine in the morning when I jogged, but Lily seldom wore hers. We were being quiet, so I asked her how they fit.

"They're nice," she said.

I looked at my feet. "I should get my dad a pair," I said.

"He would like that," Lily said. "I keep telling you to invite your parents up here."

"It's a far drive."

"They haven't been here once."

"I know, it's a far drive."

We had walked around the lake and were starting up the hill to the forest. Lily had become quiet. She was tired. I began to regret going for a walk. The coffee had roused me, made me restless, but I should have just done some push-ups and gone to bed. Instead, I was out in the darkening forest with my wife and she was upset. I knew when Lily was upset. I looked again at my feet in the running shoes. Lily had been right; my parents had yet to come see our home. But with all that was happening in the world, it was becoming difficult to see the purpose in such things. What did my parents' visiting matter?

Lily stopped and looked at me, she was almost teary-eyed. I knew we were thinking much the same thoughts. I took her hand, no words, Lily said it all in a look, and I knew she was right. It was most important, in these days, to find the purpose in things, the indelible import of meanings, as small as each might be. For without the tiny significances of moments, we would have nothing. I held Lily's hand as we started walking again. Then I casually glanced back. That's when I saw the first of them.

"There's a wolf behind us," I said, matter-of-factly.

Lily stopped and turned. The wolf was down along the bend of the lake, standing squarely in the path, staring up at us. It was a large wolf. Then we saw another. It came slowly from the brush, down the embankment into the path. It was smaller, not a cub, but thinner than the big one. They both looked up at us.

"Let's keep walking," I said.

We went up the hill. I kept an eye over my shoulder. The two wolves had not advanced after us, which was relieving, to say the least. I was unsure about what to do. The wolves were blocking our route home, and I had little desire to try to insist that they move. The best idea, I figured, was to go up through the forest, loop back, and come down again, leaving the wolves alone as best we could. My little idea probably would have worked had Lily not looked back once more.

"Oh, my God, Evan," she said, gripping my arm. "Look!"

I turned. I will always love Lily for her curiosity and her unorthodox acceptance of what other, more self-possessed people might readily discount in an otherwise unbelievable situation. And also because she made me turn around that evening. There was a white doe poised at the bottom of the hill, facing us. Its ears were turned up showing their pink interior, and its coat shimmered marble-white in the last of the evening sun. We looked silently, astonished by the brilliance of its coat, for it truly shimmered, much more than scant light through the tree line would have allowed. The white doe shone almost blue, itself the source of the light. I was astounded. Lily still gripped my arm.

All this time I had entirely forgotten about the wolves. They gained my attention again when the doe suddenly jerked its head, and I saw that there were more of them, three more, coming down out of the hills and along the path. The white doe remained absolutely still, its eyes turned to the wolves drawing closer. It seemed obvious to me then that the wolves had been tracking the doe. The first two I had seen must have gone ahead to wait at the lake. I wondered how long the white doe had been fleeing. Yet it seemed completely at rest, not at all fatigued or frightened. The wolves drew ever closer.

"Oh, my God," Lily said, her only phrase when dumbfounded, and I knew she was reaching the same conclusion about the wolves and the doe as I, only she was certainly taking it further. She saw that the wolves were going to kill the doe.

Then the wolves started. It was all quite instantaneous, really. I had only one thought – to get Lily out of the way. I grabbed her and rushed down into the brush. The white doe sprang up the hill and past us, a blue trail of light following in its silent wake. Then the wolves came over, all five running at once in a close team. I held Lily close in my arms under the brush. The moment was all of a single heartbeat, sheer terror as I held my wife and listened to the wild patter of the wolves. There was, amidst all of it, another sound.

A voice.

Sister, what's wrong? All day you have run from me.

Then the noise diminished over the hill amongst the trees. Lily sat up. We got to our feet and dusted our clothes. We looked along the path with the intent perhaps of discovering lasting evidence of the doe and the wolves. We found evidence in the tracks, light hoofprints and ragged paw marks, all together in the dirt. Without words, and this will always attest to the integrity of our bond, Lily and I started following the tracks. They lead down the hill to a short plateau and then up again. There was a curved ridge, a hill spotted with young saplings, and then another slope down to a glade. We saw the blood first.

The wolves were dead. All save for one. The larger one, the first we had seen, was still alive. It stood among the bodies of the others, upon the rocks and grass in the glade, and the ground was dark with blood. We stopped on the slope and looked. A glittering light illuminated the glade, emanating undeniably from the white doe. She stood just beyond the body of wolves at the base of another small hill. The surviving wolf looked up at her. There was blood upon its fur, and dark stains across its snout.

"It killed the others," Lily whispered. "Why would it do that?"

I said nothing. As I watched, a second light flooded the glade, casting out from the body of the wolf, and as the light spread over the rocks and grass to the trees that lined the area, we heard a rising sound. It was similar in sense and steadiness to a song, and we listened. The glade hummed with it, a low chanting howl with a constant harmonic cadence. It appeared, from all I could gather then, that the lone wolf was singing, either in exhilaration from the kill, or in some sort of supplication to the white doe.

And then there was a voice again.

That is it then. They have died. For you I have tasted their blood. For you I have made the hunt upon the hunters. Is that better? Do you still hate me, Sister?

Lily gripped my arm with both hands. My legs trembled, but I stood straight for the both of us. The white doe looked down at the lone wolf, its ears turned up as before. Then it quickly jerked its view in our direction. The lone wolf slowly turned, sniffing the bodies below, until it stood as when we had first seen it, large, staring direct and cold at us.

Is it not enough, Sister? Do you desire more, before your anger is at rest?

The wolf tilted its head, as if inquisitively, still with its eyes on us. I could feel Lily shaking. Some part of me thought to look for a stick or a rock. I put my hand on Lily's stomach and pushed her a step back. I thought to tell her to run. If the wolf attacked, I'd tell her to run, and I would try to get in its way. I kept my hand on her stomach, holding, and waited.

And then we heard a different voice.

No, Brother, the hunt is ended. Continue your song. Your song is what I love.

I released my breath, relief flooding me, but neither of us moved, save for my hand clamping onto Lily's hip and her squeezing my arm. We said nothing. The doe and the wolf remained in the glade, their light radiating in waves, a steady rhythm in sync, I concluded later, with their respective pulse. At the time I was perhaps caught in a mixed sensation of fear, shock and amazement. I don't recall exactly the path of my thoughts or decisions and, least of all, my actions. Lily described it later that I had a smile on my face. That I was holding her hip very tight, and my smile was devious and delighted. I remember none of that, only the vital realization, or rather impulsive conclusion, that these animals were *gods*.

And then I remember, though I hardly believe it of myself, I called out, "Who are you?"

The white doe looked straight at me. But it was not a deer looking at a man. The eyes I saw, and the impression I felt of being seen, of being wholly considered, was all much more invasive and intimate than any animal could instill. It was the gaze of a mind registering a voice, a question even, and regarding the speaker with interest. I waited patiently for an answer I was sure would come. Lily said my smile perked in that moment.

Then the doe's voice sounded across the glade, louder than before.

I am The Artemis. He is my brother. He is The Apollo.

The wolf looked at us, then moved coolly out from the rocks and the bodies of the other wolves, and went up the small hill to stand with the doe. Together, they regarded us.

I said, "What are you doing here?"

The voice of the doe sounded: *We are here always.*

"But why now? Why do you show yourselves now?"

Show ourselves? The doe's voice carried. *We show nothing. Only what we have always been.*

"But why have you come into our world?"

The doe lowered its head and appeared to sniff the grass. Beside her, the wolf stuck out its snout. A harder voice said: *You mistake yourself, mortal. It is your world that has entered ours.*

Lily was gripping my arm.

"I don't understand," I called.

Come, Sister, said the voice of the wolf. *The sun is down, I will sing to you.*

"Wait, please!" I called, desperately. "You have to explain!"

The doe stopped and raised her head and looked at me. Her eyes were round and black. Her voice came gently. *Dying worlds will often seek refuge and rebirth within another.*

"Dying worlds?" I repeated, muttered to myself, more like.

We will try to help, said the doe. *Soon. Very soon.*

"Come, Sister," and the wolf whipped around.

I called out to them again, but already they had turned and their light was fading from the glade. The forest darkened. The sun had been down for some time, and the air turned sharply cold. The white doe and the wolf had gone over the small hill and away. Lily and I were left alone in the dark. We said nothing. I don't remember the walk back to the house.

Inside, I went immediately to my office and sent an e-mail to Professor Galbran, explaining everything as best I could recall. It took a while, typing and retyping. My hands were shaking. Lily had gone into our bedroom.

I went to the kitchen and took the bottle of whiskey from the cupboard. I poured a small glass. Lily came out of the bedroom after a while.

"Are you okay?" I asked.

She looked at me with a heavy, disconcerting look, but was not upset. She was frightened. I poured a second glass of whiskey and held it out to her. She sipped it, and winced. We sat down in the living room together on the couch and slowly drank the whiskey and fell asleep.

In the morning I woke on the living room floor in the sunlight coming through the windows. Lily had gone into our bedroom. I stood up slowly. I could see the green of the forest from across the yard. The whole incident possessed the weight of a dream. After I washed the sleep from my face, I made a pot of coffee. Lily came into the kitchen wearing her yellow morning gown.

"How are you feeling?" I asked.

"Fine, Evan," but she stood in the kitchen listlessly, staring at me.

"It's okay," I said. "I don't know what to do either. Come here," and I put out my arm.

"No," she said, with a rolling of her shoulders that I knew and understood.

I hated when she wouldn't let me hold her. In those moments she was never upset, but rather figuring something out in her own private way. I knew that eventually, in her own time, she would let me in. But I just wanted to hold her, to comfort her, and comfort myself. All I truly had, if I had anything to keep me, was holding Lily.

I poured two cups of coffee and we drank them slowly at the kitchen table. Later, Lily went into the living room and I went to my office to check my e-mail. Professor Galbran had replied.

Evan, I know. Congratulations! It's finally happening. Go turn on your television.

Alec.

I started from my desk, but Lily was already calling me.

"Evan! Evan, get in here!"

I hurried into the living room. Lily had the television turned to the CBC news. They were playing clip after clip of aerial footage of the Shrines across the world, Alberta, Brazil, China, Siberia, each one—

"They're opening," Lily said, and gripped my arm. "The Shrines – My god – They're opening!"

I said nothing. There was nothing one could say at that moment. I opened my arms and let Lily find her place against me and I held her. On the television we watched what could be described only as the end of the world.

But that was wrong. It was the beginning.

ACKNOWLEDGEMENTS

Well, we're here and we did it! First off, we'd like to thank Michael Callaghan for seeking us out to co-edit this anthology – he made us an offer we couldn't refuse. Thanks to all of our authors, for their patience, work ethic, and keen insights and honesty, which got this anthology to be what is is right now (that is, a really amazing collection that we are both so proud of).

We'd like to thank our families. For Kelsi, her parents, Lorrie and Kevin; her brother Jake; and of course, the girls, Lexie and Stella. For Kaitlin, her parents, Anne and Rob; her grandma, Barb; her brothers Brian and Eric; and sister-in-law Felicia, for always making her feel like she belonged somewhere, no matter what. Special thanks to Jake Babad for his insight, and for letting us show our gratitude in beer and whiskey. And thanks to Battlenet, for being the one reliable chat for this book while Kaitlin was in Osaka and Kelsi was in Toronto.

And finally, we'd like to thank Dominik Parisien and Jonathan Levstein, who had to put up with the worst of us throughout this book. Through different cities, different countries, many early mornings and late nights, they were unfailing sources of support, love – and wine.

ABOUT THE AUTHORS

Nathan Adler is a writer and artist who works in many different mediums, including audio, video, drawing and painting, as well as glass. He has published the indigenous monster novel *Wrist*, had a story in the anthology *The Playground of Lost Toys* (Exile Editions), and his writing has appeared in *Redwire, Canada's History, Shtetle, Shameless,* and *Kimiwan Zine*. He is a member of Lac des Mille Lacs First Nation, and lives in Mono, Ontario.

Braydon Beaulieu is a doctoral candidate with the University of Calgary, where he studies creative writing, poetics, science fiction, and digital games. His most recent chapbook is *ERASURE: A Short Story*.

Andrea Bradley lives, moms and writes in Oakville, Ontario. By day she practices Aboriginal law and by night she attempts to sleep. Her work has been published in *Daily Science Fiction, Phobos Magazine* and the *Globe and Mail*.

Chadwick Ginther is the Prix Aurora Award-nominated author of the *Thunder Road Trilogy* and numerous published short stories. He lives and writes in Winnipeg.

Helen Marshall is a lecturer of Creative Writing and Publishing at Anglia Ruskin University in Cambridge, England. Her first collection of fiction, *Hair Side, Flesh Side,* won the Sydney J Bounds Award in 2013, and *Gifts for the One Who Comes After,* her second collection, won the World Fantasy Award and the Shirley Jackson Award in 2015. In 2016 she was awarded the $5,000 Best Story category of the Carter V. Cooper Short Fiction Awards, and that story appears in *Book Six* of the annual *CVC* series anthology (Exile Editions). She also appeared in *Book Three* and *Book Four* with shortlisted stories. Helen is currently editing *The Year's Best Weird Fiction* to be released in 2017, and her debut novel will be published in 2018.

Rati Mehrotra is a Toronto-based speculative fiction writer whose stories have appeared in *AE – The Canadian Science Fiction Review, Apex Magazine, Abyss & Apex, Inscription Magazine,* and many more. Her debut novel, *Markswoman,* will be published in early 2018.

www.ratiwrites.com   Twitter @Rati_Mehrotra

Stephen Michell is an emerging writer living in Toronto. His first novel will be published in 2017.

Dominik Parisien is an editor, poet, and writer. He is the co-editor, along with Navah Wolfe, of several anthologies, including the most recent, *The Starlit Wood: New Fairy Tales.* He is also the editor of *Clockwork Canada: Steampunk Fiction* (Exile Editions). Dominik's fiction, poetry, and essays have appeared in *Uncanny Magazine, Strange Horizons, Shock Totem, ELQ/Exile Quarterly,* and several anthologies, including *Imaginarium 2013: The Best Canadian Speculative Writing* and *The Playground of Lost Toys.* His fiction has twice been longlisted for a Sunburst Award, and longlisted for the $10,000 category of the Carter V. Cooper Short Fiction Awards.

www.dominikparisien.wordpress.com   Twitter @domparisien

Corey Redekop has publsihed two novels, the award-winning *Shelf Monkey* (Best Popular Fiction Novel, Independent Book Publisher Awards) and the award-nominated *Husk* (Best Novel, ReLit Award). His short fiction may be found in anthologies such as *Licence Expired: The Unauthorized James Bond, The Bestiary, The Exile Book of New Canadian Noir,* and *Superhero Universe: Tesseracts Nineteen.* Currently, he is cognitively mired in the thematic bog of a hypothetical third novel. He lives in Fredericton, New Brunswick.

Alexandra Camille Renwick treads international and genre boundaries, splitting time between noir, science fiction, and literary fabulism somewhere between Portland, Austin, and Ottawa. Her stories have appeared in *Ellery Queen, Alfred Hitchcock, Mslexia,* and *ELQ/Exile Quarterly,* and her collection, *Push of the Sky,* got a starred review in *Publishers Weekly.*   www.alexcrenwick.com

Renée Sarojini Saklikar writes *thecanadaproject*, widely published in journals, anthologies and chapbooks. The first completed book from *thecanadaproject* is *children of air india, un/authorized exhibits and interjections*, winner of the Canadian Authors' Association Award for poetry. She is currently a mentor and instructor for Simon Fraser University, and co-founder of the poetry reading series, Lunch Poems at SFU. With Wayde Compton, she co-edited *The Revolving City: 51 Poems and the Stories Behind Them*. Renée was recently appointed Poet Laureate for the City of Surrey. She collects poems about bees.
www.thecanadaproject.wordpress.com

Rebecca Schaeffer lives a life that is either exceedingly interesting or exceedingly boring, depending on who you ask. She gallivants around the world, taking odd jobs to pay the bills, sometimes literary writing related, but mostly translation, marketing, and paper-pushing projects. Her plays have been performed in Edmonton and Vancouver, and she was shortlisted for the 2014 Alberta Literary Awards.

Kate Story is a writer and performer. A Newfoundlander living in Ontario, her first novel *Blasted* received a Sunburst Award honourable mention. She is a recipient of the Ontario Arts Foundation's K.M. Hunter Award for her work in theatre. Recent publications include stories in the anthologies *Carbide Tipped Pens, Playground of Lost Toys, Clockwork Canada, Imaginarium: Best Canadian Speculative Writing 2015*, and *Gods, Memes, and Monsters*.   www.katestory.com

Andrew F. Sullivan is from Oshawa, Ontario. He is the author of the novel *WASTE* and the story collection *All We Want Is Everything*. He no longer spends his days handling raw meat, boxed liquor or used video games.

Michal Wojcik was born in Poland, raised in the Yukon territory, and educated in Edmonton and Montreal. He has an MA in history from McGill University, where he studied witchcraft trials, medieval monster theory, necromancers, and, occasionally, 17th-century texts about enchanted wheels of cheese. His stories have appeared in *Clockwork Canada, On Spec, The Book Smugglers*, and *Pornokitsch*.

Delani Valin is a writer living in a sleepy British Columbian valley. She enjoys vegan cookery, indoor gardening, and petting dogs. She has previously been published in *Adbusters Magazine, Soliloquies Anthology, The Sacrificial, Beautiful Minds Magazine,* and *Portal.*

Andrew Wilmot is a writer, editor, and artist living in Toronto. He is a graduate of the Simon Fraser University Master in Publishing program and spends his days writing and painting stupidly large pieces. He works as a freelance reviewer and academic editor, and as a substantive editor with several independent presses and publications. To date his work has been published in *Found Press, The Singularity, Glittership, Drive In Tales,* and *Turn to Ash,* and he was the winner of the 2015 Friends of Merril Short Story Contest. His first novel, *The Death Scene Artist,* will be published in 2018.   www.andrewwilmot.ca

Angeline Woon is a Malaysian in Ottawa, who often feels like a mermaid out of water. She edited *Flesh,* a Southeast Asian urban anthology. Recent publications include short stories in *Cyberpunk: Malaysia,* the *2016 Young Explorer's Adventure Guide,* and *Little Basket: New Malaysian Writing 2016.* Her work has been performed in theatres, broadcast on radio, and adapted for the *Dark Triptych* short film trilogy.   www.angelinewoon.wordpress.com

ABOUT THE EDITORS

Kelsi Morris of Toronto works in the publishing industry, focusing on genre fiction and graphic novels. She graduated from the University of Guelph with a degree in English and Philosophy, and used it to turn her life-long love of speculative fiction into a career of editing books, starting at ChiZine Publications, where she also helped create and launch *ChiGraphic*, CZP's graphic novel imprint. She actually enjoys reading slush, and has done so for ChiZine, The Friends of the Merril contest, and Ellen Datlow's *Fearful Symmetries* anthology. Along with co-editing *Those Who Make Us: Creature, Myth, and Monster Stories* for Exile Editions, next year will see *Over The Rainbow: Folk and Fairy Tales from the Margins,* co-edited with Derek Newman-Stille. Kelsi was also a contributing author for the Canadian Video Game Award-nominated *Lights Out, Please.* Outside of books, she finds happiness in black coffee, red wine, and dragons.   www.kelsimorris.com

Kaitlin Tremblay of Toronto is a writer, editor, and game developer. She is the author of the upcoming book *Borderlands* about the video game franchise *Borderlands,* and is the co-author of the book *Escape to Na Pali: A Journey to the Unreal* about Epic Game's 1998 hit video game *Unreal.* As a game developer, Kaitlin produced the collaborative interaction fiction anthology *Lights Out, Please,* which was nominated for five Canadian Video Game Awards. She gives talks about subversive storytelling and is a game design mentor for youth and adults. As a critic, Kaitlin has written for *Playboy, Vice, The Mary Sue, Unwinnable, Canadian Notes and Queries,* and others. Her poetry has been published in *Carousel, Rampike, (parenthetical),* and other print and e-zines. Kaitlin is currently a senior editor at Inhabit Education, a children's educational publishing company.

www.thatmonstergames.com

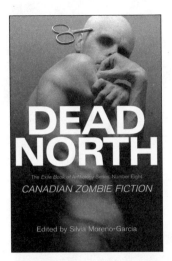

DEAD NORTH

The *Exile Book of* Anthology Series, Number Eight
CANADIAN ZOMBIE FICTION

Edited by Silvia Moreno-Garcia

FRACTURED
TALES OF THE CANADIAN POST-APOCALYPSE

Edited by
SILVIA MORENO-GARCIA

The Exile Book of Anthology Series
Number Eleven

playground of LOST toys

Edited by Colleen Anderson and Ursula Pflug

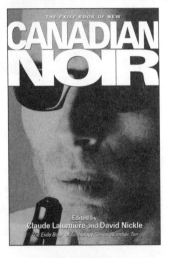

THE EXILE BOOK OF NEW
CANADIAN NOIR

Edited by
Claude Lalumière and David Nickle
The Exile Book of Anthology Series, Number Ten

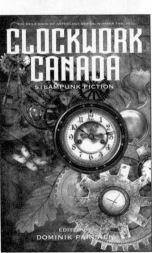

THE EXILE BOOK OF ANTHOLOGY SERIES. NUMBER TWELVE
CLOCKWORK CANADA
STEAMPUNK FICTION

EDITED BY
DOMINIK PARISIEN

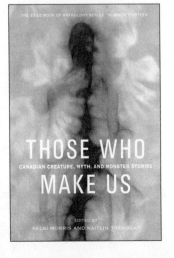

THE EXILE BOOK OF ANTHOLOGY SERIES · NUMBER THIRTEEN
THOSE WHO
CANADIAN CREATURE, MYTH, AND MONSTER STORIES
MAKE US

EDITED BY
KELSI MORRIS and KAITLIN TREMBLAY

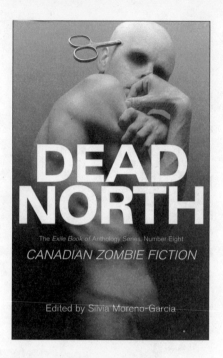

The *Exile Book of Anthology Series, Number Eight*
CANADIAN ZOMBIE FICTION
Edited by Silvia Moreno-Garcia

DEAD NORTH:
CANADIAN ZOMBIE FICTION

EDITED BY SILVIA MORENO-GARCIA

"*Dead North* suggests zombies may be thought of as native to this country, their presence going back to Aboriginal myths and legends…we see deadheads, shamblers, jiang shi, and Shark Throats invading such home and native settings as the Bay of Fundy's Hopewell Rocks, Alberta's tar sands, Toronto's Mount Pleasant Cemetery, and a Vancouver Island grow-op. Throw in the last poutine truck on Earth driving across Saskatchewan and some "mutant demon zombie cows devouring Montreal" (honest!) and what you've got is a fun and eclectic mix of zombie fiction…" —*The Toronto Star*

"Every time I listen to the yearly edition of *Canada Reads* on CBC, so much attention seems to be drawn to the fact that the author is Canadian, that being Canadian becomes a gimmick. *Dead North*, a collection of zombie short stories by exclusively Canadian authors, is the first of its kind that I've seen to buck this trend, using the diverse cultural mythology of the Great White North to put a number of unique spins on an otherwise over-saturated genre."—*Bookshelf Reviews*

Featuring stories by Chantal Boudreau, Tessa J. Brown, Richard Van Camp, Kevin Cockle, Jacques L. Condor, Carrie-Lea Côté, Linda DeMeulemeester, Brian Dolton, Gemma Files, Ada Hoffmann, Tyler Keevil, Claude Lalumière, Jamie Mason, Michael Matheson, Ursula Pflug, Rhea Rose, Simon Strantzas, E. Catherine Tobler, Beth Wodzinski and Melissa Yuan-Ines.

FRACTURED:
TALES OF THE CANADIAN POST-APOCALYPSE

EDITED BY SILVIA MORENO-GARCIA

"The 23 stories in *Fractured* cover incredible breadth, from the last man alive in Haida Gwaii to a dying Matthew waiting for his Anne in PEI. All the usual apocalyptic suspects are here – climate change, disease, alien invasion – alongside less familiar scenarios such as a ghost apocalypse and an invasion of shadows. Stories range from the immediate aftermath of society's collapse to distant futures in which humanity has been significantly reduced, but the same sense of struggle and survival against the odds permeates most of the pieces in the collection… What *Fractured* really drives home is how perfect Canada is as a setting for the post-apocalypse. Vast tracts of wilderness, intense weather, and the potentially sinister consequences of environmental devastation provide ample inspiration for imagining both humanity's destruction and its rugged survival." —*Quill & Quire*

Featuring stories by T.S. Bazelli, GMB Chomichuk, A.M. Dellamonica, dvsduncan, Geoff Gander, Orrin Grey, David Huebert, John Jantunen, H.N. Janzen, Arun Jiwa, Claude Lalumière, Jamie Mason, Michael Matheson, Christine Ottoni, Miriam Oudin, Michael S. Pack, Morgan M. Page, Steve Stanton, Amanda M. Taylor, E. Catherine Tobler, Jean-Louis Trudel, Frank Westcott and A.C. Wise.

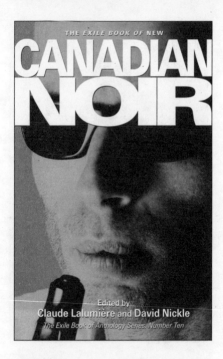

THE *EXILE BOOK* OF NEW
CANADIAN NOIR

Edited by
Claude Lalumière and David Nickle
The Exile Book of Anthology Series, Number Ten

NEW CANADIAN NOIR

EDITED BY CLAUDE LALUMIÈRE AND DAVID NICKLE

"Everything is in the title. These are all new stories – no novel extracts – selected by Claude Lalumière and David Nickle from an open call. They're Canadian-authored, but this is not an invitation for national introspection. Some Canadian locales get the noir treatment, which is fun, since, as Nickle notes in his afterword, noir, with its regard for the underbelly, seems like an un-Canadian thing to write. But the main question *New Canadian Noir* asks isn't "Where is here?" it's "What can noir be?" These stories push past the formulaic to explore noir's far reaches as a mood and aesthetic. In Nickle's words, "Noir is a state of mind – an exploration of corruptibility, ultimately an expression of humanity in all its terrible frailty." The resulting literary alchemy – from horror to fantasy, science fiction to literary realism, romance to, yes, crime – spanning the darkly funny to the stomach-queasy horrific, provides consistently entertaining rewards." —*Globe and Mail*

Featuring stories by Corey Redekop, Joel Thomas Hynes, Silvia Moreno-Garcia, Chadwick Ginther, Michael Mirolla, Simon Strantzas, Steve Vernon, Kevin Cockle, Colleen Anderson, Shane Simmons, Laird Long, Dale L. Sproule, Alex C. Renwick, Ada Hoffmann, Kieth Cadieux, Michael S. Chong, Rich Larson, Kelly Robson, Edward McDermott, Hermine Robinson, David Menear and Patrick Fleming.

The Exile Book of Anthology Series
Number Eleven

playgroUnd
of
LOST
toys

Edited by Colleen Anderson and Ursula Pflug

PLAYGROUND OF LOST TOYS

EDITED BY COLLEEN ANDERSON AND URSULA PFLUG

A dynamic collection of stories that explore the mystery, awe and dread that we may have felt as children when encountering a special toy. But it goes further, to the edges of space, where games are for keeps and where the mind plays its own games. We enter a world where the magic may not have been lost, where a toy or computers or gods vie for the upper hand. Wooden games of skill, ancient artifacts misinterpreted, dolls, stuffed animals, wand items that seek a life or even revenge – these lost toys and games bring tales of companionship, loss, revenge, hope, murder, cunning, and love, to be unearthed in the sandbox.

Featuring stories by Chris Kuriata, Joe Davies, Catherine MacLeod, Kate Story, Meagan Whan, Candas Jane Dorsey, Rati Mehrotra, Nathan Adler, Rhonda Eikamp, Robert Runté, Linda DeMeulemeester, Kevin Cockle, Claude Lalumière, Dominik Parisien, dvsduncan, Christine Daigle, Melissa Yuan-Innes, Shane Simmons, Lisa Carreiro, Karen Abrahamson, Geoffrey W. Cole and Alexandra Camille Renwick. Afterword by Derek Newman-Stille.

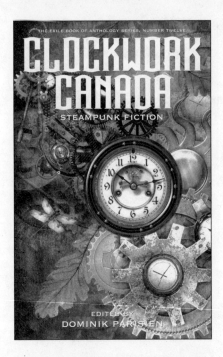

CLOCKWORK CANADA: STEAMPUNK FICTION

EDITED BY DOMINIK PARISIEN

Welcome to an alternate Canada, where steam technology and the wonders and horrors of the mechanical age have reshaped the past into something both wholly familiar yet compellingly different.

"These stories of clockworks, airships, mechanical limbs, automata, and steam are, overall, an unfettered delight to read." —*Quill & Quire*

"[*Clockwork Canada*] is a true delight that hits on my favorite things in fiction – curious worldbuilding, magic, and tough women taking charge. It's a carefully curated adventure in short fiction that stays true to a particular vision while seeking and achieving nuance." —*Tor.com*

"…inventive and transgressive…these stories rethink even the fundamentals of what we usually mean by steampunk." —*The Toronto Star*

Featuring stories by Colleen Anderson, Karin Lowachee, Brent Nichols, Charlotte Ashley, Chantal Boudreau, Rhea Rose, Kate Story, Terri Favro, Kate Heartfield, Claire Humphrey, Rati Mehrotra, Tony Pi, Holly Schofield, Harold R. Thompson and Michal Wojcik.

Exile's $15,000 Carter V. Cooper Short Fiction Competition

FOR CANADIAN WRITERS ONLY

$10,000 for the Best Story by an Emerging Writer
$5,000 for the Best Story by a Writer at Any Career Point

The 12 shortlisted are published in the annual *CVC Short Fiction Anthology* series and *ELQ/Exile: The Literary Quarterly*

Exile's $3,000 Gwendolyn MacEwen Poetry Competition

FOR CANADIAN WRITERS ONLY

$1,500 for the Best Suite of Poetry
$1,000 for the Best Suite by an Emerging Writer
$500 for the Best Poem

Winners are published in *ELQ/Exile: The Literary Quarterly*

These annual competitions open in October & November
details at: www.TheExileWriters.com